T0126406

What Reviewers Say About BOLD STROKES Authors

ை

KIM BALDWIN

"*A riveting novel of suspense* seems to be a very overworked phrase. However, it is extremely apt when discussing Kim Baldwin's [*Hunter's Pursuit*]. An exciting page turner [features] Katarzyna Demetrious, a bounty hunter…with a million dollar price on her head. Look for this excellent novel of suspense…" – **R. Lynne Watson**, *MegaScene*

"*Force of Nature* is an exciting and substantial reading experience which will long remain with the reader. Likeable characters with plausible problems and concerns, imaginative settings, engrossing events, and a well-tailored writing style all contribute to an exceptional novel. Baldwin's characterization is acutely and meticulously circumscribed and expansive. It is indeed gratifying to see a new author attempt and succeed in expanding her literary technique and writing style. Kim Baldwin is an author who has achieved both." – **Arlene Germain**, reviewer for the *Lambda Book Report* and the *Midwest Book Review*

ை

ROSE BEECHAM

"…her characters seem fully capable of walking away from the particulars of whodunit and engaging the reader in other aspects of their lives." – *Lambda Book Report*

"When Jennifer Fulton writes mysteries, she writes them as Rose Beecham. And since Jennifer Fulton is a very fine writer, you might expect that Rose Beecham is a fine writer too. You're right…On the way to a remarkable, and thoroughly convincing climax, Beecham creates believable characters in compelling situations, with enough humor to provide effective counterpoint to the work of detecting." – *Bay Area Reporter*

❧

Ronica Black

"Black juggles the assorted elements of her first book with assured pacing and estimable panache…[including]…the relative depth—for genre fiction—of the central characters: Erin, the married-but-separated detective who comes to her lesbian senses; loner Patricia, the policewoman-mentor who finds herself falling for Erin; and sultry club owner Elizabeth, the sexually predatory suspect who discards women like Kleenex…until she meets Erin." – **Richard Labonte**, Book Marks, Q Syndicate, 2005

"Black's characterization is skillful, and the sexual chemistry surrounding the three major characters is palpable and definitely hot-hot-hot. If you're looking for a more traditional murder mystery, *In Too Deep* might not be entirely your cup of Earl. On the other hand, if you're looking for a solid read with ample amounts of eroticism and a red herring or two, you're sure to find *In Too Deep* a satisfying read." **Lynne Jamneck**, L-Word.com Literature

❧

Gun Brooke

"*Course of Action* is a romance…populated with a host of captivating and amiable characters. The glimpses into the lifestyles of the rich and beautiful people are rather like guilty pleasures.…[A] most satisfying and entertaining reading experience." – **Arlene Germain**, reviewer for the *Lambda Book Report* and the *Midwest Book Review*

"*Protector of the Realm* has it all; sabotage, corruption, erotic love and exhilarating space fights. Gun Brooke's second novel is forceful with a winning combination of solid characters and a brilliant plot." – **Kathi Isserman**, *JustAboutWrite*

❧

Jane Fletcher

"*The Walls of Westernfort* is not only a highly engaging and fast-paced adventure novel, it provides the reader with an interesting framework for examining the same questions of loyalty, faith, family and love that [the characters] must face." – **M. J. Lowe**, *Midwest Book Review*

Lee Lynch

"There's a heady sense of '60s back-to-the-land communal idealism and '70s woman-power feminism (with hints of lesbian separatism) to this spirited novel—even though it's set in contemporary rural Oregon. Partners Donny (she's black and blue-collar) and Chick (she's plus-sized and motherly) are both in their 50s, owners of the dyke-centric Natural Woman Foods store, a homey nexus for *Sweet Creek*'s expansive cast of characters....Lynch, with a dozen novels to her credit dating back to the early days of Naiad Press, has earned her stripes as a writerly elder;- she was contributing stories to the lesbian magazine *The Ladder* four decades ago. But this latest is sublimely in tune with the times. " – Richard Labonte, Book Marks, Q Syndicate, 2005

Radcly*f*fe

"...well-honed storytelling skills...solid prose and sure-handedness of the narrative..." – **Elizabeth Flynn**, *Lambda Book Report*

"...well-plotted...lovely romance...I couldn't turn the pages fast enough!" – **Ann Bannon**, author of *The Beebo Brinker Chronicles*

Ali Vali

"Rich in character portrayal, *The Devil Inside* by Ali Vali is an unusual, unpredictable, and thought-provoking love story that will have the reader questioning the definition of right and wrong long after she finishes the book....*The Devil Inside*'s strength is that it is unlike most romance novels. Nothing about the story and its characters is conventional. We do not know what the future holds for Emma and Cain, but Vali tempts us with every word so we want to find out. I am very much looking forward to the sequel *The Devil Unleashed*." – **Kathi Isserman**, JustAboutWrite

THE
100TH
GENERATION

THE IBIS PROPHECY BOOK ONE

THE
100TH
GENERATION

THE IBIS PROPHECY BOOK ONE

by

JUSTINE SARACEN

2006

THE 100TH GENERATION
© 2006 BY JUSTINE SARACEN. ALL RIGHTS RESERVED.

ISBN 1-933110-48-1

THIS TRADE PAPERBACK ORIGINAL IS PUBLISHED BY
BOLD STROKES BOOKS, INC.,
NEW YORK, USA

CREDITS
EDITORS: STACIA SEAMAN AND SHELLEY THRASHER
PRODUCTION DESIGN: STACIA SEAMAN
COVER DESIGN BY SHERI (GRAPHICARTIST2020@HOTMAIL.COM)

Acknowledgments

Few writers, and certainly not this one, can write in a vacuum. I want to first thank Dr. Angelique Corthals, who, in a sense, gave me modern Egypt and through the benefit of her Egyptology, the ancient one as well. Thanks also to Derek Ragin, for providing in his own gifted and charming person the eponymous character of the novel. I am also grateful to those wise women—Lorie, Elizabeth, Ilona, Inga, and Carmen, who, out of sheer friendship, consented to critique early drafts of the work.

Thanks to Sheri for a splendid cover with real hieroglyphics and authentic tomb images, to Stacia Seaman for her deft touch with the editorial "fine-tooth comb," to Shelley Thrasher who, like the toughest buyer in the souq, haggled down my writing peculiarities to a manageable few, and to Radclyffe, for inviting me to the marketplace in the first place.

Dedication

For Angelique, my Wadjet, who began the tale as a joke,
and is the spirit that will waft through it forever

PROLOGUE:
ORIGINAL SIN

Pharaoh wept in his sleep. Everywhere before his burning eyes the beasts, the winds and waters, and the hills cried out. Pitiless, the Sun Disk rose and smote them, rendering them dumb. Then Seth, iron-eyed guardian of the light, loosed his spear upon the vanquished.

But lo, a humble priest stepped forward, an amulet in his hand, and the spear blade shattered into sparks upon it. Gathering the sparks with the power of his breath, he sucked them in—and spat them out again as words. "*Khetet! Rekhi renusen. Djedi medjatsen,*" blazed into the air and faded.

Pharaoh Meremptah awoke, clutching the bed cloth to his pounding heart. To his chamberlain he called, "Light the torches. Summon the court!" He rose in the darkness, donned the immaculate ceremonial kilt, and strode to the Great Hall. There he sat upon his throne, white-lipped and shaken, while his court assembled.

Roused betimes from his sleep, the priest Rekemheb dressed quickly while Pharaoh's messenger waited before his door.

His wife, disquieted, stood by him. "Why does the god-king summon you so early?" she asked, laying on his wide collar of lapis lazuli and tying it in the back. "The light will not come for hours."

The priest looked at his children—the girl, with ochre-stained fingers curled in a fist, and the boy smiling even in his sleep—and his heart was light. "It will have something to do with the New Year ceremonies, I am sure. Be sure to wake the children in time for the dawn."

He embraced his wife with brief tenderness. "Be full of joy today, as I am full of joy for you," he whispered. Then he turned away and hastened with the messenger along the still-dark streets to the palace. To his surprise, the doors to the Great Hall were thrown open and the court stood in attendance. Palace guards stepped to his side and escorted him down the center aisle to the throne. Bewildered, he fell to his knees at the feet of the god-king, his hands raised and open in the gesture of adoration.

Pharaoh leaned forward on his golden stool. "The gods have given me a vision this night and have revealed their chosen one. I speak his name: Rekemheb, Priest of the Temple of Hathor." Taking up a wide pectoral ornament from the hands of a servant, Pharaoh placed its chain over the bowed head. "This is the sign of thy sacred office. Go now with this on thy heart to prepare for the Opening of the New Year."

Rekemheb glanced up for the briefest moment at Pharaoh's face and caught his breath. Where he had expected strength, he saw fear.

He rose with lowered head and backed down the length of the throne room, eyes searching among the courtiers for explanation. He saw only surprise and confusion to match his own. At the door, the priest turned and hurried along the corridor. At each of the red-painted columns, braziers of burning oil cast trembling semicircles of light upon the stone. Guards stepped aside to let him pass.

As Rekemheb came to the great pylons that fronted the royal palace, he stopped at the last brazier. Drawing the chain over his head, he held the filigree gold plaque toward the flame and studied its sparkling images. At the center stood the sacred Balance weighing the heart of a man, witnessed by the gods of the underworld. Around the periphery, in shallow relief, the forty-two Judges sat enclosed in a vulture's wings. The priest's hand shook, for he held in jeweled miniature the entry into death.

"You do well to tremble, Hathor Priest," a voice said, startling him. He turned to see a man, hook nosed and gaunt, standing in the shadows. The long palette and reed case of a scribe hung from his shoulder.

"I do not know you, sir, nor that whereof you speak," Rekemheb said courteously. He drew the chain over his head again, pulling his priestly side lock up through it.

"But I know you," the scribe replied, holding his palette to his hip like a weapon. "And I will tell your story."

"My story? Of being chosen for the Rebirth of the Year?"

"Of being chosen for the rebirth of the gods. It is a great honor, and you will die for it. Yet a child of your line will bring you forth into the world again in the hundredth generation. Then you shall be witness to these things: the Balance, the Book, and the bearing of the Child. This is our hope against the Aton, rising in the west."

"The Aton? But the Sun Disk cult is gone. Its priests are scattered. Surely—"

The scribe laid the tip of a bony finger on the amulet. "Hold fast to this. It is the prophecy."

Rekemheb stood speechless as the scribe faded into the shadows and then, bemused, he descended the wide steps of the palace. The dawning city was still quiet, for every man was in his house preparing for the New Year festival. The Dog Star had appeared, and in the east, the molten sun cast the street in a comforting orange glow.

Then he saw them, stepping out from behind the granary. Two men armed with spears, and a third one who ought to have been banished along with his usurper god. The Priest of Aton glared at him with iron hatred in his eyes.

Rekemheb bolted, drawing his pursuers away from his house and family. His heart aching, he ran through alleys, along mud-brick walls, over heaps of refuse in the streets.

White-hot, the spear blade pierced his back, throwing him onto the dusty ground. He opened his mouth, desperate to inhale, but no air came. He felt only the searing, nauseating pain of the metal tearing upward through his flesh as the spear shaft fell. He lay paralyzed and choking, and he tasted the frothy blood filling his mouth. Dread hissed over him like locusts as with dying eyes he watched the scorching sun disk rise.

CHAPTER I:
GOD IS GREAT

A aalllaaaaahh uakbar!"
The faint whining cry of the muezzin that drifted toward them in the darkness told them the city was near.

"Aaallaaahh uakbar!" It came again along the breeze as, reluctantly, Valerie Foret slowed her camel. Unbeliever that she was, she had always loved the first call to prayer, imagining bearded muezzins summoning the faithful through cupped hands from atop their minarets. Now she resented it, for it brought them to a halt. She stopped the moment Ahmed did and sat impatiently while his honking camel broke first at the front and then at the hind legs and he dismounted.

The excavation foreman unrolled the prayer rug he kept on his saddle and stepped out of his sandals. Scooping up handfuls of the limestone sand, he purified his hands and feet and turned eastward. *"Bismillah Arrahman Arraheem."* With open hands cupped to his ears, he began.

Valerie rode a respectful dozen meters farther on, annoyed. She tapped with her knuckles on her knee, recalling the forced rosaries of her childhood. *Ave Marie...Mère de Dieu.* Oh hell. They should have been in Giza by now, instead of a kilometer away from the pyramids. She could see them now in the increasing light, the great tombs of Khufu, Khephren, and Menkaure. In the predawn sky that silhouetted them, they had a majesty they would lack the rest of the day, when the plateau would be crawling with tourists and vendors. Now, mute black monuments to an ancient faith, they towered over the new one.

Restlessly, she laid her booted foot over the crosspiece of the saddle, brushing off the powdery sand that had collected in the folds of her trousers. She took off her hat and rubbed her gritty scalp. Six months in the sun had lightened her brown hair at the edges and tanned her like a farmer, from her elbows to her hands. She fidgeted. So close, and so much to be done. Derek. She had so much to tell him. Things that would knock him over. And Jameela. Yes, Jameela. She tried to moisten dry lips but had no saliva.

"Y'alla bina!" Her foreman was suddenly beside her, brushing sand from the tail of his turban. "You will wish to return to the site right away, I think. I will get supplies today and have camels ready to go tonight."

"I wish we could, Ahmed, but we can't leave for two days. As for the provisions, I will get a few things at the souq, but I depend on you for the rest. I have people to visit and an opera to see."

"Opera?" A slight drawing together of his thick gray eyebrows indicated his astonishment. "You stay two days to see an opera?"

"I know that delays us for another day, but the singer is like a brother to me, and I missed his last visit here." She looked over toward Ahmed's leathery, avuncular face, which had grown familiar in the months of the project. "Besides, he's performing *Orpheus*, about a man who visits the underworld. A good omen for an Egyptologist, don't you think? By the way, you will need to hire another camel. He's coming back with us."

"An opera singer in the desert," the Egyptian replied with studied neutrality. "Very good."

Squinting in the half-light, she barely heard him. Giza, finally, had come into sight, a wide gray-brown stain behind the pyramids. She tapped her camel lightly with her goad, urging the tired beast to move a little faster. She felt excitement growing, in spite of her fatigue.

Soon the travelers arrived at the west façade of Menkaure, desert-most of the pyramids. Without looking up, Valerie sensed the edifice that filled space above them, rendering them trivial. Lines of men and boys swarmed toward them, peddlers with their sacks of postcards and plaster sphinxes. *"As salaamu 'alaykum."*

"Wa 'alaykum as salaam." They passed through them to the next phalanx of "guides" who recited a mélange of facts and fictions about the tombs, and the stablemen, who for a few pounds would snap a photo of a foreigner sitting bravely on one of their emaciated horses. She tapped her camel with her goad again, urging it faster. She hated what the site had become. There was more refuse on the ground now—soda cans and plastic water bottles and countless cigarette butts.

At Khufu she could see Giza clearly under a gray morning haze, its apartment blocks and sooty squalor encroaching like lava upon the pyramids. "It's a pity," she said to her companion. "Egypt swallows up its own history."

"There will be more history, Doctor. God is ever telling His story."

Valerie shrugged. "The Egyptians trust too much in God and too little in themselves, I think."

"*Imshii!*" A rock flew out of nowhere and thudded against her camel. The snorting beast danced sideways, and she spun around to see a boy with a sling hanging open from his hand. She thought, absurdly, of the biblical David.

"Uh!" A second stone slammed into the side of her head. Stunned, she swayed blindly on the saddle, raising her hand to her ear. Bright pain radiated through her head; infantile fears, jagged pieces of memory like shattered glass, showered down on her. Confinement, hard hands thrashing her, a stone floor rising up to meet her. "*Maman,*" the child had whimpered uselessly.

Then sight returned.

As she tottered, a bearded man sprang upward at her, his eyes bright with rectitude. She raised both arms against him, but he seized the cloth of her shirt, yanking her forcefully toward him. She toppled from the high saddle into his arms, and they fell together onto the sand. Furious, she rolled away from him, rose to her knees, and snatched her pistol from her holster. Ahmed, somehow dismounted, threw himself at a second man. A few meters away, peddlers had a third man on the ground.

Panting, Valerie struggled to her feet, still pointing her trembling pistol at her attacker, who had not risen from the ground.

He stared at her, composed, his glance intense, intimate. "You insult God," he snarled, "and your punishment will come."

Her finger tightened on the trigger.

From behind her a small hand reached out and touched her wrist. Dark fingers with milky white nails pressed gently into her skin. "Do not," a woman's voice said softly.

Valerie lowered her arm without taking her eyes from the attacker.

"Lady." A uniformed soldier suddenly stood in front of her, huffing, his carbine across his chest. "You knowing these men?"

Behind him, other soldiers reached into the roil of men and pulled them apart.

"No. Of course not. I am an archaeologist." She replied in Arabic, to his obvious relief, and pointed toward her foreman. "And this man is my *rayis*. He will confirm that we have just come in from Ghard Abu Sennan, where we are working. With government permission." She laid her free hand on her shirt pocket, suggesting the letter was there.

"Yes, Captain." Ahmed nodded to the soldier, who was clearly not an officer. "We have just come from the desert and know nothing of these men. But now, as you can see, the lady is injured and we must hurry into Giza."

"Yes, of course. Then it is the fanatics. They have been causing trouble at the tourist places. But don't worry. These will not bother you again."

"Y'alla bina!" he shouted at his men, who fast-marched the three bloodied attackers and the boy toward the causeway. Twisting in the grip of a gendarme half again his size, the bearded one turned back for a moment, his expression unreadable.

Valerie cupped her right hand over the throbbing wound on her cheek.

"Are you all right, Doctor?" Ahmed took hold of the rein and couched the camel so she could remount.

Valerie looked down and realized she still held the grip of the holstered pistol. She let it go finally, flexing her cramped fingers at her side. "My God. I almost shot him, Ahmed. I almost shot a man. This woman stopped me."

Shielding her eyes against the light of the sun, she turned around to see who had stayed her hand.

She recoiled. A vulture hulked on the lowest block of the pyramid swinging its leathery head left and right, as if noting the outcome of the incident. Savage eyes watched her for a moment, and then the beast unfolded its wings. Black feather-fingers opened at the tips as the creature hopped awkwardly off the block. Within inches of the ground, the wings beat laborious strokes, drawing its mass slowly upward. Finally the creature gained height and banked in a wide arc over the desert.

"I am sorry for this, Doctor. The extremists cry out against foreigners but they are ignorant. They do not speak for Egypt."

"I know that." She gingerly touched the cut on her cheek, frowning down at the blood on her fingertips. "I wonder who does."

Leaving the desert plateau for Giza proper, they made their way southward along the dirt road that paralleled the highway. At the familiar side path, they turned into the squalid patch that was Younis's stables, and she braced herself for the onslaught to her senses. That she had a headache and an open cut on her cheek did not help.

"Dr. Foret! *Ahlan wa sahlan!*" Rajab called out to her as he came from the stable with a bucket of what seemed to be fresh manure. His brother turned from the water urn by the roadside where he was splashing water on his face and waved as well. She waved back, touched by the boy's warmth. They were motherless, she knew; Younis's wife had died of some infection or other, and the family toiled, like millions of the Egyptian working class, in grinding poverty. She wished for the thousandth time that her university budget allowed for an act of charity.

Farther away, a third boy, still a young child, urinated into the center of an automobile tire. The tire, she noted, was one of several leading toward the taxi-garage a half a kilometer down the highway. Its sooty little black-and-white Ladas buzzed past every few minutes on the road behind her.

At the far corner of the property, but not nearly far enough, a square marked out with rocks held the stable's accumulation of dung. In the early morning its stench was tolerable, but the blanket of flies that swarmed up as Rajab emptied his bucket reminded her why she never stayed long at the stable. Today least of all.

The two dismounted by the side of the stable, and Valerie shifted her knapsack from the camel's back to her own. She patted all her pockets to make sure she had everything.

Younis emerged from the stable doorway. A man who ought to have been portly at his age, he was instead merely swollen at the middle, his arms and legs still spindly. The bales of hay along the stable wall did not stop him from smoking, and he took the cigarette from his mouth to smile at her with tobacco-colored teeth.

"*As salaamu 'alaykum,* Younis." She brushed away flies.

"*Wa 'alaykum as salaam,* Dr. Foret." He took the reins of her camel with one hand and raised the other in a friendly salute rather than shake her hand. She was relieved.

"Take good care of our girls here, Younis. Give them some extra food, a little fruit too maybe. They've been hard workers the whole time we've had them, and we'll be taking them out again in two days."

"Yes, Dr. Foret. Extra fruit. But when they see how fat you keep them, my other camels will stage a rebellion."

"Then feed them too." She laughed. "And put it on our bill."

She turned around to her foreman and pressed a bundle of currency into his hand. "You have the list of supplies for the excavation? Good. This should cover the expenses here and the purchases. I'll meet you here at dusk in two days. If I need to, can I phone you at Sammad's?"

"Yes, Dr. Foret. I will be ready. But now, please see to that wound."

"I'll be fine, Ahmed. Really, it's nothing. In two days, then." She shook his hand, adjusted her knapsack, and set off on the way back to the road. She badly needed a shower, a good meal, and some attention, she thought, and her pace quickened from a walk to a jog. As she hurried toward the taxi-garage, the two sensations came at once, confusing her: the ominous throbbing in her battered ear and the delicious anticipation of Jameela.

CHAPTER II:
OTHER MEN'S TOYS

B athed, breakfasted, and sated, Valerie caught her breath among fresh white pillows. Her earache was gone, and the handsome head of Madame Jameela al Rashidi, wife of the President of the Supreme Council of Antiquities, lay on her shoulder. Her chin resting on the fragrant hair, Valerie felt her sweat cooling and considered how to extricate herself.

The forty-year-old woman was still a knockout, Valerie thought, and still willing at a moment's notice to deceive her husband—even early in the morning. In the months of grueling, fruitless labor on the excavation, her visits to Jameela had been a relief and an adventure, with just the right amount of risk. But now this one seemed a digression. Now something more important loomed. She felt a pang of guilt as the woman stirred in her arms.

"Mmm. That was nice. Something I can think about all day long," Jameela murmured into Valerie's neck, then rose up on her elbow and blew long hair out of her face. She threw back the sheet, exposing them both to the sluggish air that wafted from the overhead fan.

Valerie glanced downward and smiled at the difference between their two nude forms. Jameela's caramel-colored body was sleek and pampered. Shaven and well-lotioned legs led down to pedicured feet with painted toenails. She herself, for all her time in the desert, was pale the length of her, all but her forearms and face, and her muscled legs were spotted with the bruises of hard physical labor. Jameela's womanly belly curved softly toward her own flat one, and the dark Egyptian breast swelled against the small white one like a hen sheltering its chick.

She did not want to be sheltered right then. She wanted to be on her way, but it was too crass to leave so soon. She closed her eyes, savoring the residual arousal of their play. Any other time, she would have stayed half the day. But now…She let herself drowse awhile, losing her train of thought. The image of a white limestone step formed in her mind's eye, filling her with joy, impatience. "Thank you, Egypt," she murmured.

"Egypt? My dear, I am the one you should thank, not Egypt. The rest of the country would be quite horrified by what we just did."

"Of course, I mean you, *Habibti*." Valerie opened her eyes, turned her head, and slid down the pillow to kiss the full breast. "Ouch! Damn." She sat up, pressing two fingers just in front of her ear.

"Oh, look, your cut is bleeding again." Jameela touched her hand. "Poor thing. Let me clean it once more." She slid off the bed, snatched a silk dressing gown from the foot of it, and swayed across the room to the bathroom.

"Don't worry, Jameela. I'm fine." Valerie glanced around the room that had once impressed her. She knew the scimitars and Bedouin weavings on the wall were all fabulous antiques, and the chairs expensive copies of Egyptian artifacts. Even the family pictures, of children posing in their school uniforms, were in extravagant gold frames. But their beauty no longer fascinated her. Now every object simply seemed to be one of President Rashidi's trophies, even his bored and restless wife.

The cheerful adulteress came out from the bathroom with a small brown bottle and a piece of gauze. "I thought the government had cracked down on those fanatics. But it just gets worse and worse. So much anger. I don't understand it."

Madame Rashidi sat down on the side of the bed and dabbed at the sore until Valerie flinched. "Sit still, now. The iodine is good for it." A lewd smile played over her lips. "And now we are both going to be sore this evening."

"Jameela, don't paint my cheek red." Playfully, Valerie moved her lover's hand away from her face. "I'll look like a clown. I've got an opera to go to tonight."

"An opera? How very nice for you. I have to play the hostess tonight at one of those dreadful receptions, shaking hands, talking nonsense about pyramids and tombs in five languages. And the men will be peering oh so discreetly at my bosoms." She leaned forward to display the coveted objects inside the silk robe. "I shall be thinking of you the whole time."

"I will be thinking of you too. Of course." Valerie kissed her quickly on the lips and rose from the bed. She walked naked to where her knapsack lay on a chair, gathering up her soiled clothing on the way.

Jameela followed her across the room and embraced her again from behind, kissing her between her shoulder blades. She reached past Valerie to grasp the shirt folded in the knapsack. As she pulled it out, it unfolded, and she held it up by the shoulders. It was an exact replica of the soiled shirt Valerie had just rolled up. "*Habibti*, don't you have anything more, well, feminine? All this boys' clothing!"

"Oh, but it's the boy part that you like, isn't it?" she teased. Valerie took the shirt from her hand. "I know that I look like one of your boyfriends. Without the beard, of course. Are you still sneaking around with that Saudi journalist?"

"Never mind him. He is not at all like you. Nobody is like you. You may be a foreigner, but those eyes are more Egyptian than any I know. And your kisses make me want to leave my husband." She leaned over and picked up a .22 caliber pistol by its holster. "But then there is this." She held the weapon up in the air between them. "What is chasing you anyhow so that you feel you have to carry a gun?"

"Nothing is chasing me. But I travel alone all the time. I don't want to be locked up someplace at someone's mercy."

"Locked up? Why would anyone lock you up?"

"Don't leave your husband, and don't worry about me, or my gun. We'll both be fine." Valerie took the pistol from the other woman's hand and laid it back on the night table. She planted another light kiss on Jameela's lips and drew on the clean shirt. "I'm sorry to leave so soon. Really. But I have to meet a friend and buy supplies for the dig site. You understand."

"You and that excavation. You still have a fantasy of being the next Howard Carter and finding a Tutankhamun, don't you? But after eight months digging in the middle of nowhere, you've got nothing more than a cut on your face. Didn't that Lord Somethingsomething—the one who financed the Tutankhamun excavation—die of a cut just like that?"

"Carnarvon. His name was Lord Carnarvon." The archaeologist buttoned her shirt, ignoring the question. "The reception tonight. Who is it for?"

"Oh, I don't know. Someone from Belgium. An academic, I think. Do you suppose you would know him?" Jameela fussed over Valerie's collar.

"It's a small country. Not a lot of Egyptologists." Valerie drew up her trousers, zipped, and buckled her belt. "Are you sure it's not a cultural minister or curator?"

"You know I don't pay attention to that sort of thing. It's just another hand to shake. I'll show you the announcement." The president's wife went into the next room while Valerie laced up her boots, disquieted.

Jameela returned holding up a folded paper. "Is it anybody important? Should we serve the good champagne?"

Hooking her holster onto her belt at the hip with one hand, Valerie took the announcement in the other. Her hand closed into a fist, bending the paper. She read the text a second time slowly, biting her lip, wanting it to be a mistake. With her free hand she slid the gun holster behind her under her jacket.

"*Merde.*" This was the last thing on earth she needed.

CHAPTER III:
FAMILY

Valerie read the announcement for the fourth time and then tucked it back into her shirt pocket. It didn't seem fair. All the euphoria of the dawn had deflated to confusion and dread. Well, Derek would help her figure something out.

She leaned one arm on the iron railing of the balcony café and studied the flow of people on the El Hussein Square below. The midmorning crowd that streamed past the El Hussein mosque was already dense, and from one side it oozed sluggishly into the Khan al Khalili bazaar. Egyptians mostly, she noted, with only a few tourists, they pressed in clumps of two and three off the main thoroughfare into the narrow side streets. Their individual voices blended into a curtain of white noise, punctuated by car horns and the bray of a donkey somewhere. The dusty air carried the scent of animal ordure, car exhaust, and cigarette smoke and irritated her nose. She was glad the open skin in front of her ear was covered by a bandage. From the narrow ledge where she sat, she leaned forward and watched for her old friend, tapping her knuckles softly on the railing.

He was late, of course. He was never not late, excusing himself on every occasion by saying he was on "black time" or "gay time" or "opera singer's time." She decided it was the last, because that was what most excused him from reality. His countertenor voice, neither male nor female, but some transcendent mixture of the two, gave him an otherworldliness, as if he were a priest in the service of some splendid god. That was why she cared for him, she supposed; he elevated her.

"*Allah yirhamuh.*" The waiter collected the empty tea glass at her elbow and set down a second one. "Another funeral. Too many this year."

"Yes," she agreed, realizing what she saw. Across the street a stream of men was pouring out from around the side of the mosque. In their midst, four pallbearers carried a simple wooden bier. Coffinless and shrouded in white, the body lay exposed. The mourners gathered around the pallbearers until, at some signal, the entire cortege flowed into the square.

A sudden movement from the right caught her eye. Conspicuous by his tank top and shorts, a pale-skinned man—journalist or tourist, she could not tell—hurried across the street. Taking up position slightly in front of the procession, he began filming with a handheld video camera.

Three of the mourners approached him, waving. One of them snatched the camera from the stranger's hand and threw it into the oncoming traffic. Outraged, the photographer lunged at the assailant, and as the two men tussled, a crowd gathered around them. The funeral cortege continued in the direction of the necropolis while the smaller crowd dragged the photographer into a side street. She stood up and leaned on the terrace railing, trying to catch sight of them. The fool. Didn't he have any sense that he was trespassing?

A hand gripped her shoulder. Instinctively, she spun around—and bumped against a wide chest.

"Well, aren't *we* jumpy today? Hello, my darling bone collector!" Large lips kissed her noisily on her undamaged cheek.

She stepped back, grinning at the handsome black man who smiled down at her.

Large eyes rimmed with lashes of extraordinary length were set above cheeks a shade lighter than the rest of his face. Together, they gave him a sort of radiance. In spite of his hair, which she thought he wore far too short, he was rather beautiful.

He pressed her back onto her chair and sat down knee to knee with her. "My lovely Valerie Marie-Ghislaine. How *are* you? And however did you get that big nasty thing on your cheek? Someone's angry husband? Well, the bandage has *got* to go." His hand, spread wide on his chest, signaled his aversion. "It's just too too…*vilain.*"

"No, nothing like that." She laughed at his concern, not for her health, but for her appearance. "More a political statement from a Muslim fundamentalist. A young one, but with very good aim, apparently."

"Other than that, you look delicious. Nefertiti face and almond eyes to die for."

"You're looking good yourself, Derek. I see you're sporting jewelry now."

"You mean this?" He held up his hand as if admiring his fingernails. At the base of his ring finger was a wide silver band, studded with tiny blue stones. "I bought this in Cairo, in fact, after the October performance. You weren't around so I had to console myself with a little self-indulgence. Does it look too sissy, you think?"

"Not at all. It looks good." She grasped his hand. "And I'm sorry I missed your Cairo debut, darling. You know I was stuck in Brussels, organizing the excavation."

He took a sip from her tea glass and winced. "Needs sugar. Yes, that was heartless, simply heartless." His voice rose in pitch. "And I was hideously lonely. But then I ran into an Egyptian friend, Auset, who took care of me. Very good care." His expression had changed three times during his speech.

"An Egyptian? You have an Egyptian friend? Should I be jealous?" She leaned back on her chair and stretched out her stiff legs, crossing them at the ankles.

"Uh-huh. A Jewish Egyptian, if you can believe it, and barely that. She lived for a long time in New York, so she's more American than I am. You'll see. She's meeting us this afternoon." He leaned his chin on one hand, supporting his elbow on the other. "But what about you, girlfriend? What trouble have you been getting into?"

"Well, to start, I moved the dig site to another location. That didn't sit well with the committee at all."

"Moved? Why *ever* did you do that?"

"You're the only person I'm telling this to." She sat up again and leaned in, embarrassed. "Anyone else would think I was crazy." She dropped her eyes for a moment. "I...I had a dream. Don't look at me like that. It was very vivid. You were in it, dressed like an Egyptian, with a priest's braid on one side of your head."

"Really? How did I look?" He ran crossed fingers down the side of his face and turned in profile.

"Pretty good, actually. Thinner. But you spoke Egyptian, and you told me to dig in the next valley. So I did."

"Oh, so now I get the blame for the trouble you're in?" His fist went to his hip.

Her smile began small, then grew as if slowly releasing some joyous inner creature. "Not the blame, dear. The credit. We found something."

"Oh!" His eyebrows shot up again, and he pressed his fingertips over his mouth. "You found a tomb?" he whispered.

"Limestone steps in the middle of nowhere? Can't be anything else."

He bounced slightly in his seat, his hands clasped in front of him. "Oh, Valerie, honey. Fame and fortune! I can hardly wait!"

"Well, there's also this." She pulled the crumpled paper from her shirt pocket and tossed it onto the tiny table. "Just got it this morning. An announcement of a reception for the new chairman and head of excavations at Brussels University. It's a disaster."

"A reception a disaster? Why?" He unfolded the paper and glanced over the announcement, pursing his lips.

"Not the reception. The man. He's one of the senior professors in my department and a religious fanatic who thinks women don't belong in the university. But more to the point, he arrived in Cairo without warning, and he'll of course want to see the dig site. This is the absolute worst moment for him to arrive."

"But you've got something good to report now."

"Not yet. I don't know what I've discovered. I've spent months digging for this thing, but until it's opened, it isn't really 'discovered.' I've got to be able to say, 'Look here. I, Valerie Foret, have found a tomb.' Until then, I've got to evade him."

"No problem, darling." He patted her hand. "After the performance, and a good night's sleep, I'll be ready to go out and play archaeologist with you. We can head out tomorrow as soon as it's cool to finish the job!"

Furious shouting from the street below interrupted them. Derek peered over the terrace railing. "What's going on? The police are all over the place."

Valerie stood up to see. The group of men that had pursued the photographer had grown larger and was spreading out into the square. The original offender was nowhere in sight; only the angry mourners tussled with police. Individuals broke away from the crowd and ran along the street under the café terrace. Several police vans had pulled up in front of the mosque, and white uniformed men with bayoneted rifles were pouring out.

"Come on," Valerie said. "We're conspicuous here. We'll be better off in the souq."

"You want to go shopping with all this going on?" Derek looked back at the street where a knot of men engaged the soldiers and were thrown to the ground.

"It's not going to stop, I'm afraid." She hoisted her knapsack onto her shoulder. "And we still have supplies to get."

"What are they so upset about? I mean, what's gotten into them?"

"That's the big question, isn't it?" she said over her shoulder.

Behind them a dark object rose up in an arc from the street. It seemed to hover in the air for a second overhead, revealing itself as a Coca-Cola bottle. Then it crashed onto the iron balustrade, spraying a shower of brown fluid and glass splinters across the terrace floor.

CHAPTER IV:
GIFTS FROM A DARK HAND

The two of them withdrew into the winding alleys of the souq, threading their way past carts, bicycles, dogs, donkeys. Merchants called out to them, announcing the quality and prices of their wares in several languages. Valerie drew Derek through narrow passageways of shops for footwear, copper and brass, jewelry, pottery, and papyrus and stopped finally before a spice merchant. Bushel baskets of dried teas, flower petals, ginger, and unidentifiable vegetation lined the front. Flies swarmed over everything.

"Tell me again why we're buying food in the souq instead of a nice clean supermarket?" He wrinkled his nose. "Where people don't throw things?"

"Don't be so American, dear." She squeezed his arm. "Enjoy the history. Besides, I really want to smoke a little *sheesha* later." Valerie turned to the bearded merchant, who already held a wooden scoop and an open paper bag. She pointed at the heap of dried hibiscus petals. *"Tneen kilo, min fadlak."*

The merchant dug into the dark red mass and scooped them into the bag. The flies swarmed leisurely over to the neighboring basket. *"Ishrin guineh,"* he said, handing over the bag. He smiled, revealing horrifying teeth.

Valerie raised her hand politely. *"Ashera guineh."* She pulled a ten-pound note from the breast pocket of her khaki shirt and laid it on the counter.

He shook his head. *"Tamantashar guineh."* He pushed the note back to her.

"Ashera," she repeated. She opened her knapsack but was distracted. In an alley, off to the side of the merchant's stand, someone

stood watching. A woman in a dark dress and black head scarf thrown over one shoulder seemed to study her.

The merchant's voice registered shock and an appeal to common sense. He held out his open hands to show he had nothing to hide. He was an honest man. She was ruining him. *"Sittashar guineh."*

"Ashera," Valerie persisted courteously.

The woman still watched from the side, intense and blatant, as no Egyptian woman would be in public. Delicate dark hands, their fingernails much lighter than the skin, were clasped in front of her.

The spice merchant lamented his debts, his ailments, his many children. *"Arba'tashar guineh."*

"Ashera," Valerie repeated, but could not focus on the haggling. She kept glancing to the side at the strange woman who stared at her and would not look away.

"Itnashar." The man made his last offer.

"Ashera," Valerie droned, wondering if the woman would approach.

The merchant shrugged finally and picked up the ten-pound note. The transaction completed, he offered his hand. The gruesome teeth appeared again as she shook hands and then packed away her bag of *karkady*.

Derek frowned as they stepped away from the shop. "What was that all about?"

"The usual. He assumed we were tourists and doubled the price. I haven't got time for all that today. I paid him the going price. Besides—"

The stranger stepped out from a doorway and blocked their path.

She looked like no other Egyptian Valerie had ever seen. Her features were sharp, her jaw and cheekbones well delineated. The long, straight nose was more Greek than Arab, and her eyes were so dark that Valerie could see no iris, only depth. Her long black hair was uncovered, conspicuous in a quarter where women wore the hijab. Under a loose black abaya, she was spare, lacking the voluptuousness of the mature Arab woman. Age and youth combined in her oddly, and she was, in a curious, severe way, stunning.

"I have something you will need," the woman said solemnly. She held up a narrow ivory box, not quite the length of her forearm, incised with a line of text and capped at both ends with gold. Attached to it by a cord was a tiny leather bag.

The archaeologist recognized it instantly: palette, reeds, and pigment bag, the paraphernalia of an ancient Egyptian scribe. "It is very beautiful," she replied. "But we are not looking for souvenirs, thank you."

"It is not a souvenir," the Arab woman said. She stared from fathomless eyes and laid the object in Valerie's hand.

"Yes, but…" She studied the box palette. It had the usual two wells cut at the top, with faint traces in them of the ochre and kohl pigments. Below the inkwells a column of hieroglyphics descended. She held them up to decipher them. "'I am the instrument of Jehuti,'" she read. "'Let each word that floweth herefrom be given life, forever.' Interesting. It is correct New Kingdom Egyptian."

"Can I see it?" Derek took the object from her and peered at both ends of it. Suddenly the gold cap came off in his hand. "Oh my God! Did I break it?" Horror swept across his face for a second and then relief. "Oh, but look. There's something inside." He pulled out a tube of papyrus and unrolled it. "It's got that picture writing."

Valerie looked past his arm at the text. "It's the Negative Confessions, from the Book of the Dead. Hmm. Beautiful work. Whoever made this is really good."

Derek pursed his lips. "Who are these guys all around the edges?"

"Those are the forty-two judges. Amazing. How much is it?"

The stranger nodded in agreement, although it was not clear to what. "There is no price. It is for you alone."

"No price? You are giving this to me? Why?"

The dark woman stepped forward, until she was just inches away. She reached out, touched the bandage delicately with the tip of a dark finger. Then she leaned in and whispered into the other ear. Valerie stood astonished, as the ache faded. The strange woman stood a moment, motionless, her hand still resting on the wound, her face close. Valerie could smell her hair, a scent vaguely like cedar, and feel the warmth that radiated from it. The woman's hip, covered by the abaya, still brushed against her faintly, ambiguously. The memory of Jameela's nude body writhing under her flashed through her mind.

Then the stranger stepped back and Valerie watched, speechless, as she turned and disappeared into the native streets.

"Well, what was *that* all about?" Derek exclaimed, tucking the palette into Valerie's knapsack. "What did she whisper?"

"She said, 'It begins now. And I will follow you.'" Valerie touched her cheek. "What do you suppose that means?"

"I don't know, girlfriend." Derek laughed, crinkling the light patches under his eyes. "But if I were you and some good-looking woman suddenly appeared and offered to follow me home, I'd be pretty turned on. Oh, that reminds me." He looked at his watch. "There's another attractive woman expecting to meet both of us in just about an hour. We better hurry up."

"Yes, of course." Valerie linked her arm in his and guided him toward the brass merchants. She looked around for any sign of the mysterious woman but saw none. Follow her home? Well, that wasn't going to happen. She had been living in a tent for the last six months. She had no home at all.

CHAPTER V:
EL FISHAWY

Laden with packages, they made their way awkwardly around chicken crates and motorbikes into the street of the jewelers. At the end of a row of tiny shops, all of which seemed to sell the same thing, they turned sharply to the right.

"Oh, loook!" Derek halted suddenly before an alley.

Shaded on both sides and with only a thin strip of sunlight along the middle, the street had been claimed as a coffeehouse. Clusters of men sat along the walls sipping from glasses and smoking hookahs while peddlers made their way back and forth among them. Here and there ragged children held out their small hands. Heavy mirrors in carved frames hung on both walls, doubling the images and the confusion in the street. From a radio somewhere overhead, the whiny strumming of the oud and the plaintive Koranic singing of Umme Koulsoum covered the buzz of conversation.

Valerie laid her hand on his shoulder. "This is it, Derek. El Fishawy. The heart of the souq. Every visitor to Cairo ends up here. Let me buy you a drink, Egyptian style."

"Oh, I love it! Looks like something from an Agatha Christie movie. Is this the place where people meet Inspector Poirot, that French detective?"

"Belgian. He was Belgian." Valerie rolled her eyes.

They fitted themselves into the line of men on the benches and chairs along the wall. An aproned waiter approached and stood silently. Valerie knew he waited for the foreigners to speak so as to decide which of his half dozen languages to use with them.

"Coffee with cardamom, please," Valerie ordered in Arabic, and he smiled. "For both of us," she added. "And *sheesha* for one."

Derek studied the walls of the street café and the ornate covered windows that ran along the upper stories of the buildings on both sides. "Wow, this place looks medieval."

"It is medieval. All but the electricity." She pointed to the rows of cables strung loosely along the tops of the wall on all sides. "It's a wonder there aren't more fires."

In a moment an old man, with the tilted gait of some lifelong disability, set the tall *sheesha* pipe down on the ground between them. From his pocket he drew out a plug of something fibrous and laid it on the clay stopper before turning away. A boy followed behind him with a small cauldron on a chain. Derek watched, clearly intrigued, as the boy picked up one of the glowing coals with a pincer and dropped it onto the wad of *sheesha*.

Valerie took a long pull on the mouthpiece and heard the satisfying gurgle of water. She leaned back on the cushioned bench and blew out a stream of sweet blue smoke. "All right, now tell me about this Auset person."

Derek crossed his legs, watching the bubbles percolate in the glass vessel. "Uh, well, there's not much to tell. I know her from New York, where she studied at Columbia. She's Jewish but her father is Arab, believe it or not. In the export business. She took me everywhere in January. We became…close." He lowered his eyes coquettishly.

A battered metal tray appeared on the table, crowded with cups and a badly chipped enameled pot. Valerie poured the spicy coffee into both their cups. "You and an Egyptian woman? In all the years I've known you, you've never looked at a woman."

"Oh, I never do. For sure. But it didn't seem to matter. She was really persistent, and…I don't know. It just happened." He picked up his cup and sipped delicately.

"Well, I can hardly wait to meet this woman who had the power to turn *your* head." She puffed again, tasting the honey-sweetened tobacco, visualizing him in the arms of some Egyptian siren. Somewhere overhead the recorded voice of Umme Koulsoum still sang of love.

"Don't worry, my sweet. You'll always be my significant other. Lord knows, we both are 'other,' aren't we? Do you think we'll ever settle down and have a real life?"

At that moment, a woman walked up behind him and laid her hands on his shoulders. Her loose, uncovered hair contrasted with the somber green abaya she wore which, for all its volume, could not conceal the fact that she was pregnant.

Obviously startled, he twisted around suddenly. "Auset! How are…" As he stood up to offer her his chair, his eyes traveled downward from her face and gradually widened in alarm. "…you?"

"Sorry I'm late." She kissed him lightly on his cheek and sat down in his place.

His eyes fixed on the woman's midsection, Derek drew over another chair and dropped down wordlessly next to her. Shock and a hint of fear played over his face.

"Yes, *Habibi*, it's yours." Auset made herself comfortable on the narrow seat. "One of life's little ironies." Turning her attention away from him, she offered her hand across the table. "And you must be Valerie. He's told me all about you! Ooh! I love your desert hat. Very Indiana Jones! He didn't mention the bandage, though."

"Uh, thank you." Valerie found herself smiling. Auset's cheer was infectious. Her speech was almost masculine in its straightforwardness, but her face and voluptuous body were all woman. Large Semitic eyes were outlined with sable lashes that needed no kohl, and her lips were full and sensual. Valerie glanced with sympathy at her old friend. The poor man was lucky to merely be seduced and not devoured alive.

Auset turned back to the still-speechless Derek, who stared at the bulge of his descendant the way a man stares at a small, dangerous animal. She laid her hand on his. "Relax, dear. It's all right! My father won't have you killed. Or me. It took a while, but he and mother have gotten used to it finally."

He grasped her fingers. "Auset. Why didn't you write and tell me? You must have known I would care."

She slid her hand out of his gentle grip. "Whatever for? You wouldn't have run back here to marry me, would you?"

"I might have. I don't know. Well, maybe not. But I'd have… well…sent money or something. A single mother alone in Egypt? Don't they stone women for that?"

She leaned back, crossing her legs with difficulty under the swelling of new life. "Well, there are a few people in Egypt nowadays who would still do that. Fortunately, that does not include my family. My father was horrified, of course, and refused to talk to me for a few weeks, but my mother defended me. When I got my own apartment in Zamalek and was careful not to embarrass them in front of their neighbors and customers, things settled down. Here, let me give you the address and phone number."

"Yes, of course. We have to talk." His eyes darted around, as if trying to pick one of the questions that hovered in the air. "What religion will you raise him in?" he blurted suddenly.

"You mean will I tell him God is called Allah or Jehovah or Lord Jesus? So that he can fight for one of them against the others?" She looked heavenward in feigned despair. "Everyone has got a story. Well, don't worry, my songbird, he will hear all of them. Just like I did."

"Uh...speaking of songbird, Derek, don't you have a performance soon?" Valerie looked at her watch.

"Oh, hell! Right!" He jumped from his chair as if jolted by electricity. "I'm sorry. There's just so much going on. I have to get made up, costumed, warm up my voice. You know." He pressed fingertips to the side of his head. "Can we discuss this some more tomorrow, Auset? I can't think just now." He kissed them both lightly on their cheeks and hurried away just short of running.

Auset laughed. "If I didn't know him better, I would have called that a panicky escape."

Valerie took a long drag on her *sheesha*. The slight light-headedness she felt finally dispelled the nervousness that had driven her all day. She leaned back and allowed herself to be studied by the other woman.

"So, you are an Egyptologist," Auset said. "You can read the stories on the walls in our tombs and temples."

"Yes, I can, when there's something to read." She blew out smoke in a long, slow stream. "A lot of them are damaged, though. By vandals, religious rivals, time."

"I know. I was in the Valley of the Kings last year to see the royal tombs. The walls are covered now by glass panels."

"Yes, to keep people's hands off the paintings. The Antiquities people want to do it in the temples too for the same reason, to stop people defacing the inscriptions. So many of the old texts are ruined now."

Auset nodded sympathetically. "I guess it's because people see the inscriptions just as decoration. They forget the temple used to be holy. Marking the walls is like defacing an ancient Torah or Koran. The glass is a good idea."

"You're the first Egyptian I've met who has shown any appreciation of the old religion. I would love to show you—" Valerie looked past Auset's shoulder suddenly and stopped.

"Quelle extraordinaire coincidence!"

A voice smooth as silk came from the peculiar man who walked toward them. He had a long oval face with wide, almost Asiatic eyes. An overlong nose dropped to full Negroid lips, conspicuous on the face of a white European. His slender upper body swelled at the hips like a woman's, although the distortion was artfully diminished by well-tailored white linen trousers. It was obvious that he dressed with attention and expense, and he had the quiet demeanor of one used to being accommodated.

Valerie stood up and pressed dry lips together. "Dr. Vanderschmitt."

"Well, Miss Foret. A surprise to find you here, of all places. I would have thought you would be at work." He inclined his head as he spoke in slightly Dutch-accented English. His voice, when he spoke, had neither volume nor emotion.

"I came in for a few days to purchase supplies." She indicated the pile of packages at the side of the table. "Excuse me. This is Auset, a friend of mine. Auset, this is Volker Vanderschmitt, a colleague in the Archaeology Department at Brussels University."

"Colleague? Perhaps you have not been informed. I have been appointed Chairman and Head of Excavations." He smiled and pursed his full lips at the same time.

"Uh, well, I never received an official announcement. As you know, I've been out at Ghard Abu Sennan, more or less out of touch." While she spoke, he turned away and surveyed the clientele of the café, as if she did not deserve his full attention. He was beginning to get on her nerves.

He cleared his throat. "Were you not aware that field operations must remain in weekly contact with the University Committee? Since you have omitted to do so I came, among other things, to find out what exactly you are doing. You see, the committee is distressed that you are digging at a site other than the one proposed."

"I explained all that ages ago. There are unmistakable indications. Besides—"

He went on, overriding her reply. "Therefore, the committee has decided it would be more advantageous to have a man—a senior scholar—directly oversee the project. That would be myself." He paused, letting her absorb the full weight of the announcement. "I will of course accompany you to the excavation site when you return. I assume that will be in the near future? Or do you plan to extend your shopping trip?"

Valerie fought against the urge to sit down, not wanting to have to look up at him. Her voice, when she replied, was tight. "Yes. Tomorrow night. At dusk. You can follow along then."

"Follow along? Ah, yes, of course. I will hire my own camel and be ready at that time. Since you speak Arabic, you can inform your team of the change in supervision."

Without looking at her superior, Valerie gathered up her packages. "Uh, would you excuse us now? We still have errands to settle." She glanced at Auset, who stood up with her, pulling her own purse strap over her shoulder.

"Yes, of course. I too have obligations." He gave a hint of a military bow in Auset's direction. "Congratulations on the blessed event."

"Thank you, Mr. Vanderschmitt." Auset laid her arm protectively over her abdomen.

"Dr. Vanderschmitt," he corrected, his eyes half-closed.

"Sorry. *Doctor* Vanderschmitt." Auset was already away from the table.

"Until tomorrow evening, then." Valerie laid several five-pound notes on the table and stepped past him without offering her hand. It was a slight no one could overlook.

❖

Vanderschmitt watched his junior colleague hurry away from him. Infuriating creature, he thought. A young European woman wearing what amounted to men's clothing and smoking a *nargileh* in front of the whole street. Despicable behavior. And her suggestion that he "follow along," as if he were a servant rather than the official head of the excavation was…unforgivable. Did she not realize what trouble she was in?

He knew her type; every generation had them. Ambitious women, contemptuous of authority and of the whole institution. Emasculating, unnatural women like Mead, Goodall, Hawkes, Fossey, who invaded the field sciences to plant their flags. Or like Monique, who thwarted men in other ways. They were a plague, exploiting men's natural desires.

Monique. He still remembered the sting of her hand on his face, the shock of looking down and seeing his white jacket flecked with his own blood.

He continued to stare at the street long after Valerie had disappeared into the crowd. No woman would ever humiliate him that way again. He was chairman of a department now; he was the authority, and she was his subordinate. If she did not yet know her place, he would certainly teach it to her.

CHAPTER VI:
HALF IN MYTH; WHOLE IN NATURE

Gluck's *Orfeo*. Such a beautiful opera with such a preposterous libretto, Valerie thought. Maybe it was just her unbandaged cheek that itched, irritating her. Her fingers crept obsessively to the spot near her ear to touch the wound. Orpheus's great aria "Che farò senza Euridice" thrilled her briefly, but then she decided it was the Orpheus myth itself that annoyed her. She was a scientist and knew what love was. Hormones, nothing but hormones, and all the rest was loneliness. Transcendent love was a myth, a cruel lie that kept the heart craving. Certainly none of *her* lovers would go into the underworld to save her. Jameela least of all.

Valerie thought suddenly of the woman of the souq who had promised to follow her. She looked around at the well-coiffed ladies and gentlemen who sat with her in the mezzanine. Well, it was clear no Arabian femme fatale had followed her there. Damn. She felt like a fool even thinking about it.

The chorus of "Trionfi Amore!" signaled the end of the opera, and she rose with the rest of the audience to applaud. When the curtain calls were over, she threaded her way back to the dressing rooms.

As always, the backstage corridor was crowded with admirers chirping their adulation of the singer. Derek was already out of his costume and in street clothes, but his stage makeup was still in place. A part of him remained in myth as he let himself be kissed and complimented. "Flowers? How lovely! Recorded? Yes, Deutsche Grammophon. So glad you could come. Roses, oooh, how sweeeeet!"

Valerie kissed him quickly and stepped past him to wait at his dressing table until he came in, still chattering and flush with excitement.

"My, how pretty you are tonight with that lovely hair all tucked up—just for me—and the teensy-weensiest bit of mascara around those heavenly eyes! No nasty bandage, I'm glad to see. And, dear Lord, she's wearing a dress! Now if only you didn't have those muscley arms, my sweet." He kissed her again.

"Muscles are what you get when you dig in the ground all day. But that's not something you choirboys would know about, is it?" She play-punched his shoulder.

He sat down before the mirror and began to apply thick layers of cold cream to his cheeks and neck. "Oh, you are *such* a bully, my dear. *Ta chère Maman* had no idea what you'd grow up to be! A pity I never met her. I'd have told her a few things!"

"No chance of that. I barely met her myself, since she died when I was six. I told you that. But I don't think Maman would have approved of you either, my little opera queen who makes babies. By the way, is Auset here tonight?"

"No, she reminded me the last time she came to one of my performances she got pregnant. I said I'd call tomorrow and we'd make plans to get together."

"Uh, you might want to make that call tonight." Valerie leaned against the back of his chair.

"Why? What's going on?" He snatched up tissues to wipe makeup-tinted cold cream from his throat.

"Derek, darling. We have an emergency. My department chairman has tracked me down and is about to take the excavation away from me."

The singer turned around to face her, Orpheus mascara magnifying his already large eyes. "I don't understand. Did you tell him you've found something?"

"No, of course not. He'll try to publish it under his own name. He's a predator, a hyena, showing up after someone else's hunt. Once he's gotten his hands on the discovery, I become invisible. We *have* to open the tomb before he gets there."

"Before he gets there? What"—his voice dropped in pitch and volume—"does that mean?"

"It means we have to leave a day before he does."

Derek threw his makeup-stained towel aside. "But the day before he leaves is—"

"Tonight." She nodded.

"Tonight?" His jaw fell behind pursed lips, and his eyebrows did a ballet from astonishment to indignation. "I…just…sang…an…entire…opera."

She picked up his leather rucksack from a chair and began dropping in objects from the dressing room table: cold cream, towel, bar of soap, toothbrush. "You've got clean socks and undies along, I assume? Good. I've already called my foreman. We'll take a taxi from here to the stable in Giza where he's waiting with the camels. I'll change there." She zipped up his bag and reached for the doorknob.

He stood dumbfounded, his scowl rendered ferocious by stage-makeup eyebrows. He looked at his wristwatch. "But it's—"

She threw his rucksack over her shoulder and opened the door. "Don't whine, Derek. Midnight is perfect. Nice and cool."

❖

Midnight was long past when the little caravan set out southwestward over the Giza plateau. Four camels padded, somnambulant. Ahmed drew ahead, leading the heavily laden pack animal and leaving the two friends to their own company behind him.

They rode without speaking, adapting the sway of their bodies to the lopsided gait of their mounts. In the quiet of the desert they listened to the chuffing of the camels, the soft flopping of the animals' feet, the creaking of the saddle frames.

Derek fidgeted on his unfamiliar seat, leaning forward, then sideways, fishing with his foot for a stirrup that was not there. "Valerie, I'm sure we look really fabulous on these camels, but my butt's killing me. Is there any special reason that we're not riding in a nice jeep?"

"Very special. No road. The sand's hard-packed here, but it gets very soft about a kilometer from the excavation and won't support the weight of a car."

"What's it like at the camp? Am I going to have to sleep on the sand? I have such sensitive skin." He touched his brow.

"Don't worry your pretty head, Derek. The workers sleep on mats in a common tent, but I have a tent all to myself. You'll be accorded the status of weakling, thus permitted to sleep on a camp bed there."

"'Weakling' is fine with me. I don't have to sleep on rocks to prove I'm a man."

"No, you don't. And since we're on the subject, what'll you do about Auset?"

"I called her while you were changing and apologized for leaving. When I get back to Cairo, I'll find out what she needs. You know, just because I'm gay doesn't mean I'm irresponsible. And, well…the more I think about having an Egyptian son, the more it pleases me. I like these people."

"I do too. But not all of them like us." She raised her hand to the barely closed wound that she had covered with her head cloth. "I told you I was accosted at the pyramids by fundamentalists. What I didn't tell you is that I nearly shot one of them."

"Girlfriend, you can't go around shooting people for that. And besides, you're asking for trouble. You're doing the Antiquities president's wife, remember?" He looked pensive. "Weren't you already getting in trouble back in school for that sort of thing? Some little Egyptian girl they caught you in bed with?"

"She was Moroccan. I forgot I told you that story. Yes, the nuns expelled her, but they couldn't send me home, so they simply beat me and locked me in a dark room for the rest of the night. I was nine years old. After that I simply made up friends I couldn't lose—Cleopatra, Hatchepsut, Ramses…" Her voice trailed off as she remembered loneliness.

"I know what you mean. Only in my case, it was Batman and Robin." He sighed. "We spend our lives looking for love, don't we? And here we are, adults, still looking. Or have you found it?"

She dropped her voice, although Ahmed was a good hundred meters ahead of them. "With Jameela? I don't think climbing through a window for a few hours of forbidden sex with a powerful man's wife counts as true love."

"Oooh, when you say it like that, it sounds delicious!"

"Yes, but dangerous. Islam is just as hostile as Christianity is to people like us. More so. They all go by the same book of rules."

"What's the answer, then? What religion would accept us?"

The nocturnal predators became audible—the shriek of a kestrel, the high-pitched yipping of desert foxes, and farther away the deeper bark of the jackal.

"Listen to them. They were here long before there was a West. Before there were pharaohs, even. The Egyptians made a theology of them."

"Vultures and jackals and snakes, oh my!"

"Don't scoff at vultures and snakes, Derek. They've survived for millennia in a searing desert. Particularly those two. They were revered as protectors of Pharaoh. That's why their heads are on his crown. Not to mention that we wouldn't dare eat them. But for a million years, they've eaten us."

"Eeeeewwww!"

"It's just the balance of things." She patted her knapsack, which hung from the horn of her saddle. "The papyrus that woman gave me yesterday lists certain crimes. Holding back the Nile flood, driving animals from their pasture, for example. Even tampering with the merchants' scales. It's all about balance."

"Hmm." Derek rode for a while without responding. "God's world as ecosystem. I like that. But who was that woman anyhow—the one who gave you the palette and scroll? Did you ever find out?"

"No, I didn't have a chance to ask around the souq."

"She was a looker, too. Do you think she was making a pass?"

"I dunno. I've been thinking about it."

"I'll bet you have, girlfriend," he said dreamily.

In the bluish desert light Valerie watched his outline slouch as he managed to doze even while in the awkward camel saddle. Suddenly a screech cut through the darkness, and a ragged form swept across the face of the moon.

"Huh? What the hell was that?" He lurched upright.

Valerie laughed. "You'd better stay awake, *chéri.* Looks like there's a vulture watching."

"A vulture? Oh, Jesus," he muttered.

She chuckled again. "Jesus? I don't think so. We're *way* out of his jurisdiction."

CHAPTER VII:
THE TOMB

*A*lhamdulillah!" Ahmed exclaimed as the excavation came into sight.

Slouched in a semitrance from the six hours of monotonous rocking, Valerie was startled by his voice. She squinted through the folds of her head cloth at the blurred ellipse of activity a shade darker than the eye-scorching sand on both sides of it and the featureless shapes moving in the distance. "It looks like everyone's already up working. That's a good sign."

"Look!" Derek awoke as well and leaned forward, rubbing his back. "They've seen us too. Someone's running out to meet us."

"It is my son," Ahmed said with quiet pride.

The boy waved both hands excitedly, and as he neared, Valerie could see that his galabaya was torn in several places.

He met the oncoming camels and then danced alongside them, breathless. "*As salaamu 'alaykum.* Father! Doktor Foret! Come along, quickly. We have found a door!"

"Good man, Ibrim! Let's have a look."

At the edge of the excavation site, the four animals knelt down first at the front and then at the back and blinked long eyelashes at the boy who took their reins. Valerie and Ahmed swung their legs over the saddle post with the ease of long familiarity.

Glancing behind her, Valerie watched Derek pry himself with obvious effort from his own mount. "You okay?" she asked.

"I'm fine, really. I'll be along in a sec." He stamped his feet and squeezed the back of his thighs, encouraging circulation, then limped behind the others.

In and around the pit, Arab workers leaned on their shovels and greeted the archaeologist as she arrived. She felt a wave of affection for the men who had labored while she was away. She offered her hand first to Hamada, Ahmed's second in command. A slender man in a wide turban from a family of Sufis, he had a mysterious authority. Though she had never heard him raise his voice, he had kept the men working intensely while she was away. "Hamada, thank you. Selim, good job. Thank you for all your work, Shafik." She met each of them eye to eye for a moment as she walked past them. "Gamel, can I use your torch? Thank you." She clicked the switch once, to test the batteries.

Valerie stepped down into the cut they had made in the chalky ground. It was obvious that in their hurry to uncover the ramp and tomb entrance, the men had dug only the narrowest channel. She felt the abrasions of the shale and limestone chips on both sides and understood why everyone's clothing looked so ragged. Finally she stood at the end of the pit before what was unmistakably a door. She pressed her hand against it.

Sealed. The lumps of clay were still pressed into the door lintel and jamb, and the priests' markings were still readable. She ran fingers gently over the priestly seal, a vertical cartouche of the Anubis jackal squatting on a platform over nine captives. It was an efficient way of suggesting harm to any who might violate the tomb.

"Have you taken pictures of the seal?" she called up to the men at the edge of the pit.

"Yes, many pictures," one of them said.

"All right then. Ahmed, have the men break it open."

The workers chiseled around the sides of the mud-brick door and pulled at it with crowbars. A section broke away; then the whole door collapsed in a shower of mud bricks. They stepped back, fanning at the cloud of dust until it settled.

Derek threaded his way down the ramp to join them. "Oh! It's just a tunnel!" He peered into the darkness.

"There's supposed to be a tunnel." Valerie stepped over the rubble, swinging the light beam back and forth, illuminating rough-cut stone walls and the floor, which inclined gently downward. At the end of the corridor, they stood before a second sealed doorway.

"Give me your tools, Ahmed," Valerie said, hooking the flashlight onto her belt. The foreman handed over chisel and hammer, and she gave a single tap with the chisel tip, knocking away a chip from the surface. "Wood covered with mud plaster. Standard."

She scraped a layer of plaster from the surface and incised a circle a few centimeters in diameter. Euphoric but exhausted, she wiped her sleeve across her face and began hammering. In three firm taps she was through.

There was a faint whoosh of air moving from one pressure to another. She sniffed carefully. "No organic gasses." She hammered around the periphery, enlarging the hole to the size of a fist. Pressing her forehead to the wood over the aperture, she peered in over the rim of the flashlight, waiting for her eye to adapt. In a moment she could see it. She felt like weeping.

The circle of light slid along a wing to a red-orange disk flanked by cobras, then to another wing. Unmistakable. The merged goddesses of Upper and Lower Egypt.

"*Bonjour, Mesdames,*" she murmured through the hole. "Have you been waiting for me? God knows, I've been waiting for you." She stepped back and covered her face again with her head cloth. "Finish the job, Ahmed."

The foreman hooked the crowbar into the wood and pushed the iron bar sideways. The door split cleanly at the center and fell in two pieces against the opposite walls. The group waited for a few moments, and then Valerie stepped inside. She turned slowly, sweeping her light beam like a lighthouse, in a full circle.

"Oh…yes," she exhaled.

The four walls were covered in brilliant colors. Scenes, texts, invocations called out to her as if they had sound. The floor was cluttered with objects, and she dared not take another step for fear of trampling on them.

She was drenched with sweat and could scarcely breathe in the dust that still hung in the air. Yet when she drew off the long twisted cloth from her head, it seemed as if a breeze wafted over her face, cooling the fever of her wound. She felt a familiarity, a powerful déjà vu, like a traveler coming home. The texts on the wall seemed private messages, and the mummy, which she knew with certainty would be there, waited for her alone.

"Oh…wow," Derek whispered from the doorway. Around him in the tunnel the men murmured, "*Alhamdulillah.*"

Valerie turned again, holding the light for a moment on each object on the floor in front of her. A statue of Osiris stood in one corner of the chamber. To his right against one wall a wooden bed stood on slender animal legs with lion heads carved at the upper end. Along the opposite wall, chests of wood and ivory were lined up, with alabaster vessels spread out over them.

One object drew her like a lure and she crouched in front of it, illuminating it with her flashlight. A river barque, of gold leaf hammered over wood, nearly a meter in length from swanlike prow to the high curved stern. At the center, the naos-cabin housed a gleaming sphere. She dared not touch it, but its sheen suggested it was solid gold. Ra in his essence and glory, and ten painted wooden gods sailed in state with him.

"Beautiful," Ahmed said softly. "This god has long spear, goddesses have horns and feathers and every little thing. Is great piece of art."

"More than art, Ahmed. This was to the ancients like a cross to a Christian. More, even." She inhaled with effort, needing air again. "This is the Barque of the Sun. The emblem of their living world."

Derek had crept into the chamber behind them. "What's this writing here, in the long columns?"

Valerie stood up from a crouch, fighting sudden vertigo. "That's a calendar, twelve thirty-day months ending in July. The last five days were just tacked on." She took a cautious step closer to the wall. "It looks like this man died then, just before the beginning of the New Year. That's curious—"

"Ho! What's this?" he interrupted from behind her. "Men kissing? Is there something you haven't told me, girlfriend?" He pointed toward a drawing of two male faces touching.

"What? Oh, that's the God's kiss. To empower the king for the New Year. It's the transfer of knowledge, not romance." She coughed dryly. "Sorry to disappoint you."

Something moved in the corner of her eye, and she spun around to shine the flashlight on it. A parrot-like bird perched on the top of the lion's bed. In the flashlight beam the bird's eyes ignited as it tilted its head, as if studying them. Then it lifted from the bed, fluttered over her head, and disappeared.

"How did a bird fly down here? And what's a bird doing this far out in the desert?" No one answered, and pivoting around made her suddenly realize how little strength was left in her legs. And the air was stifling.

"Hey, come here. You have to see this." Derek stood transfixed before the opposite wall of the tomb.

"What? Another kiss?" Rubbing the muscles above her knees, Valerie went to stand beside him, adding her light to his. Two circles danced over the scene of a king bestowing a gift upon a kneeling man. Pharaoh wore the double crown of Upper and Lower Egypt. The maternal Vulture hovered over him with outspread wings.

"Look at the guy who's kneeling. With the African features. Jeez, Valerie. Am I narcissistic or does he look just like *me*?"

She leaned on his shoulder. "He does, kind of. Nubian, probably. Owner of the tomb." She was mumbling, scarcely able to form words. Her mouth felt like paper. With a shaking hand she unhooked her canteen and took a long drink. Her heart would not stop pounding. She felt her hair hanging in clammy ringlets around her face, and she was unsteady on her feet. One more wall to see, she thought. Three more minutes.

She shone her light beam on the west wall and smiled in spite of her increasing vertigo. It was a scene every Egyptologist would know, the Weighing of the Heart in the Underworld. She took another drink of water and shook her head, trying to clear it.

Still light-headed, she stepped forward toward the Great Balance, blinking to focus her eyes in the insufficient light. The painted gods on both sides seemed to shimmer and move, their eyes registering her presence. She felt drawn into the scene itself, and she knew suddenly whose heart lay on the scale. She shrank before the unrelenting gaze of the Jackal-god and the Ibis-scribe, and she heard the whispering of the judges. She covered her eyes, murmuring, "You live on truth…and gulp down truth…Let me enter in. I am without falsehood…" Then she stumbled backward.

Familiar hands reached toward her as she heard herself condemned—and she collapsed unconscious on the floor of the tomb.

CHAPTER VIII:
REKEMHEB

W ell, it's about time, Miss Drama Queen."
Valerie awoke to the light of an oil lamp somewhere below her feet and the smiling face of Derek hovering over her. Slowly, lethargically, she came to her senses.

"I fainted, didn't I? *Merde*. In front of all the men."

He wiped her face with a damp cloth. "Don't worry about it. You actually came to right away, but you were babbling, so we carried you in here for a good long sleep. I thought I was the weak one, but I guess you don't have superpowers either."

"Is everything okay? I mean with the tomb?"

"Yes, the tomb is fine. Ahmed let everyone in to see it and then got them busy unloading the supplies. He gave them the afternoon off for a little celebration, and they kept coming by to ask if you were okay. Uh….what's the matter? Why are you looking at me that way?"

"Not you, behind you on the chair. It's the bird again, the one we saw in the tomb. Something's not right…"

Derek twisted around to look over his shoulder and shot up from the chair as if jolted. "God. What is this thing?" The creature remained, unruffled, on the back of the chair.

Derek leaned toward it, peering at its head. "It doesn't have a beak or feathers on its head, just a little dark face." He swallowed hard. "My face."

The bird bobbed up and down as if agreeing and walked sideways along the chair back. Then, as if startled, it lifted off the chair and swooped out through the tent entrance.

"It can't be." Valerie sat up on her cot. "God help us. It just can't be." She took hold of her friend's arm. "Derek, listen! It came for us. I know it came for us. We have to follow it!"

He shook his head. "What are you talking about? That makes no sense."

She pounded her feet into her boots without lacing them and stood up. Snatching a flashlight, she stumbled out of the tent, stepping awkwardly over flapping shoestrings. The creature hovered a few meters away, defying gravity.

"Just grab another light and come on!" she hissed back into the tent.

Derek emerged and the creature fluttered on toward the excavation. It circled once, as if looking to see if anyone followed, and descended the ramp into the tomb.

Valerie took a deep breath. "Listen. What we just saw, I think… well, it looks like…" She inhaled deeply. "A Ba-bird." To give her trembling hands something to do, she knelt down to finally lace her shoes. "A dead man's soul."

"A dead man's soul? With my face? Excuse me? I may be out of my element here, but I'm pretty sure *I am not dead*!"

"No, No! It can't be *your* Ba. What am I saying? It can't be anyone's Ba. It's a myth." She lurched to her feet again. "Come on. Just follow the damned thing!" She dragged him by the elbow toward the hole in the desert floor. "And if you're running, you can keep your knees from shaking."

"If that's your encouragement speech, it needs work," he said, huffing alongside of her.

They reached the narrow channel to the tomb and were slowed immediately by the sharp limestone. "Ow!" Derek grunted. "I just tore my shirt." At the foot of the ramp, before the entrance, a figure curled up in a blanket startled awake.

"Ahmed, did you see the bird fly past you?"

He stood up. "Ah, Dr. Foret. You are well again. *Alhamdulillah.* A bird? No, I saw nothing. Is something wrong? Should I call the men?"

"Thank you, Ahmed. That's not necessary. But you can go back to the tent. Now that I'm rested, I want to look around in the tomb again. There's no need for you to stand guard. Go and get a good night's sleep."

"Are you sure? All right, Doktor. But please call me if you need anything." He shuffled up the ramp, throwing his blanket over his shoulder.

Their fear dissipated by the delay, they stepped over the rubble that once was the doorway and hurried along the stone tunnel. Valerie noted that the men had cleaned away much of the dirt that had been underfoot and was grateful. At the entrance to the tomb chamber, they stopped and shone their flashlights inside.

The not-quite-bird waited for them. Perched at the head of the lion bed, the creature half opened its wings once. At the moment they stepped into the chamber, it rose from the bed and flew into the wall.

"Where the hell did he go?" They shone their flashlight beams along the edge of the ceiling, rotating to illuminate all four walls.

"Look!" Derek lowered his beam to the picture that took up much of the wall space behind the lion bed. "There he is, in the painting!" He focused his light on the painted animal perched on top of the Balance.

Valerie shook her head. "That's ridiculous. There's got to be a hole in the wall someplace. Something that we missed before." She stepped back, perplexed.

"I don't see any hole, but I do see the Ba thing," Derek insisted. "Right there in the middle of that scene."

"That's the Hall of Judgment scene, in the Duat. But that doesn't explain—"

"Duat? What's that? And why is there a balance?" He stepped closer. "Look, this guy here on the end in a white skirt, he has the same face as the bird. My face. Man, my face is all over the place! What the hell is going on?"

"Slow down. Let me explain," she began, and her shift to the voice of the lecturer had a calming effect on them both. "The Duat is the hereafter, where the heart of the deceased is weighed against the feather of justice. The figure there in the kilt is the deceased or, rather, his Ka spirit. The Ka and the Ba have the same face because they're both the dead man. But put your mind at ease, Derek. It's not you. Look, here's his name, right beside it. Rek-em-heb."

"Rek-em-heb," Derek repeated, as if savoring the strange new sound.

She shone her flashlight again along the juncture between wall and ceiling. The bizarre creature had to have landed someplace. She was determined to find it and the explanation for its existence.

"Yes. Rekemheb. He's about to enter the afterlife, but only if his heart is light. He'll be judged by the forty-two judges all around the Hall." She turned around and shone the light beam on the juncture on the opposite side of the chamber. "Maybe it has a nest."

"But why does this Ka guy look so much like me?" Derek persisted, leaning close to the image.

"He's probably Nubian. Maybe your ancestors were too."

"How would I know?" He shrugged and pronounced the name again. "Rekemheb."

Behind Anubis, the painted figure of the Ka opened his eyes.

Valerie took hold of his arm. "Say it again, Derek."

"Huh? What's happening?" His voice rose in pitch.

"Say it!" she hissed.

"Rekemheb," Derek said tentatively.

She squeezed his arm tightly.

"Rekemheb. *Rek-em-heb!*"

The figure brightened, became luminescent, and the fragrance of fruit and flowers wafted over them. They stepped back a pace as the glowing figure turned out of profile and stepped onto the tomb floor before them.

"Rekemheb," it said.

CHAPTER IX:
REVELATION

Silence. Long moments of stupefied silence. As if dream-paralyzed, Valerie's muscles would not move. The wounded side of her head pounded fiercely, and her disbelieving mind would not compute. Finally fragments of perception filtered through, like insects through a screen, separately, too few to be interpreted. Nubian features. Side lock. White kilt down to the ankles. Sandals. Slowly the particles aggregated to a whole, forcing her to a frightening logic.

He was a living Ka.

She panted through dry lips, waiting for light or rescue to come, to banish the illusion. She could hear her own labored breathing as her thumping heart signaled flight. If there could be a Ka, then there must also be…

Derek's flashlight crashed to the stone floor, startling her and saving her from the terrifying conclusion.

The impossible thing tilted its head in the same way as Derek had moments before and repeated, as if talking to an infant, "*Rek. em. heb.*" He laid a shimmering hand on a shimmering chest.

She inhaled deeply. "Val," she croaked. A useless sound that elicited no response. Then she repeated, "*Val. er. ee,*" imitating his gesture.

The apparition took no notice, fixing his gaze on the dumbstruck American whose eyes were wider than she had ever seen. The glowing figure reached out a hand to touch him on the shoulder.

He flinched away. His voice barely had tone. "What…is…it?"

Valerie replied in a soft monotone. "I…think it is his Ka. The…uh, spirit of the man entombed here."

"Riiight." His eyes riveted on the spectre, Derek knelt and picked up his flashlight. He held it out, pressing its broken On switch. He pressed it again and again, the dead thing wobbling uselessly in his hand.

The Ka spoke again. Several words. His voice was slightly detached, almost musical, as if on a gramophone record. Slightly staccato sounds, not unpleasant.

Valerie realized suddenly that she understood, and the realization was a comfort. Something about him fit into her science. "He's speaking Middle Egyptian, Derek," she whispered. "For God's sake. I understand him."

"Uh-huh." He was still in a stupor.

"He's talking to you, Derek. I think he said…'Grandchild.'"

The Ka spoke again, slowly, as if taking pains to be understood, and Valerie struggled to separate out the sounds. He repeated himself, giving her time to comprehend.

When she grasped the sense of what she was hearing, she laughed softly. "I should have guessed. He's asking your name. Tell him."

The singer regained his composure. "My name. Yes. Uh…" He pointed at the center of his chest and said, "I am Derek."

The spectre repeated "Ayemderak" and nodded with satisfaction.

"Close enough," Derek murmured.

The spectre continued talking and Valerie listened, frowning in concentration, trying to match sounds to words she had only ever seen written. "I believe he said he is pleased that you are fat."

Derek finally tore his eyes from the spectacle and looked down at himself. "What? He said fat? I'm not fat. Tell him…I am considered handsome."

"I think he means prosperous. But why don't I ask him why he calls you grandchild?" She searched her memory and spoke in short, stiff phrases, recasting ceremonial language she had never heard into small talk.

The Ka listened, frowning slightly, and then replied.

Valerie listened in turn, reversing linguistic direction. "'You are…child of my child…foretold in the…prophecy of the jewel. 'No,' she corrected herself. "'Of the amulet. You are the…hundredth generation.'" She realized what she had just translated and turned back to the glowing entity. "Prophecy? Amulet?"

"The gift of Meremptah." The Ka stepped to the opposite wall and laid his hand on the scene of Pharaoh bestowing an amulet on the kneeling figure. "At the New Year, the Great King made this gift to me."

Valerie nodded, remembering. The amulet. Of course. The only object on the tomb wall painted in gold. Her head throbbed, and she pressed her hand over her ear as she struggled with the unfamiliar words. "Where does your mummy lie?"

The Ka raised both his hands in apparent joy. He reached up to touch the image of the Ba at the top of the Balance. "Here within." The transparent finger tapped on the wall. "Touch here," the Ka said, stepping aside.

Obediently, Valerie stepped forward and studied the human-headed bird. Seeing it close-up, she realized that it bulged slightly from the surface of the wall, like a blister. She tapped on it as the Ka had done. When nothing happened, she pressed harder with two fingers. Suddenly, the image gave way, and within the wall they could hear the gritty sound of a sliding bolt.

With the rumble of stone against stone, the painted image of the mummified Osiris edged outward from the wall like a puzzle piece and slid toward them into the chamber. "Look, the God of the Dead is himself the door! These people had a sense of poetry."

She knelt down as soon as the opening permitted it and shone the flashlight beam into the darkness behind it. The two of them peered in together. Light sparkled back at them from a thousand places, like birds fluttering.

"*Pu...tain,*" she whispered.

The two of them put their shoulders to the Osiris door, forcing it farther outward on its arc. Finally Valerie could press herself through the opening into the burial chamber. She crawled in, setting her flashlight in front of her, then stood up. "Reassure me I'm awake, Derek."

"No," he muttered, crawling in behind her. "I'm sure we're not."

The large pieces were set along the floor: chests and caskets, shrines large and small mounted on sledges, a cow's head in life size, a crouching leopard with agate eyes, seated human figures. Upright against the wall were oars, priestly standards, and fans that clearly once held feathers.

Two long tables that ran along the walls held rows of bowls, goblets, plates, and vases. At one end sat flasks and unguent jars, in animal shapes. At the other were trumpets, sheathed daggers, sandals, and figurines, and before them in rows, elaborate pectorals, collars, buckles, bracelets, rings. The funeral trappings of a prince.

Valerie sensed the Ka beside her, then saw his soft glow.

"I was favored by His Majesty," he explained, matter-of-factly.

She looked up at the painting on the wall. Ten gods stood on a shore in a row, hands raised as if in horror toward two figures in a river barque. "The Barque of the Sun," she said, "but it is not the way I have seen it before."

"It is the Barque of our dark dreams." the spectre replied mysteriously.

She studied the ancient river craft, curved extravagantly upward at both ends, and searched for meaning. The solar disk that surmounted the boat's central shrine was painted red, and before it at the prow Seth the Defender raised his harpoon. In front of the boat, a huge serpent spiraled upward from the water, its jaws agape. The harpooner took aim at the adversary, but his long camel head uncharacteristically faced into the chamber. It seemed to Valerie that he glowered down at her, and the brightly painted eyes followed her wherever she moved.

"Seth and Apophis are so large. And look, Jehuti has his own text next to him. '*Rekhi renusen. Djedi medjatsen.*' That's not any Egyptian that I know."

"I also do not know them," the Ka replied. "The words were dreamt by my lord Meremptah."

"Meremptah. Of course. I *knew* it was nineteenth dynasty." She directed the light beam toward the great dark object at the center of the chamber and heard her own sudden inhalation.

An undisturbed sarcophagus, the fervent dream of every Egyptologist. And she was the first to set eyes on it, after thousands of years. She shone her light on the four clay jars at its foot, on the carved jar heads of man, baboon, jackal, and hawk. "And the canopic jars are intact too."

They approached the object reverently, and Valerie ran her fingers lightly along the upper edge. It was wood, she noted, finely finished and painted on all sides with the spells of the Coffin Texts.

"You may open it. It was thus prophesied." The Ka directed his reply to the uncomprehending Derek, who stood at the foot of the sarcophagus. Valerie translated for him and set the flashlight down to free both hands.

The sarcophagus lid lifted easily from its base, revealing an inner mummiform coffin. The seam between the upper and lower portions of the coffin was clear, and Valerie inserted her knife blade. "It goes against all my training to break into a coffin this way," she said, tilting the blade gently upward, "but so does talking to a Ka."

The tiny aperture gave forth a faint pffft, and she suddenly smelled a mix of resin, camphor, and mold. Taking hold of the cover with both hands she slid it downward along the axis of the coffin, just enough to expose the head. She expected gauze or a desiccated face and was prepared for the horrors of decomposition. She laughed.

The face of Derek Ragin looked up at them from the coffin with wide kohl-rimmed eyes. Only the painted side lock of braided hair showed that the mask was an Egyptian priest, three thousand years dead. Narrow strips of linen held the mask in place around the head. Wider strips encircled the throat and were wrapped in geometric patterns down to cover the rest of the mummy's body.

Derek looked over her shoulder. "I'm dreaming, for sure, and seeing my own self dead."

The Ka pointed a glowing hand toward the wrapped cadaver. "The prophecy is there, on the king's gift. The words of the Scribe."

Valerie slid the coffin cover a few centimeters farther down and peered inside. Below the Derek-mask a stunning jeweled pectoral lay on the gauze of the mummy's chest.

The Ka clasped his hands, as if to suppress his own excitement. "Take it up. It is for you to read."

She reached down carefully, fumbled for a moment unhooking the chain from around its neck, and raised the heavy gold plaque to the light.

"It is the Judgment Hall scene, the same image as in the painting in the anteroom." Perplexed, she turned the object over. "There are a few hieroglyphs here. '*Djamu nu thau—shet mekhet.*' The hundredth generation. Then, '*nefer renepet.*' The glorious new year." She laid the ornament respectfully back on the mummy, tucking it under a layer of gauze.

The Ka looked from one mortal to the other. "The scribe said I would be taken from my tomb by my descendant." He gestured toward Derek. "That I would witness the Balance, the Book, and the bearing of the Child. Then Aton would rise in the west."

"Balance, Book, Child? What does that mean? How can the sun rise in the west?"

"I do not know more. But Pharaoh knew, for the god had given him the dream. He wrote it on papyrus and told the wrong that must be righted."

She peered again into the sarcophagus, directing her light to the four corners. "I don't see any papyrus."

"It is given to the good gods and lies beneath the Sun God Ra. Apophis is the key. I have read it and it is written in my heart. It tells of the great shame that caused the fall. '*Khetet*,' it says. 'Before my burning eyes, the beasts, the winds and waters, and the hills cried out.'" The Ka paused suddenly and listened, as if detecting some distant sound. "I must go. Cover me again, please. Protect my mummy from the touch of Seth."

The priest lost opacity and began to fade, from the feet up, smiling all the while, until there was only empty space where he had been. In the silence, a small pebble fell from the opening of the chamber and Valerie jumped.

"Oookay." Derek, who had been silent the whole time, finally spoke. "Are you going to tell me what just happened?"

Valerie pressed her hand to her ear. "I'm not sure. In the dark, you know, and in all the dust. You saw it too, right? It said…he said…he had been waiting for you, his descendant." She shone her flashlight again on the four walls, where the images were two-dimensional and motionless. "And that it was all written down on papyrus someplace."

"Do you think anyone is going to believe us?"

"I don't believe it myself. It's just too crazy." She closed her eyes for a moment. "I'm exhausted. I need to get out of here."

Derek looked around. "I…don't know. It seemed real to me. But maybe you're right. There's not enough air. Let's go back up and talk."

They made their way out of the burial chamber to the anteroom. "I think we should keep the burial chamber hidden a while longer. Until we can figure this all out." She pushed the Osiris block back into the closed position. "Right now I'm having doubts about my own sanity."

Valerie packed dirt once again into the crack to conceal the separation and moved one of the chests directly in front of it. "If any of the men come down here, they should overlook this. At least for a while. Now let's get out of here and just think about this."

They began the ascent, laboriously, toward the entrance. A circle of radiance at the top of the tunnel revealed it had become morning. As they plodded slowly upward, a figure stepped into the light and stood in blurry silhouette. A figure wearing boots and trousers.

"*Putain*," Valerie muttered.

They stepped together out into the harsh light to face him.

"Dr. Vanderschmitt."

CHAPTER X:
HYENA

The pale scientist stood at the top of the narrow channel that had been cut in the desert floor. As the two emerged from the dark, he stepped down onto the ramp and they could see his full lips pressed together, his unshaded eyes half closed. A small dark man, obviously his guide, stood behind him.

"You should not have evaded me, Miss Foret," he said in a quiet monotone. "I might have recommended that you stay with the excavation, perhaps in an administrative capacity. But I am afraid this speaks for your removal from the project." Valerie heard a quiet satisfaction in his voice.

The Arab workmen watched from a distance. Except for Ahmed, none could speak English well enough to follow the stranger's remarks, and Valerie sensed that their silence revealed a single common concern. Who was now in charge?

She glanced around the site for a moment and seemed to consider what to say. She forced herself to smile. "You are right, of course, Dr. Vanderschmitt. I acted hastily. I didn't want you to come out here until we were certain that we really had something." She shot a glance at Derek, whose faint nod reassured her he understood.

"But of course you found your way out on your own. I am pleased to tell you there is indeed a tomb, as you can see, which we have just now opened, and it is full of artifacts. It is a stupendous find the team has made, a great coup for the university. You can be very proud."

She gestured toward the tomb entrance. "Let me show you around." Effecting a smooth transition from adversary to agent, she started down the ramp. The new chairman followed without speaking.

She continued cheerfully in the tunnel, showering him with data, measurements, digging schedules, to keep him from repeating his ultimatum. Finally they were at the antechamber.

He stepped, obviously awestruck, into its center and turned in a circle as Valerie herself had done, sweeping his flashlight over the four walls. She knew exactly what he felt, and for a moment she regretted hating him. They could have shared the discovery as colleagues. Then she remembered it was not hate but fear that he had called up in her. Sharing was the last thing he intended.

"Excellent. Excellent. Yes, indeed. Have you determined whose tomb it is?"

"Well, you can see for yourself." She shone her flashlight onto one of the walls, providing no information. He walked around the tomb, pausing for a moment in front of each group of artifacts. Derek came in silently and stood next to her. Vanderschmitt halted finally before the wooden Barque of the Sun, the obvious centerpiece of the antechamber. "Remarkable," he murmured, delicately touching one of the two figures at the prow with the tip of his finger. It was the figure of Seth. She knew exactly the temptation he felt, the overwhelming urge to pick up the exquisite golden dolls and examine them. She was relieved to see that he did not.

"And have you found the burial chamber?" His glance swept across her like a moving spotlight, to more interesting things.

"No, but we assume it would be here, behind the south wall. I was going to have the men start looking tomorrow. I've been working them pretty hard these last weeks." Her tone remained neutral, cooperative.

Vanderschmitt studied one of the scenes, sweeping his flashlight back and forth over it. "Ah, Pharaoh Bestowing his Gift. Excellent. We can date the tomb by the identity of the king. Have you found his cartouche? Well, here we are. The kneeling man here appears to be the tomb owner."

Valerie did not reply. Every discovery of his was a negation of her own, every gloating word a theft of her achievement. He was a parasite, consuming her.

He leaned in again to study the text while with his free hand he drew a small automatic camera from the case that hung on his shoulder. "Ah, yes. Here it is." He read laboriously. "'Lord of the two lands, beloved of Ra…Meremptah…bestoweth the gift…upon his servant…'"

Vanderschmitt continued to snap photographs until the film ran out and he returned the camera to its case. Without looking at her he said, "I shall inform the university and the Egyptian government immediately, of course. However, you will return with me to Cairo. After we have registered the find with the Department of Antiquities, we will telephone Brussels to discuss the continuation of your assignment." He turned and began to walk up the tunnel toward the surface.

Valerie fell in step with him, and Derek followed close behind. At the entrance she spoke again, unaffected, cheerful. "Yes, of course. But at the same time you will surely want the work to continue. While you are in Cairo, I could start the men searching on the rear wall for the hidden entrance. When you return in a few days, you should have your burial chamber."

The new supervisor squinted out at the desert that he had just crossed, obviously weighing risks, benefits. She could almost hear the questions going back and forth in his head. Could he trust her? She was allowing him to win glory while she did all the work. But did he dare to leave her alone now, after threatening her?

Derek broke the silence, reaching out his hand, man to man, to the academic. "Forgive me, Dr. Vanderschmitt. I am only a guest here and have not yet officially congratulated you." His voice, Valerie noted, was several notes lower than usual. The handshake, she was willing to bet, was equally virile.

Vanderschmitt looked down through bored eyes. "Who, may I ask, are you?"

"Oh, I am sorry. Derek Ragin. I'm a friend of Dr. Foret. I was performing in Cairo and Dr. Foret invited me to assist in preparing the site for your arrival. I already knew of your work in archaeology, but now, well, what a brilliant discovery you have here. Or will have when you open the burial chamber. You must let me know when the time comes to publicize it in the general media. I could even give you the name of my publicist."

Vanderschmitt stood confused for a moment by the flow of words. "Eh, thank you, Mr. Ragin. I quite agree. It is a marvelous thing. I had not thought of a publicist. But perhaps you have a point. And of course the search for the sarcophagus should go on while we are in Cairo."

"Uh, well, yes." Derek scratched a spot at the back of his neck. "But then there is always the risk of theft, isn't there? I mean, I'm sure these men are honest. They should be, at least. But they are also dirt poor. And they'd be all alone out here." He lowered his voice even more and leaned in discreetly. "With priceless artifacts."

Vanderschmitt looked around at the tattered Arab team which stood, somewhat bewildered, waiting for instructions. "I take your point, Mr. Ragin. Well then, Miss Foret, on second thought, it appears prudent to leave you active for a few more days at the excavation. You speak Arabic to the men, I understand. You can explain the transfer of authority while I am gone. Then, when I return, we can discuss the nature of your future involvement."

Valerie tilted her head in feigned deference, even surprise that he could have doubted her. While he gave orders to his dragoman, she watched him reach into his case for his camera and insert another roll of film. In the open case, she could see a row of film canisters tucked into elastic loops.

He closed the case and said over his shoulder, "Abdullah, I am changing the schedule. But first I need you to come back with me into the tomb. We must create a record of the walls and artifacts."

"Would you like us to assist you, Dr. Vanderschmitt?" Valerie asked.

"No. That will not be necessary." The new Head of Excavation waved her away as he descended again into the tomb to have himself photographed.

CHAPTER XI:
LEAP OF FAITH

So, what do we do now?" Derek sat down on one of the cots and watched Valerie move about the tent.

"About getting rid of Vanderschmitt and saving my career?" She poured water from a pitcher into a tin basin.

"Getting rid of Vanderschmitt? Well, that would certainly be my first choice, but I was thinking in more practical terms." He reached for his backpack. "That was a good stall for time out there, by the way."

"Yeah. Thanks for your help, too." She splashed water on her face with a cloth, dabbing carefully around the cut with trembling hands. "But I don't know what to do when he gets back in two days."

"Uh, actually, I meant, what should we do about the mummy?" He drew out a tiny mending kit from his backpack and held it on his lap. "I mean about Rekemheb."

"About that thing." She dried her face with a cloth and sat down on the camp chair, her foot tapping. She folded her towel and then unfolded it. "I don't know, Derek. I...I'm having doubts." She rolled the towel up from one corner.

"Doubts? How can you have doubts? You spoke to him!" He unbuttoned his shirt.

"Well, no. It's possible that I didn't. I fainted yesterday, remember? Just after I had a hallucination. And I have a headache that never goes away. I could have some aftereffect from that blow I got at Giza. Not to mention that we were both exhausted."

"What are you saying? That it never happened?"

"I'm saying that I'm a scientist. I believe in brain damage and hallucinations, but I don't believe in ghosts. I can't accept that I talked to a Ka. And his speech. It was too familiar. It sounded almost like…

well, like Flemish. If I was going to create a linguistic delusion, I might use that one." Her voice trailed off.

"Well, I'm an opera singer, and I have no trouble believing in Kas, angels, ghosts, whatever. If it stands in front of you talking, it's real." He took off his shirt and draped it across his knees.

Valerie stopped rolling her towel. "What are you doing?"

"Mending my shirt. I tore it running after you last night. Why?"

"I just never saw a man with his own sewing kit."

"Valerie, darling. Do you *know* how many times I've had to repair a torn costume, minutes before going onstage?" He broke off a length of thread and drew it through his lips. "Tho, Ba and Ka are the thame perthon?" Squinting, he poked the moistened thread through the eye of the needle.

"Yes, in the mythology, they're the same person. Just different aspects. There are others, too, his shadow and his light, that dwell in the underworld. All of them depend on his mummy, though. If it's destroyed, they disappear too. According to the mythology."

"So, what will happen to them when Vanderschmitt finds the mummy? I mean, how does that work?" He closed the rip in the shirt elbow and began sewing with tiny stitches round and round. "According to the mythology, I mean."

"I…I hadn't thought of that." She chewed her lip.

"What?" He bit off the remaining thread and dropped the needle back in the mending kit. "Hadn't thought of what?"

"Vanderschmitt doesn't usually do excavations. I don't even think he's ever been in the desert before. He's a forensic Egyptologist."

"Which means—" He stood up and put his shirt on again, admiring his work.

"He dissects mummies."

Derek stopped buttoning. "He'd do that to Rekemheb? But he wouldn't if he met him, his Ka, I mean."

"Vanderschmitt is an arrogant bastard, but he's still a scientist. Even if he saw what we saw, he'd say the same thing. There is no Ka. We were suffering from lack of oxygen." She tapped her knuckles on her knee. "And he would dissect the mummy."

"And destroy Rekemheb?" Derek tried to pace, stopped at the tent wall after two steps. "No, no. Out of the question. He asked us to protect him, and we will." He sat down again. "And what about the prophecy? The 'hundredth generation' thing. We haven't even considered that."

She pressed her forehead into her hands. "Prophecies, on top of everything else. Gods. I feel like I'm in some cheesy movie."

Derek reached over to the pan and splashed some of the water on his own face. "At least he doesn't know about the burial chamber yet. That buys us some time."

"Time to do what?" She opened her hands as if waiting to catch something.

"Take Rekemheb out of the tomb. His mummy, I mean. Hide it someplace. The tomb doesn't need it! It's full of gold, for God's sake. Your university will have a spectacular find, and the Egyptian government will have a hoard of treasure. Who's gonna care about one dried-up mummy?"

"Out of the question. Waay out of the question. Moving the mummy without permission is a major offense. A crime. It would end my career."

He sat beside her on the camp bed, which groaned under their combined weights. "Valerie, darling, why are you still trying to be an archaeologist?"

"I *am* still an archaeologist. We uncover mummies for science and history. We don't steal them. It's not like an opera, in which the tenor makes some grand heroic rescue. It would be pillage, pure and simple. It would destroy everything I've worked for. And I told you I don't believe in a hereafter."

"First of all, you obviously don't see much opera. The tenor usually dies. As for ruining your career, I think Mr. Vanderschmitt is pretty much on his way to doing that already. You have *got* to look past your personal ambitions here for a moment." He clasped his hands together. "It's like…like we're the shepherds in the field seeing the Star of Bethlehem, and you're still worried about the sheep. This…" He gestured toward the excavation pit. "This isn't archaeology anymore. It's religion!"

She stood up, took a step, and then spun around. "Religion? I'll tell you what I think about religion. I was in chapel once, at school. I saw one of the boys kneeling on the steps near the altar. He was praying, and a beam of sunlight shone down directly on his head, making his hair glow."

"Oh, how beautiful. Like a blessing."

"Yes, that's what he thought. But it was *not* a blessing. It was sunlight, damn it. Natural sunlight shining through a cleverly placed window. And the boy knew it too, because he kept sliding along on his knees, staying under the light. I watched him for ten minutes as he slid, staging his own benediction. And then it hit me. That's what religion is. The believer kneeling, praying, begging to a natural thing and calling it God." She turned back and washed her already-clean hands again in the basin.

"I don't know what you're so worked up about, sweetie," Derek said, conciliatory. "I'm not asking you to be baptized again, just to remember that we talked to a ghost. They usually come from somewhere. Down my way, we call that the hereafter."

"I don't accept the hereafter. For me, life is the earth, an oxygen- and water-rich sphere hanging in space. Living things appear, mature, and die. End of story." She threw back the tent flap and stormed out toward the excavation. At the tomb ramp she halted. "What's going on here?"

Across from her, four men paced slowly, pallbearer-like, bearing a wide wooden plank up the narrow steps from the tomb entrance. Tied to the center of the plank, tottering precariously, the Barque of the Sun rose from the tomb into the light of day. Workers standing on both sides murmured as it caught the sunlight.

"Oua'f!" she shouted to the men. "Stop! What the hell are you doing!" She called toward the foreman at the bottom of the ramp. "Ahmed. Who told the men to move the artifacts?"

The men halted, and the tiny god-figures wobbled in their slots along the sides of the barque. Something small and curved fell soundlessly to the ground. The foreman hurried toward her with his hands held out. "I am sorry, Dr. Foret. But the other doctor has ordered this."

"Get on with it!" a voice barked from behind the four men. They continued their slow pacing up the ramp toward a table that had just been set up. Vanderschmitt came up behind them. "Ahmed, go back down and stand guard. I don't want anyone near the gold when I am not there."

Valerie moved toward him, both hands open. "What are you doing? Aren't you concerned that the heat will harm the wood? After three thousand years in a cool, dark place?"

"No need to be hysterical, Miss Foret. It is all in good hands now, and I would appreciate it if you would refrain from countermanding

THE 100TH GENERATION

my orders. An object of this quality has got to be photographed and documented, a fact which you seem to have overlooked. You cannot possibly have expected to leave such priceless artifacts exposed to this class of Arabs."

"This class?" she felt herself begin to sputter. "I know these men, and—"

"You would be of greater use to this project if you would assist in identifying the objects rather than interfering with my efforts to protect them. You might start by getting a camera and taking more pictures." He took up position at the side of the examining table and peered through the lens of his camera, snapping frequently.

"Do you even know the theological value of this artifact? It's an extraordinary portrayal of the gods of incalculable value. Horus is at the prow, with his brother and adversary Seth right next to him. That's unheard of."

"Yes, yes. Horus and Seth. Of course." He held the camera up to his eye and focused the lens, grimacing.

"Not only that, but look at who is attending. These goddesses are Hathor and Isis; behind them are Shu and Tefnut. Then Ma'at and Jehuti, and at the rear the 'two ladies,' Nekhbet and Wadjet."

"Your guesswork is not necessary, Miss Foret." He advanced the film and snapped several more pictures from different perspectives. "We'll leave the research to the graduate students, won't we?"

She fell silent for a moment, absorbing his insult and surveying the faces of the men who had been her workers for nearly half a year. They were paid by the university and had to do what they were told, but she could see they didn't like it. Only Ahmed's young son was animated and cheerful as he crept toward the table from behind the senior scientist. Reaching his small dark arm past Vanderschmitt, he touched something on the deck of the barque.

"Get away from that, you little thief!" Vanderschmitt spun around. Seizing the boy by the shoulder of his galabaya, he yanked him backward. The child toppled back onto the stony ground with a soft "Uh!" Two of the workers helped him to his feet and signaled that he was all right.

Valerie turned back to Vanderschmitt, who had his eye to the camera again. "The boy was not stealing. And besides, you cannot strike them. Not for any reason," she said to his indifferent back. "It's an offense here, just as it is in Europe."

He held the camera at his chest for a moment and spoke without looking at her. "Miss Foret. These men work for me now, and you will not interfere with my management of them. You've been playing fast and loose with us this entire year. But that is over now. Have I made myself clear?" He resumed snapping pictures, stepping between her and the barque.

She stared at his back for a moment and at his wide hips, speechless with fury. She toyed momentarily with the thought of confronting him further, of even having him beaten up and ejected from the site. The men would do it for her, she knew, and it would almost have been worth it to lose her job over it. "Yes, very clear."

She hurried over to where the boy sat holding his knees to his chest. "I'm sorry, Ibrim," she said in Arabic. "I apologize for the bad manners of this man."

Ibrim looked at the ground. "I did not steal. The little toy fell from the boat, and I tried to put it back."

"The little toy?"

"I was afraid they would step on it." He opened his hand, revealing a miniature bronze snake the length and thickness of his own smallest finger. The snake's head was carved from lapis lazuli, and its tail had been hammered into a square. It hung for a second from the child's moist palm before dropping into her hand.

"Thank you, Ibrim. I promise you, I will tell your father how you did a brave thing, and the other men will tell him too."

She wandered back to the table where Vanderschmitt had reached the end of his film roll and knelt on the ground. While he rewound the film with a rapid, petulant wrist movement, she leaned over the barque and studied the deck, looking for the spot from where the Apophis snake might have fallen.

"I have to get more film," he said crisply. "Keep everyone away from here. I will be back in a moment."

He marched back to his tent, and she strolled in a circle around the golden barque, holding the tiny bronze peg between thumb and forefinger. She looked along the outside, then between the god-figures, then around the periphery of the naos. Finally she saw it. A tiny square hole, scarcely a centimeter in width, had been stamped just behind the naos. She reached over and inserted the peg, pleased to feel the perfect fit. "Apophis is the key," the Ka had said. She smiled at the discovery.

It was a lever.

She pressed it gently backward. Suddenly the entire center part of the barque, the naos and the solar orb it sheltered, lifted up on hidden hinges. She took hold of it with her other hand and tilted it gently back, like the lid of a chest. In the cavity beneath were the ruined remains of what had once been a rolled papyrus.

She dared not touch it, although it would be impossible to rescue in any case. It was already merely a pile of flakes. And so she simply rotated the entire barque to catch the direct light of the sun. It was just bright enough for her to read the fragment of text that ran along the top flake. She translated the fine New Kingdom text and nearly dropped the delicate lid back in place. "'Before my burning eyes, the beasts, the winds and waters—'"

"What's that?" Derek had come up behind her and looked over her shoulder as she closed the lid over the hidden cache.

"Rekemheb's words," she said somberly. "And the death sentence to my career."

"Abdullah and I will leave at dusk tonight, after we have photographed everything." Vanderschmitt had returned, brushing dirt from his sleeves and trousers. "It should not take more than a day to file the papers with Antiquities, contact Brussels, and so forth. In the meantime, I require you to look after things." He paused, letting her appreciate that it was an assignment, not a resumption of authority.

"I will direct the men to continue looking for the burial chamber, as we discussed." She nodded, full of cooperation.

"No. There will be no more digging. I have decided to close the tomb again until I can return with proper security measures. I have got to procure an iron gate, mortar, etc. In the meantime, it is far too dangerous to leave those artifacts exposed. You must seal off and guard the entrance for the next two days. The foreman, whatever his name is, can stand guard at night. I will have made a photographic inventory, so that if anything is missing, you will of course be held responsible."

A voice spoke from behind her with courtesy and warmth. "Of course, Dr. Vanderschmitt. I will block passageway immediately. Is not a problem." Ahmed joined them and stood shoulder to shoulder with Valerie. He inclined his head in a gesture of exaggerated servitude she had never seen before.

"See to it, then." Vanderschmitt resumed photographing as Valerie and Ahmed walked back to the tent. When they were out of earshot of the other man, the foreman stopped.

"Doctor. How long must we now work for this camel's ass?"

Valerie shook her head. "For a long while, I'm afraid. But you can help me to…cause him a few problems."

"I will do anything you ask, and so will the men." The tone of his voice suggested that "anything" included a great deal.

"You've been bringing Mr. Vanderschmitt his tea, haven't you? He's used to you being in his tent."

"Yes. He drinks a lot of it. Every few hours."

"Good. Try to smuggle out his camera bag the next time he's in the latrine. I need it only for a few moments, and you can carry it back when you fetch the tea glass."

"It is done, Dr. Foret."

❖

It took only a few minutes for Valerie to open the six black canisters and exchange their spent film for unexposed rolls. Replacing the canisters in the same order in the bag, she handed it back to Ahmed, who slipped away again to return it.

"Won't he know what we've done when he has the film developed and it's blank?" Derek asked.

"Probably. But it'll be too late to take new ones."

"And Rekemheb's mummy? Are you ready to save him now? Remember, no one knows it's there. No one but us."

Valerie stared at the ground for a moment, chewing on her lower lip. Then she said quietly, "Yes."

"All right, then. Now, how do we get him out of the camp?"

"Well, Vanderschmitt will leave tonight and be gone for at least two days. We can take the mummy out of the tomb at night and let the men discover an empty sarcophagus the next day. It would be very odd, since the funerary objects are all there, but we might pull it off. The big question, however, is where do we take the mummy?"

"I've been waiting for you to ask." Derek paused theatrically, his small smile fraught with meaning. "He can stay with relatives."

CHAPTER XII:
CRUSADERS

Riding eastward with the sun on the horizon behind him, Volker Vanderschmitt buttoned his jacket against the cooling air. Four hours' sleep was not enough for a man before starting out in the desert again, and he was exhausted. It was a hardship he was willing to endure, however. In another twenty-four hours, he'd make history.

He imagined the faces of his colleagues when they got the news. They'd congratulate him, even the ones who didn't like him. He'd be photographed, interviewed, broadcast all over the world. All those years of academic drudgery would finally be rewarded. He would be a star in the archaeological community. He could leave Brussels now for a chairmanship at one of the big universities. He could even return to Cambridge, the old denigration erased by his new glory.

He settled himself on his camel seat, drawing up one leg. Monique should see him now, the spoiled bitch. Monique, who had corrupted him and then lost interest. She had even refused to see him afterward, wouldn't return his calls. Until, recklessly, he had brazened his way into her husband's party. What was the man again, the old fool? Antiques dealer? Vanderschmitt felt his throat tightening as he recalled the confrontation.

All he had wanted was to draw her aside, tell her that she had changed him and could not simply leave him. But she had made a public spectacle of it. Before a room full of his Cambridge colleagues, she had slapped him hard enough to cause a nosebleed. As he stood there, his own blood spotting his white linen jacket, she had whispered, "You are pathetic." Humiliated, he had not replied, but simply walked quietly from the room, seething with a rage that had not left him for thirty years.

He had left Cambridge at the end of the term and spent months unemployed and bitter. She became the symbol of the world that had rejected him, and of a moral and intellectual relativism that he came to despise. There was a Bohemian licentiousness, a sort of anarchy in the disciplines too, where everything was waffling and compromise, and nothing was clear. And the women, with their "alternative" interpretations of everything, were the worst—vessels of inconstancy.

He needed certainty, the sense of an absolute truth at his back and under his feet. A year later, after he had nearly ruined himself in sullen drinking, religion finally gave it to him. Truth had come to him one night while he was sleeping off a binge, in a dream of exquisite clarity. He stood on the prow of a ship sailing toward a shore where wild things lived. The very landscape writhed and surged with them. Behind him, though he could not see it, was some great force, something noble and pure that sought to vanquish them. He had been chosen as its guardian and so was weaponed. Righteousness welled up through his veins and poured into his arms so that he sent a spear glittering toward the monsters. "The earth falls down before him," his dream self cried as the shaft exploded against the foe.

He had awakened, his heart still pounding, his lips mumbling a childhood memory of scripture: "I am the way, the truth, and the light." It was the revelation that saved him, that gave him back the moral clarity of his youth and inspired him to start all over again in Brussels.

It also freed him from women, from wanting to be attractive to them. And so when his body began to soften into androgyny, it did not matter. Monique, his friends had told him, had left England after he did, though they could not say to where—to hell, he hoped.

He shook himself back to the cool, dark present and patted the camera case that hung at his side. Now heaven and hard work had rewarded him. Great things were about to happen.

❖

Valerie sat watching the two figures shrink and fade into obscurity on the eastern side. When they were out of sight, she turned her stool around to face the west.

Derek came up to stand beside her. "Wow. Look at all the colors. Shades of pink not even a drag queen would wear."

"It's beautiful, that glow right on the horizon, but always a little depressing too. At moments like these I understand the Egyptians' dread at seeing the Sun Barque drop into the underworld."

"Hmm. I don't see it myself, Val. But I bet Rekemheb did. It would have been scary, wouldn't it?"

"Yes. Twilight was ominous. But the sky was always full of portents."

At that moment a jet sliced across the red sky. A military plane— its speed gave it away—thundered northeastward, tearing her from her reverie.

"Enough brooding." Derek squeezed her shoulder gently. "Come on. We'd better get started."

She stood up, laying her hand on top of his, trying to dispel her misgivings. "Are all the men in the workers' tent?"

"Yes. Ahmed asked if you needed him, but I said we were going into the tomb to photograph some more and he could go to bed. So, sweetie, it's now or never."

Valerie took a final look at the strip of orange that still smoldered in the west like a distant conflagration. "May the gods be with us. The law certainly will not."

They hurried across the open space and reentered the tomb. Their single flashlight trailed along the tunnel floor as they descended to the first chamber.

Valerie stopped in front of the sun barque that had been returned to its original place among the artifacts. Little pieces of numbered cardboard hung from all of them. She picked up one of them and read the scribbled notation. *Nr. 14. Ivory chest. Vanderschmitt.*

"*Salop*! He's put his name on everything. Well, we'll have to do something about that." She pressed with her clenched fist on the Ba image on the tomb mural, and once again the Osiris door sprang toward them. With their combined effort, they dragged it fully open. The Ka was already sitting on his sarcophagus, as if he had been waiting for hours for visitors.

Valerie startled again at the sight of him.

"See, I knew he was real." Derek couldn't resist saying it.

"Rekemheb." Valerie drew the Ka's attention from his descendant, with whom he seemed obsessed. "I found Pharaoh Meremptah's papyrus. You did not tell me that it was in the Barque of the Sun."

"Did it answer all your questions?"

"No. It had disintegrated. But never mind. We are here for another reason. We must remove your mummy to a safer place."

"Praise to the good gods and to Hathor." The spectre raised both hands. "It has begun, then, the prophecy. I shall be carried in my descendant's arms." He evaporated cheerfully, as if to go and pack his bags.

"Well, that part was easy, at least," Derek remarked as they slid aside the lid. "He must know something we don't."

"Derek, he knows a whole world of things we don't." They lifted off the lid of the inner coffin, and she poked the gauze-covered cadaver in several places on the chest and legs. "His body's solid and well wrapped. It should hold up to being carried. Here, take him around the shoulders, and be sure to support his head."

She held the bundle around the legs while Derek raised the upper end and supported it with his shoulder. Suddenly he jerked violently, nearly dropping his end of the load. "Oh, my God! What the hell was that? Something just slid down inside my shirt. Get it out! Get it *out!*"

"Stay calm." She directed her flashlight at the lumpy shape in his shirt and the length of chain hanging from between his shirt buttons, then breathed a sigh of relief. "It's the amulet. I unhooked the chain, remember? Hang on to him. I'll get it." Balancing her end of the burden carefully, she pulled the wide gold plate out from inside his shirt, slipping it into her own shirt pocket and buttoning the flap.

They bore the mummy of the priest through the chambers of his tomb, setting it down only momentarily in order to close the burial chamber door. When they lifted the remains of the priest again, Valerie felt the precious object weighing in her shirt. Mixed with the other sounds—the trickling of sand from the broken doorways, their panting, and the shuffling of their feet—she seemed to hear a faint buzzing, like the murmuring of an excited crowd on the other side of a wall.

❖

"Dr. Foret?" A voice called softly from behind the tent canvas.

"Ahmed!" Valerie stepped outside into the darkness and drew the tent covering closed behind her.

He stood with his hands clasped in front of him. "You work at such a late hour. Shall I send the men back to assist you?"

"No, no. That's not necessary." She raised a hand. "But listen, Ahmed. My friend and I must leave the excavation tonight. I fear that Mr. Vanderschmitt will do something that will cause problems for the tomb, and I must go to Cairo to prevent it."

He laid his hand over his heart. "I will go with you."

"No, Ahmed. No need. The way is due east, and I have traveled it many times now. But I do need you to get rid of these." She held out six film capsules and dropped them into his hands. "Throw them into the latrine. An excellent insult."

He put the objects in the pocket of his galabaya. "Oh, that will be a great pleasure. We will add camels' insult too." He did not leave, but stood waiting.

Valerie considered for a moment, then took a breath. "Ahmed, when you go back into the tomb tomorrow, you will make a great discovery."

"Discovery? More than yesterday?" He seemed to consider for a moment as well. "Dr. Foret. Do not make me wait another day to take revenge on this dog of a man. Whatever you are doing tonight, please let me help."

Valerie studied the earnest face of the foreman who had worked for months at her side, directing the men with an understanding of both her needs and theirs. He had proven himself a hundred times. "All right, Ahmed. Listen. We've discovered the burial chamber. The sarcophagus is empty, but the chamber is full of artifacts. We must go back and photograph everything so the government has a record."

He pressed his gnarled hands together in front of him, as if in joyous prayer. "Surely, God is great. Oh, Dr. Foret. I am so happy for you. How can I help?"

Valerie loaded film into her camera. "When I'm in Cairo, I'll go to Antiquities and amend the registration to say that you and I have made the discovery. But after we leave tonight, you must close the burial chamber again until someone from Antiquities returns. Do you understand the danger?"

"Yes, and I am honored that you would speak to me so, Dr. Foret. Now let us to stop wasting the time."

❖

Ahmed registered approval. "Ah, you replace the little papers that Dr. Vanderschmitt has put on. This is a good thing."

"Yes, but as far as you are concerned, you know nothing about it, all right?"

"Whatever you say, Doctor. Here, let me take the new pictures of you with treasures. You can give to Egyptian government and to your school."

"That's the plan. But we must do it methodically, according to the numbers we've put on the objects. Start here at the entrance and photograph along the tables and wall, until you've made a full circle. And don't forget the small things on the floor."

She placed the new numbered cards against the artifacts, and he followed, photographing every object from a distance and from up close. For nearly an hour they worked together in the dusty air, the only sound the snap of the shutter and the whirr and click of the automatic advance.

Finally Valerie knelt by the hidden entrance. "And now for the best part, Ahmed. You will be the first Egyptian to see this room in three thousand years." She pulled open the Osiris door and waved him through the narrow opening into the burial chamber.

"*Alhamdulillah!*" he whispered. "This is a great thing. After all your work, Dr. Foret."

"No, it was your work, Ahmed. You and the men had to dig in limestone for so many months. I promise you, I will tell the world your name. But after we photograph everything, you must close it up again until the Council of Antiquities comes to see it."

"Of course. And what should I tell them when they come? Mr. Vanderschmitt will be with them, yes?"

"Tell the truth, or most of it. It'll be easy to remember. Well, you might forget about our changing Mr. Vanderschmitt's little tags. But most importantly, you should say that we discovered this chamber together, you and I. It'll be true enough."

He chuckled, a high, light "hee hee" she had never heard before and that did not match his somber face. And then he touched her elbow, which he had also never done before, and drew her over to the empty sarcophagus to take the first picture.

After two hours they were finished and returned to the tent where Derek had all their bags packed and the mummy concealed in two of the camp blankets. Before the tent, the boy Ibrim held the reins of two camels.

Ahmed checked the security of the saddle bindings and nodded approvingly. Then he excused himself suddenly. Valerie waited nervously by the tent with a small canvas bag under her arm, wondering if she had misjudged him. She was after all committing a crime, and it must certainly be apparent that she was running away. Had he grasped the grave danger she was putting him in?

After a few moments the foreman returned with something tightly folded held to his chest. When he stood before her, she withdrew a wad of Egyptian pound notes and handed it to him. "This is the money due the men this month. There's some extra too. After you pay them their salaries, you can distribute the rest as you see fit."

Ahmed lowered his eyes, taking the payroll. "Thank you, Doctor, for your trust. I think that you do a good thing tonight." He pressed his cloth bundle into her hands without explanation. "*Ma' as salaamaa,* Doctor," he said, and took his youngest son by the hand. He walked away whispering something to the boy, and neither one of them glanced back.

"*Ma' as salaamaa,*" she murmured after them, looking down at the folded material in her hands. It was his good galabaya. Exactly what they needed.

CHAPTER XIII:
FORTH INTO THE WORLD

Scarcely twenty meters out, Valerie felt a twinge of regret and looked back. The tents, the water tank, and the gaping hole of the tomb entrance seemed forlorn in the moonlight.

Something caught her eye. A figure had stepped out from behind the smaller tent. Someone in a dark robe, with loose uncovered hair that fell to the narrow shoulders.

A woman in the camp? Impossible. There were no other women, unless one had followed her out there. Her heart began to pound. "Wait!" Valerie called out suddenly. "I have to go back. Just for a moment."

She turned her camel and nudged it back toward the camp. The figure was no longer visible, but Valerie circled the tent once and then a second time, obsessed.

"Dr. Foret!" The figure stepped out from inside the tent. "I was looking for you."

"Oh! Hamada. I didn't recognize you." She laughed nervously. "I've never seen you without your turban. Why were you looking for me?"

"The men are worried. We do not want to work for this man Vanderschmitt."

"I am sorry, Hamada. I cannot help that he is in charge now. What will happen now I do not know. Please tell the men how much I value their work. I have left money with Ahmed to pay everyone well. I will tell the world your names."

She turned the camel again, first angry at herself, then despondent, and heard the voice behind her say, "*Inshaa'Allah*, Dr. Foret."

She tapped her camel on the flank and caught up with Derek, who had advanced some distance into the desert. Wisely, it appeared.

As she neared, she saw the faintly iridescent form of the Ka hovering beside him and the Ba perched on the camel's rump behind him. Derek sat awkwardly, holding the rigid mummy diagonally in front of him. Ahmed's galabaya hung down over its gauze-wrapped feet, and a *khaffia* covered the masked head. A relief that the foreman was so tall.

"What was that all about?"

"Nothing. Just another of the workers I had to talk to." She changed the subject. "But I see you two are getting to know each other."

"Well, he hasn't said anything yet. He just keeps smiling at me."

The apparition apparently noted the arrival of his interpreter and began to speak. "May you be light of heart, Ayemderak. Whither do you come?"

Valerie dutifully translated as both camels began the journey eastward.

"He's asking where I'm from? That's cute. Just like in a bar." Derek looked over the shoulder of the mummy and said, "From very far away." He shifted on his saddle, trying to find a comfortable position. "Weird, to talk to you this way. I mean over there when I'm holding you dead in my arms right here."

Valerie intermediated between the two, faltering at first, then with greater ease, as long as they spoke of simple things. *And still,* she thought to herself in the silences, *I'm having a conversation with the dead. I'll wake up from this dream soon.*

"Yes, I have become all my parts," Rekemheb explained. "Here I am mummy, Ka, and Ba. In the Duat dwell also my light and my shade and my immortal name. But what of you? Do you have wife and child?"

"Uh. Well, not a wife. Not exactly. But a woman, a dear friend, carries my child." Derek kept his face slightly behind the head of the mummy.

Uncanny, how similar they were, Valerie thought. If the Ka was real, perhaps the kinship claim was true. Impossible. All of it. More likely she was dreaming and lacked the imagination to keep them separate.

"Ah, the Child! Of course." The Ka of Rekemheb clapped his hands. "The birth prophesied by the god. And what is the name of the woman who bears the next son in our line?"

Valerie translated numbly.

"*Our* line?" Derek laughed. "Uh, well, I suppose it is. Her name is Auset."

The Ka raised his hands skyward. "Praise to Ra and Hathor! No woman could be better chosen."

Valerie explained. "He's excited because Auset is one of the names of the Mother Goddess also known as Isis and as Hathor. She's sort of the Egyptian Virgin Mary, without the virgin part."

"Ah, well, that fits Auset," Derek quipped. "But that reminds me. I've got to try to contact her. She's our only hope right now." He extracted a small cell phone from his pocket. "Can you use these things way out here?"

Valerie shrugged. "I think the Egyptian military uses them, or something like them. Give it a try."

With the dexterity of one who did it frequently, Derek dialed a number with his thumb and held the tiny object to his ear. "Ah, ringing. Guess it works," he said, nonchalant, as if he were ordering takeout.

Rekemheb watched intently as Derek spoke into the small dark phone and repeated, "Auset, Auset."

"Does he pray to the goddess through the little stone?"

"Stone? Oh! The cell phone. No, he does not pray. He talks to her who is far away, and she replies. It is not the goddess, but the woman named after her. Well, I will explain later."

She turned to Derek, who had tucked away the cell phone. "That was quick. What did she say?"

"She'll meet us tomorrow in Giza, at the camel stable with a car. She's invited us for lunch."

"Lunch? You talked about lunch? Did you mention Rekemheb? Did you tell her that we need to hide a mummy in her flat?"

"Uh, I told her to come in a company truck, there'd be an...uh... artifact. I just thought that after she's seen Rekemheb's Ka and the little Ba thing, we won't have to convince her that we aren't crazy. Once she sees he's real, she *has* to agree to the rest."

Rekemheb looked back and forth at the two speaking English and seemed to accept that not everything would be explained to him. When they paused in their conversation with each other, he spoke in his clipped, Flemish-sounding Egyptian. "Ayemderak, my grandchild. How do you serve the gods? What is your profession?"

Valerie mediated again.

"I sing," Derek said simply.

"Sing?" The priest repeated the word in English and wafted closer to his descendant. "In the temple, as I do? You too are a lector priest?"

"Yes, I have sung in temples and churches. But not like a lector priest, whatever that is. I usually perform on a stage, before people. We call that a concert."

Valerie translated but the Ka still looked perplexed. "You sing to amuse the people? Like a slave?"

"Oh no, a concert is a like a….a big ceremony, but without God. A singer is greatly valued in this time. Sometimes he wins glory."

The priest seemed relieved.

Derek shifted the mummy so that its head rested on his other shoulder. "There is something I must ask you, Rekemheb. It has been troubling me since I saw you in the tomb. Please do not laugh at me. And not you either, Valerie. I have to know this."

"Know what?" she said. "So ask already."

He exhaled slowly. "Rekemheb…is Jesus there in the afterlife?"

"Ah, yes." Valerie shrugged. "An important question for a Christian. Well, for everyone, actually."

The Ka frowned. "Djesesh? I do not know this name. Perhaps he is in the Duat of the Greeks or the Persians."

"You mean there's more than one hereafter?"

Valerie repeated the question in Egyptian.

The Ka nodded. "Yes, many."

Derek looked up at the stars. "All the religions are true? How can that be? That's impossible. Who's in charge? Which is the real God, the one that looks after us?"

Valerie transmitted the question.

The ancient priest puzzled for a moment, obviously trying to make sense of the question. Finally he spoke. "The gods do not look after us. It is we who look after them."

Ahead of them a three-quarter moon was rising on the horizon, illuminating the travelers bluely. From somewhere overhead a falcon shrieked.

"Horus greets you," the Ka of Rekemheb said cheerfully.

CHAPTER XIV:
BLESSED AMONG WOMEN

There it is." Valerie pointed down a dirt road between broken mud-brick walls. "The stable where we met Ahmed two nights ago. Remember?"

The camels lumbered down the last stretch of dry road to the stable. At the side of the building, she dismounted and drew back the threadbare rug that covered the entrance. The odor of the stabled beasts was strong, yet as Derek came through the doorway, bowing low under the lintel, the half dozen other camels honked in protest at the smell of the mummy.

"What should we do with Rekemheb? We can't let the stable boys see him."

"There's an empty feeding trough over there. We can put him there." She reached up and carefully slid the mummy out of Derek's arms. With more rush than reverence, she laid it in the trough and covered it with a scattering of fresh straw.

"Ahlan wa sahlan, Doktor." A boy of about fifteen came in. The reeking stain on the bottom of his galabaya suggested he had just cleared the night's manure from the stalls.

"Rajab, hello. Look, we'd like to be left alone for a while—to talk business. Can you come back later for the saddles? When we're gone?"

"No broblem," he said cheerfully in Egyptian English, using the phrase every child in Egypt could say but not pronounce. Valerie pressed a few bills into his hand and urged him to the doorway.

Derek looked at his watch. "Eleven forty-five. We're early. Damn." He grimaced, breathing through his mouth. "I sure hope she arrives soon. This place is way more than my nose can handle."

Valerie leaned against the stable wall and fanned away flies with her fedora. "Is Auset usually late?"

"I don't know." He shrugged. "I was always later."

Scarcely had he spoken when a car horn sounded, and they went together to the door of the stable. Ahead of her, Derek drew back the rug.

Over his shoulder, Valerie saw what had just pulled into the stable yard. "Ah, *merde*. What the hell are we going to do now?"

Dust still settled around a blue pickup truck, its rear section uncovered and empty. Al Fakhir, Inc. Exporters was painted on the side in Arabic and English. Auset, visibly pregnant in spite of the loose abaya that covered her, came around from the passenger side of the cab. A moment later the door on the driver's side opened, and a bulky Arab in western clothing emerged.

"You didn't mention she had a friend," Valerie said through closed teeth.

Derek sighed. "I had no idea."

Auset surveyed the stable surroundings as she walked toward them. She brushed imaginary dirt from her hands, although she had not touched anything. "So, what's going on here?"

No one answered.

"Oh, sorry. Derek. This is Yussif, our company driver." She looked back at the man who stood just behind her. "Yussif, this is Derek, the father of my child."

The swarthy Arab scowled. He was taller and beefier than most Egyptians, and his ample girth would have been better served by a galabaya than by the trousers he wore. The three-day beard growth that Arab men favored emphasized the ferocity of his expression. Auset's two men nodded coolly at one another, declining to shake hands.

"And this is Valerie, Derek's archaeologist friend I told you about," she went on, ignoring the bristling males. Before Valerie could speak, Auset turned back to Derek and demanded, "Now where is this 'extraordinary artifact' of yours, and why did you drag us way out here to get it?"

Derek pressed his lips together for a moment, then nodded faintly, as if agreeing with himself. "Auset. You seem to be a very levelheaded person. I think you can recognize a morally complicated situation when you see one. Am I right?"

Auset narrowed her eyes. "What's going on, Derek? What have you done?"

He raised a hand. "No, no. It's nothing that we've done. Well, it is sort of something we've done. Or rather were compelled to do. It's *very* complicated. You must promise to reserve judgment until you know all the facts."

Auset's voice dropped in temperature. "Perhaps you could start by telling us what the hell you're talking about?"

Derek's eyes darted toward the brutal-looking truck driver, and he hesitated.

Auset saw the direction of his glance. "Look, whatever is going on here, if it involves me, it also involves Yussif. So talk." The driver did not comment, but crossed his arms over his large chest.

Derek exhaled, as if he had been holding his breath. "All right. I guess it's truth time. Come in here, both of you. I want you to meet Rekemheb."

"Who?"

The two Egyptians followed him into the last stall of the stable, where the feeding trough hung. Derek lifted away handfuls of straw until a black painted mask smiled up at him. Then he brushed away debris from the rest of the upper body.

Auset put her fists where her waist would have been. "A mummy? Is this a joke?"

"No. I mean, yes, it's a mummy, not a joke. It's my ancestor, I think."

She pressed two fingertips between her eyebrows. "You stole a mummy that you think you're related to?"

Valerie came to her friend's defense. "We didn't steal a mummy. We rescued it. And it isn't *it*. It's *him*." She pointed over Auset's shoulder.

The two Egyptians turned around and flinched simultaneously. Auset took a step backward, and the burly Arab put his arm around her without touching her. Both stared awestruck. In the corner of the stall stood the radiant figure of the Ka.

"Auset, darling." Derek reached out one hand to the woman and the other toward the apparition. "I'd like you to meet my ancient ancestor, Rekemheb, Lector Priest of Hathor in the reign of Pharaoh Meremptah."

The two modern Egyptians said nothing.

"Yes, I know." Valerie's voice was sympathetic. "We reacted the same way. It takes a while to grasp that he's real. It sort of messes up everything else you believe."

His face still registering fear, the husky driver stepped forward and reached out a hand toward the enigma. When his fingers penetrated the surface of the glowing chest he flinched again. "Is true, then. This man is not…like us. If this is one of the dead, God forbid, what does he seek among the living?"

"Well, that's the big question, isn't it? And we've been working on that ourselves. But I'll ask him again in your words," Valerie said, and spoke to the Ka.

"It was the living who came to me, as it was written," the apparition replied.

Valerie translated again and then she added, "He means me, of course. I took him from his tomb. But the bizarre thing is that he was waiting for us."

Auset's scowl increased. "Look, I don't know what's going on here, Derek. If you and your theater friends are pulling a prank, I'm the wrong person for it." She rested a hand on her swelling abdomen. "And this is certainly the wrong time."

Derek and Valerie looked at one another, perturbed. Plan A had failed and they had no Plan B. Derek raised both hands. "Auset, please. Just listen for a minute."

"Auset." A soothing voice repeated the name with a strange accent. All eyes turned again to the apparition, who bowed slightly from the waist. "Great Lady, Justified by Ra, most beloved of the Goddess. Surely, my grandchild has chosen the noblest of women to be the temple of the future."

Valerie translated, carefully selecting superlatives.

Auset looked at the Ka and then at Valerie. "Is he saying that or are you making it up to placate me?"

"No, I swear it is him. Myself, I don't think you're all that noble."

The Ka took a step forward and knelt before Auset, his hand pressed upon his naked chest, his priestly side lock dangling handsomely. "Auset, whose very name is that of the Great Mother, you have been chosen from among all women. All of heaven honors you with this child and asks only that you shelter the mortal substance of his ancestor."

Valerie repeated the speech, emphasizing the word "honor." Could flattery succeed where reason failed?

Auset looked back and forth between Derek and Valerie. "This can't be real."

"Unfortunately, he seems to be," Valerie replied soothingly. "And we can explain him, but we need to take him someplace safe while we do. We *cannot* stay here."

Auset shook her head. "This is just too weird. Yussif, am I going crazy here?"

The Arab, who had not taken his eyes from the priest, expressed no opinion.

Finally Auset threw up her hands. "This place smells like the toilets of hell. If we're going to discuss that thing, you'll have to bring it out to the truck." She spun around toward the door. "I'm never going to get the smell of camel poop out of my clothes!"

"Wait," Valerie called, stretching out the one-syllable word. "There's another…uh…thing you must see first."

Auset stopped suddenly and closed her eyes. "There's more?"

Derek cleared his throat, clasped his hands, rubbed his palms nervously. "Yes. One more thing. But it's no big deal, really. It's just that feathered creature perched on the edge of the stall. Right over there."

Auset turned and glanced carelessly toward where he pointed. "Is that all? It's just a parr…Oh, my God! It's got a little human head!" She recoiled. "It's grotesque!"

"No, look! It's Rekemheb's face, don't you see?" Derek was talking faster now. "It's his Ba. His soul. It goes along with the Ka, sort of. You just have to get used to it."

Auset leaned forward again to inspect the creature, which half opened its wings and then shivered, rocking back and forth on wrinkled claws. "Ba?" she asked weakly.

Valerie took over the argument. "It's rather like a messenger and…well, it flies around. I always thought of it as a variation on the soul myth, but well, obviously, it's not. A myth, I mean."

Auset had lowered her eyes again. "Is there anything else?" she asked very quietly. "Any other demon, jinni, ghoul, or succubus I should know about?"

"No." Derek shrugged slightly. "That's it, basically."

"Well then…" Auset enunciated carefully, as if to a deranged child. "Ask all your new friends to come along to the truck," she said, and walked out of the stable.

Outside, the truck had baked to a dangerous heat in the noonday sun. Gingerly, Derek and Valerie laid the mummy in the center of the flat bed of the truck and climbed up alongside of it. They crouched, clutching their knees, taking care not to let their skin touch the blistering hot metal. As the truck pulled away from the stable, sunlight struck some shiny object and reflected onto the side of Valerie's face. She covered it with her hand and found the old wound swollen and suppurating.

The Ka, which sat next to his mummy, looked at her. "The sun disk smites you. Have a care."

CHAPTER XV:
WIDENING CONSPIRACY

The transfer of a long and bulky bundle from an export truck to the third floor at 233 Ahmed Sabri Street attracted no particular attention, and when it was done, the four of them came into the living room with glasses of cool water. Valerie threw herself down on the sofa and covered her eyes with her forearm for a moment, as if to avoid dealing with the impossible for a few minutes longer.

Derek stood in the middle of the room and glanced around. "Oh, I love your decor!" He noted the several bedrooms and the carpeted side room that opened to a balcony. "Sort of Ottoman, but eclectic."

Auset did not reply.

Derek coughed. "Okay, I'll get to the point. Would you be able to put us up for a while? At least until we can…you know…figure things out?"

She sat down heavily across from him. "And what might you be trying to figure out? How to get away with this? I can overlook the fact that you've tracked camel dung over my floor and put a cadaver in my guest room, but stealing a mummy is a felony."

Derek opened both hands, presenting his case once again. "Auset, darling, I've told you. He's not just a mummy. He's the ancestor of our baby!"

"Our baby?" She rolled her eyes. "Oh, please." She leaned back and crossed her legs, a movement that required some concentration. "Be reasonable for a moment, Derek. Surely you realize the danger you're putting us in. We could all go to prison. I don't understand why you had to take this mummy out of its tomb. And those other…things. Where are they, by the way?"

"They stay with the mummy," Valerie contributed weakly. "And those 'other things,' the things you can't account for, are the reason for this whole situation."

Valerie dabbed with her cuff at her sore ear. "Auset, you're doing exactly what I did when I first saw them, refusing to accept the Ka and the Ba as real, reasoning around them like a hallucination which you hope will go away." She rested her forehead in her hand for a moment. "I didn't want to accept them either, but if they are real, we have to protect them. Volker Vanderschmitt, whom you've met, would destroy them."

"They can't be real." Auset struggled to her feet again and lumbered into the kitchen. For several moments, they heard only the sound of running water. Then she came back with a damp washcloth carefully folded.

Valerie took it gratefully and held the cool cloth to her cheek. After a moment, she sighed. "So here we are, with a mummy and two supernatural creatures that are challenging our credulity to the utmost," she said. "How much longer do you think we can pretend they're an illusion?"

Auset sighed. "All right, assuming they are real, what exactly do you propose to do about them?"

"Well, to start, we can try to stay out of jail and salvage my career." Valerie drew the film canisters from her shirt pocket. "We can take these pictures to Antiquities and at least claim that the sarcophagus was empty. Pillaged in antiquity and so forth. No one will be looking for a mummy. That would give us a little breathing space to hide him in some other place."

"I have good friend," a thickly accented voice said.

All heads turned toward Yussif. Valerie had almost forgotten him, the sullen stranger in their midst whose closed and bearded face she could not read. The Arab continued unemotionally. "This man is photographer. I can take film to him right away and tell him is emergency. He can make pictures very fast—for tomorrow." He stood up.

Valerie was reminded again of how big he was. Enormous, an unknown factor, a potential—and serious—problem. Nothing in his eyes or in his manner told her otherwise. "Yes, I suppose that would be…good." Reluctantly, she handed over the canisters of film.

"Yes, it would be good," he said impatiently, dropping them into his trouser pocket. As he went to the door, his eyes darted one more time around the room, lingering for a moment on Auset, and then he left.

Valerie closed the door behind him and turned back to the others. "Auset, I'm sorry. I have to ask you this. Can Yussif be trusted? How well do you know him?"

The Egyptian struggled again to her feet. "I know him better than I know you. He's worked for my father's firm for years. In fact, Yussif is the only one here I do trust. What's your problem with him?" she said over her shoulder as she made her second trip into the kitchen. "Is it because he's a Muslim?"

Valerie looked at the washcloth in her hand. "To be honest, yes. This cut on my face is from Muslim fundamentalists. You know they don't like archaeologists. We glorify the old heathen culture, and we're decadent Westerners. So, on top of all my other problems, I don't want to quarrel with Islam."

"Yussif is not a fundamentalist." Auset came back with a fresh bottle of water. "And he isn't a child, either. He will make up his own mind about Rekemheb. So, for that matter, will I. I think you're exaggerating the religious issue here." She filled Derek's empty glass.

"Not if the Ka is real," Valerie countered.

Derek glowered. "The Ka *is* real."

"So why isn't he here explaining himself? This would be a good time for that." Auset turned around, looking up at the corners of the ceiling. "Can you conjure him up whenever you want?"

Derek followed her glance. "You act like he's some sort of party trick or an annoyance. He's from the hereafter, for God's sake. Why isn't anyone getting that?"

"Whatever." Auset sat down finally. "I don't want to argue any longer. You two have been up all night, and frankly you look like hell. Get some rest and we'll talk about everything later. Derek, you'll have to share the room with the mummy, but I take it that's fine with you." She turned. "Valerie, you can camp out in the little room by the terrace. You don't mind sleeping with just a pillow on a carpet, do you? Good. And for now, let's clean that cut with some disinfectant. At least there's one problem I can fix."

❖

Awakening suddenly, Valerie read her wristwatch by moonlight. *One in the morning. Is that all?* She lay fuzzy headed for a while on her mat by the open terrace door, feeling the evening breeze waft over her. Sleep would not return, so she clicked on the lamp at her elbow.

There they were, next to each other on top of her knapsack, the two artifacts that taunted her. She lifted up the palette box and ran her finger over its golden cap. A priceless object, but why had she been given it? Who was the woman who had almost-kissed her?

The amulet was just as puzzling. She picked it up and turned it restlessly in the light, reading the hieroglyphs for the tenth time. Drill, vulture, owl, child and man, and the triple stroke: the word "generation." Then whip, loaf, and curl: "100th." The inscription stirred nothing in her memory of spells and incantations. And the text at the bottom was beyond her altogether. *Rekhi renusen. Djedi medjatsen.* She could pronounce it from the phonetic hieroglyphs but knew no such words, not even in Old Kingdom Egyptian. A pity the philologists would never see the amulet before it went back to its owner.

And what was Rekemheb, the phantom that kept appearing, against all law and logic? Derek had been able to accept him immediately, but then the singer had always had one foot in the fantastic. He would have adapted to a leprechaun or saint, Martian or ghost. But she was not an opera singer; she was a scientist, she reminded herself yet again, and could not adapt, in spite of the arguments she kept making to Auset.

A pettier emotion that had been nibbling at the edge of her consciousness since they had fled the excavation suddenly surfaced. Resentment. She realized she was annoyed, even jealous, that Rekemheb showed no interest in her. After nearly a year of labor, her spectacular discovery had suddenly become Derek's affair. Her life's work was at risk for some inexplicable event that belonged to him and not to her. She loved him like a brother, but she did not care to be a mere actor in someone else's fate.

The ivory palette, at least, was hers, though its relevance was obscure. "It is for you alone," the woman had said, then almost-kissed her. Where had she gone, the woman who had promised to "follow"? She could almost smell the fragrant hair again, almost feel the provocative pressure of the stranger's body leaning lightly against her.

She lay back, tucking her right forearm under her head, and stared up at the ceiling. It was time to visit Jameela again.

CHAPTER XVI:
FOOD FOR THE SPIRIT

The first call to prayer awoke her, as always, and Valerie began the day gratefully with a hot shower. The vigorous scrubbing she gave herself and the sunshine that poured into the bathroom while she toweled herself dry lifted the depression of the night before. The moist, bright air of the bathroom seemed to promise they would find a solution.

When she emerged dressed in nearly clean clothes and squeezing handfuls of her hair in the towel, Derek was slouching by the bathroom door in his boxers. His still-puffy eyes indicated that he too was not yet inclined to conversation. She kissed him quickly on both cheeks, Belgian style, and stepped past him into the kitchen.

Auset was already preparing breakfast. She moved about efficiently in sandals and a blue galabaya, her hair hanging loose down her back. A modern Mary Magdalen, grinding coffee beans.

"I'm sorry if I woke you," Valerie said. "I should have been quieter."

"Oh, no. I always get up early. Hunger, you know. I was about to make breakfast for all of us. You can set the table."

Valerie folded the towel over the back of a chair and opened the glass door to the cupboard. "Hmm. I wonder if we should set a place for the Ka. They eat, you know, according to the mythology."

Auset paused in her work and shook her head. "The Ka? Oh, right. The ghost. I was hoping I'd just been dreaming. But I guess not. Do you suppose he will uh…materialize this morning?"

"Well, I'm a little new at this myself but, supposedly, if you're offering food, he'll appear."

Auset resumed preparations, laying out disks of pita bread. "Well, maybe you could ask him how he likes his eggs."

Valerie chuckled. "That and a few thousand other things."

The door to the bathroom opened and Derek stepped out in a pleasant cloud of steam. Around his hips he had tied a white bath sheet that hung to his ankles. Valerie grinned at the sight of her friend who, but for the absence of a priestly side lock, was suddenly the image of Rekemheb. He came into the kitchen and kissed both women, smelling of soap and toothpaste. "I have to talk to you guys. Something strange happened last night."

"Strange? You don't say!" Auset broke eggs into a bowl.

"No, I mean even stranger than everything else. I was in bed, ready to fall asleep, and Rekemheb came to lie down next to me. I thought, 'Well, that's nice.' But then he touched me with his whole body, and something amazing happened. It was the most powerful, wonderful thing I've ever felt. It was ecstasy, and I had a sort of vision.

"I was a minister, like my stepfather, but instead of a white collar, I wore a linen kilt like Rekemheb's. I was holding his necklace. You know, the one we found on the mummy. All around me there were angels, but they were animals, not people, and they were in a panic because this great ball of fire was coming toward us.

"It shot out a bolt of lightning toward me, so I started singing, I can't remember what. The lightning struck the necklace and everything turned into sparks. They were even coming out of my mouth. I was confused, though. It seemed like I was in heaven, but I couldn't tell what side God was on."

Auset leaned over and watched the flame ignite under a pan. "Isn't a nice Christian boy supposed to know that?"

Derek wrinkled up his face. "There was, well, too much God. I mean, everything was claiming to be God, and I had to save one side from the other."

"Hmm. Sounds to me like a certain opera singer is having delusions of grandeur. All those heroic roles are going to your head," Auset said.

Valerie took silverware from a drawer. "Singing fire, heh? Oookay."

Derek pursed his lips. "I can see I'm not being taken seriously here." Grasping the front of his towel-kilt, he pivoted and returned in long strides to the guest room.

When the two women were alone again in the kitchen, Auset set down the kettle. "Okay, Valerie. Woman to woman. What's going on here? I promise not to be angry if you tell me it was some kind of trick so I would help you steal a mummy."

"I wish it were. It would be so much easier if it were all a hoax. I wouldn't have to accept that an ancient religion seems to be real. That opens up such a chasm."

Auset clasped her hands in front of her. "Valerie, whatever it is, I am not getting pulled into any religious cult, least of all a primitive one."

"I can assure you I feel the same way. I was tormented by child-hating nuns far too long to ever want religion in my life again." She shook her head. "It's a prison."

"Exactly. I've got religion all around me, and I'm sick of it. My Muslim father and my Jewish mother both come from conservative families, believe it or not. Fortunately, both of them broke away from orthodoxy enough to fall in love with each other. But I probably have relatives on both sides who would gladly stone me to death for getting pregnant by an infidel." She scrambled eggs with vehemence.

"Derek's parents too, I suppose. They're born-again Christians."

"Dogma and politics have become the same thing here. My mother's relatives in Jerusalem are always going on about God's gift of Palestine—all of it—to the Jews. And my father's relatives are equally convinced that the only truth is the Koran. And the killing gets worse and worse. In Egypt, too. I don't know where it will all end."

"Hey, girls. Guess who's coming to dinner." Derek stood in the doorway in clean shirt and tailored pants. A slenderer, bare-chested version stood translucent behind him.

Auset sighed and nudged Valerie with her elbow. "That phantom that we don't believe in? Ask it if it wants breakfast."

Valerie spoke to the apparition. "Rekemheb, will you join us at table?"

The Ka inclined his head decorously. "We have waited long to sit at table in our kinsman's house."

Valerie translated to the others as the two men took their places. The Ba fluttered in behind them, lighting on the back of Rekemheb's chair.

"Interesting. First he claims my child and then my apartment." Auset walked around the table with the frying pan, ladling yellow-white curds of egg onto each plate.

Rekemheb stared with concentration at his plate. Perched behind him the Ba held the same intense expression on its tiny man face. After a few minutes, the Ka sat back in his chair as if finished dining, and the Ba began to preen his feathers.

Derek looked in disbelief at the untouched plate and then put a forkful of the uneaten egg in his mouth. He grimaced, swallowing reluctantly. "It tastes like…nothing. He ate the flavor!"

Valerie paused in chewing toast. "Ah, that would explain a lot about ancient food offerings."

Auset chuckled. "A man who can eat his cake and still have it. I like that." She stirred her coffee and studied him, seeming to see him for the first time. "Sooo, to what do we owe the pleasure of this… visitation?"

The Ka listened as the question was repeated in Egyptian, folding his hands like a schoolboy on his lap. "The scribe said I should not rest, but be brought forth by a child of my lineage. That the Aton should rise in the west and that, in the hundredth generation, I should witness the Balance and the Book and the bearing of the Child." He smiled down at the swelling between Auset and the breakfast table.

"Well, that's a pretty complicated program. And the 'bearing of the Child,' I take it, is my contribution. Well, I can tell you right now that I am absolutely not—" A knock at the door forestalled the ultimatum. "Oh, that will be Yussif." Auset got up from her chair.

She returned in a moment, and the Arab followed stiffly behind her, carrying a folded newspaper and a manila envelope. He greeted Valerie and Derek, glanced furtively at the glowing Ka and Ba, and sat down at the maximum distance from them. Without introduction, he handed the envelope to Valerie. "I ask my friend to make good ones very large. I hope is okay."

She tore open the envelope and leafed eagerly through the package of photos. "Artifacts…good. Furniture…good. Osiris statue…not too bad. Wall paintings…really good. Oh, look. This is the best." She handed it to Derek.

An earnest young woman stood at a three-quarter angle before the wall of artifacts. Her frayed shirt, its sleeves rolled to the elbow, revealed the dirt of the day's work. Shoulder-length hair was pulled back carelessly behind her head, and strands of it hung over her ear. Discernible behind the objects was the painting of the Barque of the Sun; a practiced eye could make out the figure of Seth with his hand raised. On the other side of the frame, one end of the sarcophagus could be seen, open and empty.

"This is the one I'll send to Brussels," she said with satisfaction. "This one will bring Misterdoctor Vanderschmitt's hijacking to a screeching halt."

Yussif looked down at his hands on the table. "Maybe not." He slid the newspaper over to her, without glancing up.

"What's this?" Valerie slowly unfolded the *Cairo Times* onto the table.

There were two stories, side by side. The bigger story, four columns wide, grabbed her attention first. TOURISTS ATTACKED AT KARNAK, it read, and she automatically skimmed the first paragraph. A European tour group was set upon by three Sudanese terrorists. Several fatalities among the tourists. Two assassins captured by Luxor security forces; the third escaped.

The story held her interest for a moment, until her eye traveled to the right of the page. In two columns, over the full-faced photograph of Volker Vanderschmitt, a smaller headline declared: BELGIAN ARCHAEOLOGIST FINDS SEALED TOMB.

She exhaled slowly, laying her forehead in her open hand. "He couldn't wait."

"Is more. Please read whole story," Yussif said, his eyes still on the table.

She read on, tapping softly with the knuckles of her tightly clenched fist as she read the details. She read the final paragraph aloud.

"'The Supreme Council of Antiquities Office has called a televised press conference on Tuesday at 11:00 a.m. at which Dr. Vanderschmitt is expected to provide a detailed description and photographs of the discovery.'"

Everyone at the table fell silent while the clock ticked in the living room. Finally Derek reached over and took hold of Valerie's forearm. "Don't do it, please. You're playing with fire."

"*Putain,*" she murmured at the newspaper.

CHAPTER XVII:
A WORD TOO FAR

The building on the Sharia Fakhri was as imposing as the name of the organization it housed: The Supreme Council of Antiquities. The long avenue running from the guarded entry gate to the splendid grand portal gave the arriving visitor ample opportunity to appreciate it. Four stories of successive archways in pale stone curving over glass windows suggested enlightened authority that looked back over time.

In the cavernous interior, the four floors were laid out in galleries around a central hall that rose up uninterrupted to the roof. Pale limestone walls and marble balustrades on all sides reminded of both cathedral and fortress and were clearly designed to inspire awe in the beholder.

Valerie was in no mood for awe. She hurried up the marble staircase to the second-floor conference room where a young man in a white uniform checked credentials at the door. With a faculty ID card from the University of Brussels she brazened her way in. Vanderschmitt had just finished his presentation—with drawings only, she noted—and the first question was posed. "When do you expect to find the burial chamber of the tomb?"

Vanderschmitt blanched noticeably as, stepping over video cables, the breathless Valerie joined him at the head of the room. Respectfully, congenially, as if the two colleagues had worked together for years, she turned the microphone toward herself.

"Dr. Vanderschmitt, please forgive me for arriving late. But I will be pleased to answer that question." The chairman placed his hand over the microphone and whispered, "What the hell are you doing?" There was a murmur of confusion in the room.

Ignoring his hand and the pressure of his arm against her shoulder keeping her from the podium, she continued speaking. "Good morning, ladies and gentlemen. I am Dr. Valerie Foret. My colleague Dr. Vanderschmitt has perhaps neglected to mention that I was the archaeologist in charge who made the discovery of the tomb some days before he arrived. I am pleased to announce that in the meantime, while Mr. Vanderschmitt was on his way here, my team has uncovered the burial chamber as well."

There was a buzz of approval; two or three people applauded.

Vanderschmitt's hand slid from the microphone and he stepped back, defeated.

"As we had hoped, the burial chamber also contains a large number of fine funerary objects although, extraordinarily, the sarcophagus was empty."

Hands shot up with questions but Vanderschmitt interrupted, seizing the microphone. "Thank you, Miss Foret, but I have already discussed the artifacts of the tomb and their New Kingdom date."

Valerie walked away from the podium, drawing the cameras and the eyes of the audience along with her. It didn't hurt, she knew, that a young female archaeologist made better copy than a pedantic pear-shaped man. With the voice she was accustomed to using over the clatter of shovels on limestone, she continued her report. "The entrance to the burial chamber was through a mechanically sophisticated device concealed within the tomb wall. This would explain why Dr. Vanderschmitt in his brief visit overlooked it. The importance of this find cannot be overestimated. It not only provides a tomb household comparable to that of Tutankhamun, but also reveals something about New Kingdom technology and engineering."

Vanderschmitt was silent.

Flashbulbs flickered and a voice called out. "How do you account for the empty sarcophagus?"

Valerie continued in the same tone of authority. "The mummy seems to have been removed centuries, if not millennia, ago. While the absence of a mummy is unusual, it is not unheard of and can be attributed to any number of events—dynastic rivalry, local rebellions, etc. In any case, the artifacts, of incalculable value to the Egyptian government and to the world, remain untouched."

A second journalist stood up. "Dr. Foret. Why a single isolated tomb out in the desert and so far from the Valley of the Kings?"

"One ought not to speculate at this early date, but rivalries at court could account for the tomb being set so far away from known tomb areas. Personal enemies could still harm a man after his death by destroying his mummy and thus depriving him of the afterlife."

"Dr. Foret!" another voice called. "Could you identify the tomb owner?"

"Yes. The tomb inscriptions and paintings indicate that the entombed man was a lector priest, that is, a chanting priest—and a Nubian. An unusual combination. More details will of course emerge in the coming weeks. There is a fascinating story here, ladies and gentlemen, right at our fingertips."

Vanderschmitt held a frozen smile.

From the rear of the room a young Saudi in a red *khaffia* stood up. "Given the richness of the tomb, would you say you are this decade's Howard Carter?"

Valerie suppressed a smile of her own. "I would never presume to. However, there is an interesting parallel with Mr. Carter's discovery of Tutankhamun—in that in both cases the initial discovery was made by an Egyptian child. Mr. Carter's water boy Hussein was the first to uncover a stone slab of the tomb, and at my excavation, Ibrim, the son of my foreman Ahmed Nassar, came upon the first limestone step. Unlike Howard Carter, however, I have collaborated with my Egyptian assistant to catalog the artifacts. After all, the treasures belong to the Egyptian people, don't they?"

"And what does that treasure consist of, Dr. Foret?" The Saudi, who looked familiar, seemed to enjoy holding the floor.

"Now we're getting to the point, aren't we?" Valerie held up the manila envelope she had brought in with her. "I have prepared a list of the objects discovered in the burial chamber as well as a series of photographs of both rooms. I will of course leave these at the disposal of the Council of Antiquities along with the names of the Egyptian workers who were indispensable to the discovery." She walked back to the head of the table where the President of the Council sat.

Fuad al Rashidi was a man of about sixty, rotund and balding. A face that probably had once been handsome had become fleshy from age and too many state dinners. No wonder his wife had lost interest in him, she thought.

"Dr. Rashidi. These photographs give you a rough idea of the contents. In addition to the usual funerary items, there is also a splendid golden sun barque." She handed over the pile of photographs. While Rashidi leafed through them with little grunts of admiration, Valerie allowed herself to glance over his shoulder. The president's wife sat demurely in a cushioned chair against the far wall. Glancing back at her, Madame Rashidi smiled and fondled the end of a necklace that hung over her discreetly covered bosom.

Valerie studied the Saudi journalist who had just spoken and sat down again. Under the precisely trimmed goatee the man's face was youthful and smooth, and it bore a remarkable resemblance to her own.

President Rashidi stood up and took the microphone. "The Council wishes to congratulate Dr. Vanderschmitt and Dr. Flora on their discovery. While the University of Brussels has had our full support in this undertaking, I am pleased to hear our friends confirm that antiquities remain always and ever under the control of the Egyptian people. My position is well known, and the Egyptian government will vigorously enforce this policy so that the pillaging of the previous century will never be repeated." He paused for a moment to look at the top picture of the golden barque.

"Given the obvious value of the newly discovered objects, my office will immediately dispatch a team to secure them. To you journalists I would say feel free to publicize, through this office, the progress of the excavation, but make clear to the world that security will be extremely tight. Access to the site will be permitted only with governmental authority, and any effort to remove objects of any sort will be severely dealt with."

He turned to where Vanderschmitt had been standing and, briefly befuddled at not seeing him, turned back to Valerie. "Once again, Dr. Flora, congratulations." He held out his hand.

"Uh, that's 'Foret.' But I thank you, President Rashidi." She accepted the handshake. "I am sure that Mr. Vanderschmitt would be glad to accompany your team to the excavation site. I myself must return to Brussels for a few days. A…family emergency. But I should be able to return shortly, and I look forward to working with your team. It is my opinion that there are no additional chambers to be discovered, although Mr. Vanderschmitt may wish to determine that himself."

She looked around for Vanderschmitt, but he seemed to no longer be in the room. No one remarked on his absence, and the entire audience of journalists and governmental officials clustered around the table where the photographs were spread out. She edged through the crowd and eased out of the room.

Just outside the door, she felt a sleek hand take hold of her upper arm, and she looked over her shoulder. "Jameela." A pleasurable warmth spread through her.

"Congratulations!" The president's wife leaned over and placed an ambiguous kiss at the edge of her lips. "But you were here just three days ago. Why didn't you tell me you had found something? And now even your colleague has left without explanation. What was going on in there?"

Madame Rashidi's lips were lipsticked with precision in the color of feverish, swollen flesh. Valerie couldn't take her eyes from them. "Mr. Vanderschmitt's arrival was unexpected. A complication…that I must still deal with." Valerie glanced around, still saw no sign of him. "I have urgent business, but I should be back in a few days, a week at the most. Can I call you?" she added in a quiet voice.

The beautiful lips came together in an *O* of regret. "I am sorry, Valerie. I would so love to celebrate with you, but I am rather tied up right now. You understand." Jameela's glance slipped sideways in the general direction of the conference room where the Saudi journalist was visible.

"Yes, yes. I understand. Of course." Valerie raised a hand in agreement.

At that moment, Fuad Rashidi summoned his wife back into the conference room, and Valerie stood in the empty corridor. It was a good moment to leave. She strode toward the central hall and reached the top of the wide marble staircase.

A familiar white suit blocked her way. Volker Vanderschmitt's face was tight with rage, and his normally thick lips were compressed to pale, thin lines. "What the hell did you think you were doing in there?"

"Doing? You mean, taking credit for the discovery which I and my team had in fact made?" She walked around him and took the first step down.

Hovering over her, he said, "You forget that you and 'your team' work for me. This little mutiny will have repercussions, I can assure you."

"You are threatening me?"

"You cannot remain part of an institution whose authority you defy. The proposal was to dig at Qaret el Dahr, but on your own initiative and without permission you moved the excavation. Such behavior is not professional."

"Discovering the richest tomb in eighty years sounds pretty professional to me. It seems to me that the problem is not my failure, but my success." She took the next step down.

Abruptly he seized her by the arm and spun her back around to face him. "Your success?" His eyes narrowed. "Success is earned, not stumbled upon. You flounce in expecting washing facilities and security while you blunder about, and now when you get lucky, you want sole credit." He snapped his fingers loudly. "You demand your little rights, then bypass all authority. Well, I am the authority here, and you will not bypass me. I have had it with your sort."

She shook her arm free of his grasp. "*My* sort? So this has nothing to do with the excavation, and everything to do with me. A woman has invaded the wilderness of manly men and taken away the mystery. And the prize."

His glance traveled from her face over her canvas jacket and down her field trousers to her boots. "Dressing like a man does not make you one. And stumbling upon a find does not make you a scientist. You are unnatural and a corruption of the profession."

"How charmingly obsolete you are. Claiming to know what is natural and unnatural. Technology is unnatural; so are clothing and medicine. Civilization itself is 'against' nature. Your biblical argument is pathetic and you are pathetic."

His hand shot out suddenly and cracked against the side of her face.

Astonishment and sudden bright pain radiated through her head. For the second time in three days, she held her hand over a ringing wounded ear.

"Thought you were clever, didn't you, sabotaging my film?" he said, unperturbed. "But your own photographs have exposed you."

"What are you talking about?" She tried to conceal her confusion.

"Canopic jars, Miss Foret. You forgot about them. Where there are canopic jars, there is a mummy, and grave robbers take gold, not cadavers." He took a step down and stood eye to eye with her. His long horse face softened to a smile. "You have the mummy, don't you? And I will bet you have even been foolish enough to bring it back to Cairo." He shook his head slowly.

"Oh, Miss Foret. I have found you out. I don't know your reasons for this folly, but those admiring reporters inside will have to change their headlines now, won't they? And President Rashidi will have his men on you in a minute."

Her mind reeled, mixing rage and fear. "You can go to hell," was all she could manage. She spun away and hurried down the rest of the staircase, feeling his glare like a spear aimed at her back.

He called down the stairs after her. "It's over, Miss Foret. As an archaeologist, you are finished. And shortly I will have you in jail."

She pushed open the door to the street into the blinding heat of the Cairo afternoon, wondering if he would pursue her. He had a reason now and the force of the state behind him. The professional duel had escalated into open warfare.

CHAPTER XVIII:
MEMENTO MORI

Her ear rang. Madness. Sheer madness to provoke him that way when so much was at stake. What had she been thinking? She had imagined exposure would let her snatch the prize back from him. But it had just made things worse. Vastly worse. And now she had endangered all the others too.

She hurried down the street, indifferent to the crowds that brushed her, the noise and choking air of traffic. She searched her memory to recall if Vanderschmitt would have any way to trace her to her friends. No, he had seen Auset at El Fishawy that one time, but her last name was never mentioned. He had met Derek, but could not connect him to Auset. Yes, the two of them—and the mummy—were safe as long as she did not lead Vanderschmitt back to the apartment.

She quickened her pace until she was almost running, directionless. Where could she go now? Who could help her out of the pit into which she had jumped?

Sammad. Of course. Sammad knew how to get in or out of anything. She looked around and realized she had no idea where she was. No matter.

She flagged down a black-and-white taxi. "Midan Al Hussein," she said, leaning back in the dilapidated seat, breathing heavily. Her head was throbbing. In a few minutes they were at Hussein Square, where she hurried across the pass over the highway into the shabby butcher's souq where tourists were a rarity. In the afternoon heat, the animal odors were pungent, and she winced as she passed the chicken cages piled up just before the cloth-sellers' market.

There it was, at the bend in the alley, one of half a dozen anonymous tiny cafés in the local souq. A young man stood behind a tiny counter near the brick oven where charcoal smoldered, sipping tea from a glass. He stared toward the far corner, where a television on a high shelf broadcast an Egyptian soap opera at great volume. In spite of the heat, all four tables were populated with men sipping coffee and puffing *sheesha*. Apple-sweet tobacco smoke enveloped her as she stepped through the doorway. "*As salaamu 'alaykum*, Khalil," she said hurriedly. "Is Sammad here today?"

"Yes, miss. In the back. Go on in." His glance sprang back to the television screen, where young lovers quarreled intensely.

She pushed aside the heavy curtain to the rear and stood for a moment, letting her sun-blinded eyes adjust to the darkness.

"Good afternoon, Dr. Foret," a hoarse voice said. The blurry form of a short, paunchy man in a dark galabaya took on clarity. He had a strong presence by virtue of his girth, and his prominent nose, which on a tall man would have been conspicuous, approached the grotesque. It always made her think of a vulture.

"Have you got a few minutes for me, Sammad? I have a business proposition for you."

"Of course, Doctor. Here, sit down." He motioned to the closest of the dozen tables that ringed the room of his "nightclub" and then sat down in front of her with his business smile. Without commenting on her need for it, he took a slightly rumpled handkerchief from his side pocket and offered it to her.

"Thank you, Sammad." She held it to the thin trickle of blood that had formed in front of her ear. "I'll get to the point. I need something smuggled out of Egypt. Something large."

"Smuggled out?" He tapped a pudgy finger on the wooden table. "We are better at 'in' than 'out,' but it can be arranged. How large? A suitcase? A refrigerator? An automobile?" He lit a cigarette, an American cigarette, she noticed. Presumably his own merchandise.

"A mummy."

"*Inti magnoona*?!" His cigarette hand went up in the air. "Do you know what you are asking? Antiquities has inspectors everywhere. No, no. The shape is too difficult to conceal."

"Sammad. You know I'll pay whatever it costs."

His eyelids lowered, covering his instant calculations, and he inhaled again from his cigarette. "Where would you want it shipped, assuming we could manage it?"

"New York. It would have to be New York."

"Oh, perfect. Why don't you simply ask for the head of the Sphinx?"

"I'm desperate, Sammad. Can you do it? I can't pay everything up front. I'll have to do it in installments. But you know you can trust me."

"Do I understand you correctly? You want me to transport an impossible object to an impossible place, and you want me to do it without any money. Dr. Foret, I think you are too used to getting your way in the souq."

"It's an emergency, Sammad. A lot is at stake. I can't explain now, but…"

The businessman suddenly looked past her at the doorway she had come through, and she turned to see what distracted him.

Khalil stood there, holding the curtain closed behind him. "Effendi, the police are here, with a foreigner. They are looking for you, Doctor." His eyes darted toward her and then darted away.

"Damn. That didn't take long." Valerie stood up. "How can I get out?"

With a smooth matter-of-factness, as if hiding clients from the police was a frequent and unavoidable occurrence in his line of business, Sammad tilted his head toward the rear. "Over there. Through the kitchen. Tell the cook you have to go to the carpet shop." With practiced ease, he slid out from behind the table, reignited his business smile, and waited until she was at the door before pulling back the curtain.

Valerie closed the flimsy wooden panel that functioned as a door and ran along a corridor to the kitchen.

A hirsute man stood at a table cutting up a joint of lamb into cubes, a stubby cigarette between his lips. The long ash broke off as he raised his head.

"Sammad said you could show me to the carpet shop," she said breathlessly.

"Carpet shop? Yes. This way." Setting aside his carving knife, he went around the table to the wall. With a single vigorous tug, he pulled back a cabinet set on tiny wheels and revealed an opening in the wall, about a meter high. She scrambled through and felt the cabinet roll back behind her, as muffled voices, sudden and angry, sounded in the kitchen.

Directly in front of her, a narrow wooden staircase, scarcely more than a ladder, was hammered into place between the two walls. She clambered up the steps to a wide second-story court where women and girls were washing carpets. They glanced up only briefly as she shot up in their midst. One of them, a crone enveloped in chador, pointed a black-draped arm toward cotton bales piled on the opposite side.

"*Shukran.*" Valerie staggered toward the bales, pivoting behind them to an opening identical to the one from which she had emerged. She went down the second ladder in leaps and slipped along the wall of another court, behind a row of drying carpets. At the end, the gate to the street was mercifully open.

She emerged on the wide Sharia el Muizz as, with almost comical precision, a city bus stopped in front of her in the middle of the street. She plunged into the traffic around screeching cars and jumped onto the bus seconds before it moved into the intersection.

Diesel fumes, cigarette smoke, and the smell of oily hair assailed her, and she tried to bury herself in the crowd of passengers. But a dozen sets of eyes stared at her, the men disapprovingly, the women, their faces half-covered by hijab, more discreetly. All the faces said the same thing: what are you doing here?

What the hell *was* she doing? And where the hell was she going? She inhaled deeply, dry mouthed. Her head ached.

Two men stood on the bus steps hanging onto the top of where the door once had been. Between their chests she caught glimpses of the thoroughfare. The bus rumbled past mosque, archway, and madrassa, and each time it stopped more people climbed in, packing ever more tightly around her. The hot bodies breathing the scarce air seemed the embodiment of her fear. Even standing still, she felt her heart pounding, and she was suddenly desperately thirsty.

"*Arafa,*" the driver called out finally, and Valerie realized where they had come. She was swept along with the crowd oozing from the bus and kept her eyes on her feet to avoid being stepped on. Finally in the light, she looked up at the medieval gateway to the great southern necropolis, Cairo's city of the dead.

She made a wide circle around the bus to see if any government vehicles had followed. The several dark cars outside the cemetery seemed innocent enough, but she could not be sure. She followed the other passengers as they dispersed along the dusty paths and alleys of the necropolis. Cairo's main burial site for over a thousand years, she knew, had also become Cairo's most notorious slum, housing thousands of the poor in its labyrinthine paths. Would the authorities follow her here?

Her eyes burned, for she looked westward toward the late-afternoon sun. Chiseled dark against it was a landscape of mausoleums and tombs punctuated by obelisks and minarets. Some were miniature palaces with their own minarets, others simple stone mastabas. On the poorer side, still others were simple mud-brick domes, like bread ovens.

The thought of ovens reminded her of her parched throat. "*Minfadlak*, where can I find water?" she called to a man who walked just ahead of her.

He turned partway around and pressed his lips together, in the midst of a dense black beard. "Go away. You do not belong here."

Valerie stopped, rebuffed, and watched him stride on until a woman and a child came out to greet him. On both sides, other figures emerged like phantoms from the tombs to meet the arriving men. Drawing fingertips across dry lips, Valerie realized how she must look to them, foreign and intrusive. She could not think of what to do.

Then, just in front of her, a figure emerged from a mortuary. Covered in black, like death itself, a woman came to the path and stopped. She turned around, facing her, and seemed to wait. Valerie walked toward her. "*Masaa' il kheer*. Please, is there water here? I need water."

A loose veil covered the woman's head like a hood and, silhouetted against the low afternoon sun, her features were indiscernible. She leaned on a stick, but when she spoke, her voice was robust. "Not here. Our Bishr brings it from a long way. But there is tea. Bishr!" she called out with sudden authority.

At the sound of his name, a small grotesque man came from behind the wall, wiping his hands on baggy pants. A bandy-legged dwarf, his lionlike face surrounded by an unbroken line of hair and beard, panted from the exertion of walking. The woman raised one arm to shoo him back. "Bishr, tell Meskhenet to make more tea. We will have a guest."

The dwarf stopped in his tracks, wiped his hands again, and retreated, rocking back and forth, into the complex.

"Oh, thank you. Tea would be very good." Valerie's voice was hoarse.

"This way," the woman said, and went ahead of her toward a stone pathway leading to an inner court. While behind them the sky still held a pale pink light, inside the mausoleum court it was already dark. The dwarf was lighting a kerosene lantern.

Valerie's eyes were drawn first to the western end of the court where an elaborately carved stone mastaba lay. At the other, under a high archway, a thin, white-haired man sat on the remnants of a rug. "My name is Nira," the woman finally said, "and this is Jehut."

The old man greeted his guest with the solemn courtesy of a caliph and waved her over to him. In front of him, a young girl squatted over a charcoal stove on which a kettle of water steamed. "Meskhenet," the hostess said. "And this is Bishr."

Meskhenet looked up briefly and then returned to pouring boiling water into a copper carafe. The dwarf Bishr waddled over to the old man and dropped down awkwardly next to him. He breathed with obvious difficulty, resting his tongue on his lower jaw like a dog. Then he leaned over to move the lantern nearer to the stove and sat up, placing his stumpy hands on his knees.

Together, the two objects gave off heat and light, and the group sat in a circle as if around a hearth. A bizarre family, Valerie thought, if indeed they were one. The girl could have been a grandchild. As for the dwarf, it was impossible to tell if he was a handicapped offspring of the couple or a wretched creature they had adopted into their household. She wondered how the four of them managed to survive.

Valerie accepted a glass of scalding tea and waited with concentrated patience for it to cool. She licked dry lips. "My name is Valerie, Effendi. I thank you for inviting me into your home." She looked across the court toward a limestone arcade carved with calligraphy. Under the arcade, she could see a sleeping room where pallets had been laid out and baskets held folded clothing or linen.

The patriarch glanced at where she looked. "Here men unfold their carpets next to the bones of sultans and caliphs from every age, and their children play between the tombs."

Valerie sipped the steaming tea, astonished at the refinement of the old man's speech. Like a museum guide or professor of history. How did such a person end up squatting on a rug in a cemetery?

"Yes. It is both the richest and the poorest part of Cairo, isn't it? But who is this resident here?" She pointed toward the sarcophagus at the lower end of the court. "With whom do you share your home?"

Jehut set aside his tea. "This is the house of Emir Husaam al Noori. He was killed, so the story goes, in the destruction of Jerusalem by the Crusaders. Presumably by one of your Christian ancestors." He gestured toward the sleeping room. "His story lies within. A volume of most beautiful writing."

"Ah, then it is Husaam al Noori whom I should thank for sheltering me in his house," she said lightly.

Jehut smiled, pressing his fingertips together. "No, my dear. This tomb bears only the story of the Emir, not his substance." He looked up at the calligraphed arcade. "This empty monument was created by his scribe and companion, Sharif al Kitab, who is resident, or at least a part of him, in a modest tomb in the rear. His head lies there, and we do not disturb it, although the stone of his sarcophagus is broken." He signaled Meskhenet to offer the guest some of the pita that had been toasting over the charcoal.

"In effect, you are the guest of a scribe."

Valerie took the smallest piece. "A nice way to put it. As a scientist, I do quite a bit of writing myself. Studies, reports, articles. I don't know if that would make me a scribe."

Jehut nodded. "A fine profession."

"I suppose." She glanced toward Nira, who sat on her left. The woman's face was still obscured, and Valerie wondered briefly if it would be impolite to move the lantern closer.

The old man held up something long and thin, like a marsh reed. "Writing conquers time and the death of men. An idea once written down by the ancestor is thought out to its conclusion by his remote descendant, though it be centuries later."

The tea was finally cool enough for her to drink in gulps, and she slaked her thirst. A wave of relief passed through her. "Um, I don't think there's much conquest in my writing. I just tell people about Egypt."

Nira leaned forward to drop a few crumbs into the coals, and the mysterious face was briefly illuminated. It was not so much beautiful, Valerie saw, as...compelling. A moment later, the lean aristocratic Arab face withdrew again into shadow.

"Precisely so." Jehut brought her back to the conversation. "Sharif al Kitab served his master by telling his story. But now it is the voice of the scribe that lives, and the Emir is held captive in his words. Is not the scribe then the master?" He paused, letting his remark sink in. Then he smiled again. "Perhaps you will one day write about us."

Valerie set down her glass and wiped her fingers delicately across her lips. "Yes, maybe. Right now I am not writing. More like running. The police appear to believe I have stolen something."

The old man raised his hand in some sort of signal. The dwarf got to his feet on one side of him, the young girl on the other. Together they lifted him to his feet.

"I must retire now. If the police come, do not worry. They do not stay long in the city of the dead. Good night." With his hands on the shoulders of the mismatched children, he let himself be led into the sleeping room.

"Good night," Valerie replied to his back. Her thirst finally gone, she began to feel her exhaustion. The pain in her head had subsided to a mild dizziness, and she could easily have stretched out on one of the pallets and gone to sleep.

"Is it the police that trouble you?" Nira slid closer.

In the warm lantern light, Valerie stared at the somber face as long as she dared, studying the exquisite groove that descended from between the nostrils to the bow of the lips. Full, but not voluptuous, the mouth opened slightly at the corners under the swelling of the muscles. They gave the impression of youthful sensuality in a face that otherwise hinted of great age. In fact, she bore an extraordinary resemblance to the woman in the souq. But that made no sense.

"The police? Yes, of course, but that's only a part. You see, a few days ago I was very happy. I had made the discovery of a lifetime. Then I was hit by a stone and suddenly everything fell apart. A vicious man who used to be nothing to me now has power over my life. He is the one who has sent the police after me."

Valerie searched the other woman's face trying to make sense of it. Like Jehut, she did not seem to belong among the misfits of the necropolis. Valerie could not imagine her belonging anywhere. "There are...other things too. Things I can't explain."

Nira moved the last few inches toward her and laid a hand lightly on her back. Under the sleeve of the abaya, Valerie felt sheltered, as if by a wing.

"He is unimportant. You have another story and it is not his."

"Well, yes. We sort of had that out this morning. But I don't even really know what my story is. The life I had and believed in has been snatched away from me and nothing else put in its place."

Nira leaned slightly against her shoulder. "Go away from this man, into the desert, if you must."

"But I've just come from there." Valerie wanted to whine.

Long fingers curled around her hand, and she grasped them back. The ageless face came closer, and the stranger's lips were suddenly over the wounded ear. Valerie could not tell if the other woman was about to whisper or to kiss her, but it scarcely made any difference; Nira held her in a near embrace and she could have stayed in it forever. The woman smelled of cardamom and cedar, and Valerie inhaled the fragrance with closed eyes. She waited for Nira to act and felt the quiet rising and falling of her chest as she breathed.

The night sky lit up suddenly, and Valerie startled. On the other side of the wall, the sound of tires on gravel revealed it was from automobile headlights.

Nira drew back. "I think you must leave now. Come. I will show you where to hide."

A car door slammed and Valerie lunged to her feet. Nira snatched up the lantern and ran ahead of her to the back court. When they turned the corner, Valerie saw with a shudder where she was to hide—in the tomb of Sharif al Kitab. One end of the low stone sarcophagus was broken and lay flat like the lid of a spaghetti box. By the lantern light, Valerie could already see the skull of its inhabitant. She knelt down reluctantly.

Nira knelt in front of her, taking Valerie's face in both hands. "Do not be afraid," she whispered, and suddenly pressed warm lips on Valerie's mouth.

Shock, fear, and sudden arousal set her heart pounding, and Valerie held the kiss, letting dangerous seconds pass. Finally, the sound of footfall and men's voices propelled her into the hollow space. Nira set the stone back in its place at an angle, leaving a crack at the side.

For a moment Valerie felt terror at being immured alive. Then her fingers found the crack, and she understood that she had only to push back the slab to be free. The trickle of air streaming over her cheek reassured her, and the silence outside confirmed she was well hidden. She could endure a few minutes of confinement in darkness and in dust.

Saracen dust, she realized, giddy with exhaustion.

"Sharif al Kitab." She murmured nonsense to herself, to keep the fear at bay. "Is that your head that presses so un-Islamically against my breast? Sorry to intrude in your tomb, poor Yorick. Where do you suppose the rest of you is? Still in Jerusalem, you think?" Pleased with her witticism, she closed her eyes. Or perhaps they were already closed; in the pitch blackness, it was the same. Feeling the cool night air trickle over her face, she tried to imagine she looked out into open space and fell into a light sleep.

An army of Crusaders pursued her, and the grim knight who carried the banner of Christ was Vanderschmitt. She fled before them into Holy Jerusalem and joined the Saracens on the wall. Pierced by an arrow, Husaam al Noori fell into her arms and she held him while he died, his head leaning against her breast. Below the platform, rigid in their righteousness, the Crusaders crashed through the gates with iron battering rams. Over the invading army the noon sun shone fiercely, and the spears and arrows that blazed down on the defenders seemed to fall from vengeful heaven. Suddenly the banner knight stood over her. Helpless where she crouched, she saw his sword curve in an arc and come down on the side of her head.

Valerie awoke into the terrifying darkness. She thrashed in panic, hitting her hands against the stone, and the slab behind her head fell away with a thud. The patch of open night sky, lighter than the tomb, brought a sudden gust of air, and she scrambled toward it.

She struggled to stand up on cramped legs and listened, bewildered. Silence all around; the police must have gone. But why hadn't Nira come to fetch her? By ambient light she could discern the vague forms of walls and gateways, and so she groped her way back to the central court where the family had sat.

No one. Nothing. No charcoal stove or lantern.

"Nira? Jehut?" She called out softly. Then again more loudly. "Nira?" No response. Only the sound of dirt trickling as some night rodent dislodged it from between stones. She remembered her Zippo lighter and took it from her pocket, relieved. She flicked the wheel over the flint, and a sudden dry spark flashed and caught the wick. An inch-long flame appeared, bobbing silently up and down within its metal collar.

Holding the light in front of her, she moved along the arcade to the sleeping room. Still nothing. Only tattered rags, folded under disintegrated straw. She walked in a circle around the court and then to the spot where they all had sat. But her little flame revealed neither ash nor bread crumb. Where there was dust, it was undisturbed and bore no footprints other than her own.

Shivering, she made her way out to the main road of the cemetery. To the right, farther into the necropolis, she saw the bare-bulb lights of denizens who patched together electrical connections. On the left the tombs were dark, but it was no more than two hundred meters to the cemetery gate through which she had come. Lit by city lights from the other side, it gave off a soft smoky halo. She hurried through it, emerged onto the city street, and shook her head at the comforting banality of half a dozen taxis waiting for business. Patting her trouser pocket to make sure she still had money, she waved to the closest of them. "Zamalek," she said. "Ahmed Sabri Street. And hurry, please."

In the dark backseat of the taxi she pressed fingers to her lips. She was not crazy; someone, something, had kissed her. She wondered what the hell it was.

CHAPTER XIX:
FLIGHT INTO EGYPT

"Where have you been? I've been worried sick! And you're covered in soot! What happened?" Wide-eyed, Derek stepped back and held the door open.

She brushed past him and dropped her knapsack on the floor. "We have to get out of here!" She walked into the living room where Auset watched television.

Derek followed. "We know that already. But what happened to you?"

"Shh!" Auset waved her hand behind her without turning away from the screen. "News report."

"About us?" Valerie asked, alarmed.

"No, Palestine. Suicide bomber. A woman blew up part of a settlement."

Valerie shook her head. "Israel will retaliate soon enough."

"Already has. They're bulldozing the houses in her street right now. Or maybe that's what made her do it in the first place." The three watched the images of collapsing walls, soldiers holding back thrashing women, old men weeping. The coverage turned to the settlement. More of the same.

Stone-faced, Auset turned off the television. "So, what happened to you?" she asked over her shoulder. "Derek was frantic."

"I was so worried that I made Auset call Antiquities," he confirmed.

Valerie looked up, alarmed. "You called them? You didn't tell them your address, did you?"

"Of course not," Auset said. "We just asked when you left, and they said right after the presentation. Although now that you mention it, they did keep asking who I was. I didn't tell them that either. So are you going to tell us what happened? You're a mess, and look. Your cheek is bleeding again. Derek, be a dear and get us a washrag."

Valerie sat down wearily on the sofa and leaned back with closed eyes. "Vanderschmitt knows we have the mummy. The bastard actually smacked me and then went to fetch the authorities. I got out of there fast, but I spent half the night in the necropolis, some of it in a tomb." She pulled herself upright. "Auset, I'm sorry. It was a mistake to bring Rekemheb to Cairo. We have to get him out of here somehow."

Derek came back with the cloth. Auset folded it expertly and dabbed it against Valerie's inflamed cheek. "We're ahead of you there," she reported. "Yussif has relatives in the Dakhla Oasis. Mango and guava farmers. He called them today, and they agreed to let us use a corner of their land. For a year if necessary. That will give you time to find a more permanent place."

Derek's eyebrows went up. "Was that okay? I mean, I don't want to interfere, but I'm sort of permanently involved in this. I also kind of suspected there would be trouble if you got in Vanderschmitt's face."

Valerie winced, both at the touch of the wet cloth and at the memory. "More like he got in mine. But you did good. Moving Rekemheb is exactly the right thing."

"That's what we thought. Don't worry. Rekemheb understands that he has to stay out of sight when other people are around."

Valerie pushed away the cloth. "That's enough. Thanks. But listen. I'm not sure Yussif should be involved in this. Neither should you, Auset. It's not your problem, and there's no reason to endanger you."

Auset crossed her arms in the narrow valley between her bosom and her belly. "We discussed that. But while you were gone, Rekemheb has been talking to us. Well, trying to. He and Derek have found a way to communicate—in a primitive sort of way. I've gotten used to him, and you know what? You're right. If the Ka is real, then all the rest follows."

"And Yussif? What's his connection?"

"Will you lay off Yussif, please. He came up with the whole idea of El Dakhla. He's the only one who can drive the truck and provide a plausible reason to my father for our going there. Besides, I want him with us." She wiggled to the edge of the sofa and stood up, adamant. "So. We either do this all together, or not at all."

Valerie rubbed her forehead. "I guess it's all together, then."

❖

Yussif returned shortly before midnight, his sleeves rolled up, carpenter-like. He brushed grit or sawdust from his palms and announced, "Everything is fix and truck is ready. We have plenty of water and long box in the back to put grandfather. Plenty of packing cloth to cover him."

Valerie studied the Arab, but he remained inscrutable. His English was too strained, too unsubtle to reveal him, and his thick beard concealed expression.

"'Grandfather.' I like that." Derek laid a hand on the thick shoulder. "Thank you, Yussif. And whatever this trip costs, in supplies… anything…I'll take care of it."

"Is nothing." He looked at the floor and then at Auset. "I leave note to your father to say I drive to Luxor for alabaster. We must to bring some back when we return."

"Yussif, you've thought of everything. I'm not much good at this myself," Auset said, dropping pomegranates into a large paper bag. "I've never smuggled antiquities before."

Valerie looked at the amulet and the ivory scroll box she was wrapping in her shirt. "Smuggling. Yeah. That's what they'll call it, won't they?"

Derek came into the room, carrying the mummy diagonally across his body as if he held a very large baby. "Don't worry, Valerie dear," he soothed. "There are times when you know you're doing the right thing. Yussif, would you get the door for me? Thanks." He looked back over his shoulder as he went out. "It'll be all right in the end. I'm sure."

"That's the trouble with you, Derek. You believe in salvation," Valerie said as the door swung shut. She put on her gun belt, sliding the small pistol around to the back of her hip, under her field jacket. "I don't."

"I know what you mean." Auset added a second bag of fruit to the first. "No matter how hard I try, I can't make him cynical."

Valerie sighed. "Cynical? I stopped being cynical a few hours ago, when I was lying in a grave. Now I just feel like I'm jumping off into empty space. Dark, empty space."

Auset picked up a grocery bag in each arm. "Yeah? Well, imagine what it feels like to jump with a baby on the way."

❖

The truck rumbled southward along the Nile. Slouched in a half-sitting position, Derek fell into a doze. Irritated by the vibration of the truck bed, the breeze that whipped loose strands of hair across her face, and the discomfort of knees pressed against the makeshift casket, Valerie could not sleep. She inventoried the supplies. Gallon bottles of water, bags of nuts, fruit, and dates. Wooden poles wrapped in canvas behind her back—probably a canopy, she thought, for when the sun came up. Packing quilts for pillows, seats, or mattresses. Well done, Yussif.

Then she brooded, her arm thrown across her knapsack where, for lack of an alternative, she kept the artifacts. Two strange women had appeared since she was stone-struck, and one of them had kissed her. Who were they, and why were they doing this to her? She was beginning to long for a simpler time, when she labored fruitlessly at the excavation and came back once a week to the arms of Jameela. Success was proving to be a disaster.

She stared, grainy eyed, at the ribbon of road that curved out behind them, watching the lights of the few vehicles that came on the highway and then turned off again. All but one.

Derek stirred in his half sleep, leaning to one side to tuck another layer of quilting under his right buttock. It did not seem to add to his comfort, and in a few moments he was fully awake. "My booty's numb. Can't feel a thing back there." He peered down at the radiant dial on his wrist. "You can't sleep either, huh?"

Valerie rubbed her knees and shifted again. "Look back there. See those tiny headlights way behind us? They've been following us since Cairo, and they seem to be getting closer. They can't be from a bus, not at this hour, out here in the middle of nowhere. I don't like it."

"Are you sure it's always the same lights?"

"Pretty sure. No, very sure. I've had nothing else to look at for hours now."

"You think it's Vanderschmitt? How can we find out without stopping?" he asked. "That would sort of defeat the purpose of running away, though, wouldn't it?"

Valerie knocked on the window at the back of the truck cab, and Auset slid it open. "Looks like we're being followed," she shouted over the noise of the wind and the truck motor.

"You think it's the Antiquities people?" Auset called back over her shoulder.

"Whoever they are, they're getting closer. We can't outrun them, and along this road, we can't hide the truck. Any ideas?"

The two in the front conferred. Then Auset twisted around. "Yussif thinks we should stop and let them catch up. There's a village up ahead. You can see the minaret."

Valerie leaned quickly over the side of the truck and saw a cluster of mud-brick houses squatting gloomily by the side of the highway. One or two second-story windows held light. Otherwise the only sign of life in the village was the simple minaret lit up with rings of green neon at its far end. She clambered back to the cab window. "Yeah? Go on."

"You and Derek should take the mummy and hide someplace in the village. We'll let the other car catch up. If it's Vanderschmitt, he'll stop. But there'll just be Yussif and me here, importers on the way to Luxor to buy alabaster, right? When they're gone, you can come back."

Yussif shouted over his shoulder, "You must to do it quickly. Soon they are close enough to see you."

"Okay. Say the word," Valerie yelled, yanking open the lid of the coffin-crate.

"What is the word?" Yussif called back, obviously confused.

"Say anything! Say *Go!*"

"Anything! Go!" The truck lurched to a stop suddenly by the side of the road, just before the first few houses of the village.

"Right!" Derek slipped his arms under the mummy and lifted it easily. As soon as he cleared the crate, Valerie threw in mats and blankets, covered it again, and jumped to the ground behind him. He was already loping toward the village, a graceful dark phantom against the lighter sand.

No streetlights. That was good. They plunged into the first dark street, making as much distance as possible from the road. Soundlessly they crept past crumbled walls and crouched finally behind a wheelbarrow and construction debris. At the sound of another vehicle stopping, Derek peered out from behind the pile. "It's a car, all right, not a bus. Two people are getting out. I can't be sure, but I think one of them is wearing a white uniform."

"*Merde!*" she hissed. "Antiquities. Come on. We've got to get out of here."

They crept out from hiding and ran down another purgatorial alley, ever closer to the center of the village. Impossible to run quietly; someone surely had to have heard them. At the sound of a shutter opening, they crouched again between a wall and a dark mound.

"Oh, great," Derek whispered. "Here we are behind a dung heap in a mud village, in the desert of death. Could it get any worse?"

A dog began to bark.

"Guess it could!" Valerie leapt to her feet. Men's voices became audible and they fled again, around corners, down alleys, trying doors, trying gates. Locked doors everywhere. Locked against what, she wondered.

Finally they stood breathlessly before a large double door. Mercifully, the handle turned, the door creaked open, and they stumbled inside. They stood for a moment, panting, their backs against the wall, hearing footfall approach and then pass by. One minute. Two minutes. No one burst in after them.

Derek shifted his bundle to the other shoulder. "Where are we, I wonder?"

Valerie fumbled in her pockets, pulled out the Zippo lighter again, snapped it open. Holding the flame overhead, she walked forward a few meters and stopped before a crudely plastered wall where a red plastic frame hung on a string. Inside the frame, on yellowed paper, Arabic calligraphy curled. "Uh-oh."

"What?"

She followed along the wall and found the expected alcove the height of a man. On the other side of the alcove a second text hung in another red plastic frame. "'God is great,' it says. Oh, *merde encore.* It's a damned mosque!"

"Watch your language, then. We're in a place of worship," he hissed.

"Well, if the imam comes in here, he won't be worshipping!" she hissed back.

"What's an emom?"

"Shh!" A door creaked.

They pressed themselves against the wall again. As one of the double doors slowly opened, Valerie looked around for another exit but saw only the narrow door on the other side leading almost certainly to private quarters. They were trapped in a mosque with a stolen mummy, violating two religions. She imagined jail.

"Muuuuuuuh."

Her head snapped toward the sound. Jutting through the crack between the two doors, the white head of a cow turned slowly toward them. The beast blinked at them with bovine serenity, and Valerie exhaled slowly. Out of sight behind the animal's rump, several men cursed. After a few moments of tussling and bumping against the door, the cow looked once more at them with apparent dismay and backed out of the dark interior. An unseen hand pulled the door of the mosque shut.

They stood rigid against the door, listening to the men drag the balking chattel back to its pen. Long minutes of silence followed, broken finally by the soft sound of male chuckling.

Valerie turned angrily to Derek to hush him and saw the faint greenish halo around the mummy. "Rekemheb!" she whispered with quiet annoyance. "Not now!"

The laughter continued. "Have no fear. You are not found. The farmers have withdrawn, and the two men you flee have gone away again in their machine. I have seen it. Your friends search for you now."

"If you could see so much, why didn't you warn us about the cow?" Valerie grumbled.

"That was the goddess who smiled at you. Hathor, looking after her servant."

"Ah, finally!" Derek stepped past her and with his free hand opened the door a crack. "Nobody in sight. I think the coast is clear." He edged the door farther open and cautiously ventured out again into the alley.

Valerie followed him, whispering in the direction of the mummy, into which the Ka had disappeared again. "Hathor? I don't think so. A cow can't smile. There was definitely no smile on that cow."

CHAPTER XX:
OF GODS AND KINGS

Valerie dozed fitfully, her eyes shaded by her hat from the glare of the rising sun. The sound of polite coughing woke her, and she lifted the fedora with her thumb. Rekemheb sat on his coffin in front of her, and Derek, stretched out alongside the coffin, snored softly, apparently in deep, untroubled sleep.

Groggy, she uncapped her trail bottle and took a drink of water to remove the foul taste in her mouth and clear her head. It helped only a little, so she poured a bit into her hand and rubbed it over her face. The evaporating water cooled pleasantly. She looked at Rekemheb again.

In the full morning light he was almost opaque, with only a slight translucency, like wax. He sat on his casket, one leg drawn up in front of him, the other folded beneath him. The figure that he made—she smiled inwardly—was the hieroglyph for "priest."

"We go toward Thebes," he said matter-of-factly.

"No. Southwest from there, to an oasis. Don't worry. You will be safe there."

"I do not worry. Not at all. My grandchild Ayemderak has explained this new journey and this…" He gestured toward the truck cab. "This roaring chariot."

"'Roaring chariot.' That's a good one. Wait. You can talk to Derek? In English?" She glanced with admiration at her friend who still slept, his head thrown back and his mouth slightly open.

"N-klesh? Yes, we speak his language and mine, together. It is difficult, but my heart is light to hear his voice. My grandchild told me of this quest which he undertakes for me." He gestured again, this time in the direction they traveled. "Have I understood him correctly?"

Valerie shifted her weight to the opposite hip, which ached slightly less from the rumbling metal truck bed. "Not exactly. It is not only Derek who undertakes this, but all of us. And it is not so much a quest as…well, panicked flight."

A soft frown clouded the priest's face. "Then we flee the followers of Aton? I feared as much."

"I am not sure what you mean by that. The one who dogs us is a sort of religious fanatic, it's true. He follows us for vengeance, but also out of a belief that there is an absolute law about things—and that I have violated it."

Rekemheb gave a wan smile. "You need not explain. I know this sentiment. I saw it in Sethnakht, who stood with others of his sort against our temples. But they were nothing but assassins in the name of their One God."

"Assassination? There's plenty of that going on right now, all over the Middle East. Men of certainty killing each other. Well, some for greed and some for dogma."

The Ka looked out over the desert as if surveying the land. "That is why the gods have sent you to me."

Derek sat up from his rumpled pallet and rubbed circulation back into his face. "I can't believe I finally fell asleep in spite of everything." He looked up at the entity perched on his casket. "Well, good morning. Have you two been chitchatting? What about?"

"The reasons for this trip, Vanderschmitt, fanatics in general. Rekemheb knows them from his time too."

"Did you reassure him that he's safe now?" He reached for his own bottle of water, drinking generously, and then poured some on a handkerchief to rub over his neck.

Valerie shrugged. "I'm not so sure of that myself. He was entombed for over three thousand years, after all. How can we promise him that much protection again?"

Derek reached across the space between them and squeezed her arm. "Stop worrying, girlfriend. We'll find something. Have faith." He reached into the recess of his backpack and drew out a tiny bottle of lotion.

"Faith? Now there's a word that has me reaching for my gun. Faith just means you have no evidence."

"Sorry! I was trying to comfort, but I guess I hit a nerve." He rubbed the lotion over his face and hands, taking particular care around his lips.

Valerie looked at her own dry hands. "And besides, faith in whom? In Jesus? Allah? Jehovah? Faith in what? That we'll all be saved? That Elvis lives?"

The Ka tilted his bright head. "Are these your gods?"

Valerie turned her head suddenly. The Ka had understood her remark without translation.

Derek was unfazed. "Uh, yes. Jesus, Allah, Jehovah are all gods. *Netcheru*. Only Elvis is not." He laughed softly. "He's just a king."

The Ka persisted. "This Elvis. Where is he king?"

Derek suppressed a smile. "Used to be in Memphis."

"Egyptian, then," the Ka concluded, nodding.

"Enough about us, Rekemheb." Valerie leaned forward, her elbows on her knees. "You have told us nothing about yourself."

The Ka returned to pure Egyptian, and Valerie was just as glad. It pleased her to hear the ancient language come alive and reveal its staccato music. Rekemheb laid his open hand over his heart. "Me? There is not much to tell. I was a simple priest, the son of captive Nubians who grew up serving Egyptian gods. When I became a man, I was appointed to the temple of Hathor. This was in the time of Ramses."

"Ramses the Great." She rested her chin on one hand. "A name that rings through history. Did you ever see him? Speak to him?"

"I saw the Great King only at the solemn festivals…and of course at his funeral." The Ka paused for a moment. "That day, filled with solemn grief and fear, is bright in my memory, for I accompanied His Majesty down the Nile to his tomb at Thebes." Rekemheb looked toward the somber west.

"It seemed, but for the beating of the drums, all Egypt had grown silent. On that day the king joined with the sun and became the new Horus. His thirteenth son, Meremptah, became Lord of the Two Lands."

Derek studied the priest while Valerie translated into English. He nodded. "I can just picture it, Rekemheb, and I love the drama, but what has that to do with Valerie and me, and with Auset being pregnant?

What are we all supposed to be doing now?"

Rekemheb opened his hands. "I do not know. The gods will reveal themselves when it suits them. I know only what the scribe spoke. The Balance, the Book, and the Child. These were the gods' hope against the Aton rising in the west."

Valerie shook her head. "That doesn't make sense. Aton is the sun disk."

Derek looked up through his eyebrows. "And the sun rises in the east, right?'

"No, I mean the reference to Aton itself. It shouldn't occur in Meremptah's time. The One God was an innovation of Akhnaton, a century earlier. When he died, the idea died with him." She turned to the priest. "Didn't it?"

"It did not die. The cult of Aton was forbidden at the court, but it continued among the people." His wax-like face darkened slightly as he looked directly at her. "It was their priest who murdered me."

The truck careened around a sudden curve, swinging them to the side, and Valerie exclaimed, "Look up ahead! A military checkpoint. I think we're in trouble."

The truck pulled up to a dilapidated guard station, the paint peeling away from its outside wall. Three soldiers in white uniforms far too large for them came forward with battered automatic rifles.

Yussif leaned out the truck window and chatted cheerfully with two of them, about the condition of the road, about the crazy foreigners who would pay a king's ransom to be taken to Luxor. But, *Alhamdulillah*, it was a way to make a living.

He held out a crumpled pack of French cigarettes, shaking out one for each. Through the window at the back of the cab, Valerie could see that Auset had put on a silk veil that covered all but her eyes. The Muslim wife, silent, pregnant, all but invisible.

A third soldier came around to the back of the truck. "*Sabah al kheer.*" Valerie wished him good morning. The soldier mumbled a reply, glanced briefly at the wooden crate at her feet, and then seemed to take great interest in Derek. "*Gawáaz sáfar!*" he ordered.

Derek looked at him blankly. "*Besport,*" the soldier repeated, trying an alternative.

"He wants to see your passport," Valerie explained.

"Why only mine?" He jerked the document from his pack and handed it over, obviously piqued.

The soldier opened it slowly. "American?" He turned the pages, scrutinizing every stamp and port of entry.

Derek nodded. "Uh-huh."

Another officer came around to the rear of the truck and took the passport, perusing it with the same thoroughness. "Amereekan, heh?"

"Yes. Still." Derek held an unconvincing smile.

The second officer closed the booklet and tapped it several times on his open palm. Then, as if deciding the whole matter had ceased to be interesting, he handed it back and both soldiers walked away.

The truck jerked slightly as Yussif put it into gear, and it pulled slowly away from the guard station.

Derek blew air out slowly in relief. "Wow. That was scary. I wonder how many more times we're going to have to do that." He slid his pass back into his knapsack.

Out of sight of the road station, the truck pulled to the side of the road and stopped. Yussif came around to the rear with a map in his hand.

"What were those soldiers looking for?" Valerie asked. "Why the pass check with Derek?"

"Assassin. They look for him all over, and Derek looks like from Sudan."

"Oh, great. I come all the way to Africa, where I'm a suspect because I'm black."

"Yes. And is worse in south part of Egypt." Yussif looked down the road they were traveling. "This highway has more checkpoints, many more."

"What is the alternative?"

"That is what I come to show." He opened up the ragged map and spread it out on the truck bed. Valerie came over on her knees and looked down on it, trying to read the Arabic place names as Yussif traced the route with his finger.

"We are here. Main road on west side of Nile has military every twenty kilometer. Down here is El Dakhla. I think is much better to drive on other side."

Valerie turned the map around and traced her finger along the proposed route. "You mean here, past El Amarna. Yes, that's a good idea. It'll also give us an opportunity to stop and look at one of Akhnaton's stelae."

Derek looked up. "Do you really think we should stop for sightseeing?"

"It's not sightseeing. Rekemheb's prophecy speaks of Aton, who was important only during the reign of Akhnaton, over a hundred years before Rekemheb's lifetime. Our route runs past several of Akhnaton's stelae, and they might tell us something."

Derek shrugged. "It's going to be hot walking around at midday."

Yussif scratched the side of his beard. "El Amarna is also Islamist. People do not like foreigners in Middle Egypt. Is maybe not so good for you to walk around."

Valerie tapped a tiny spot on the map. "You can drop us off near the stela right here and then make a rest stop in this village nearby. We won't stay more than an hour."

"As you wish, Dr. Foret." Yussif folded up the road map.

"Don't worry about us," she said to the driver's back as he climbed into the truck cab. "I'm not a dumb tourist. I speak Arabic. I can take care of myself."

Derek pressed his fingertips together. "Please, God. Don't let those become famous last words."

❖

Valerie and Derek dropped from the truck bed with a soft crunch onto the pebbly sand below the cliff.

Valerie walked around to the cab window. "Go on to the village, Yussif. Derek and I have got plenty of water, and we'll be fine. We'll come along in about an hour. You should wait near the village well, wherever that is. In a place that small, there can be only one."

"Less than an hour, I hope." Derek wiped his sleeve across his face as the truck rumbled away. They began the climb up to the stela complex. "So. What's this?"

"We're looking at one of the fifteen stelae that Akhnaton ordered carved on the rocks around this plain. All of them say roughly the same thing, that Pharaoh dedicates this new capital Akhetaton to the One God, the Sun Disk."

Derek stopped at the foot of the inscribed cliff and leaned over, panting and gripping his knees. He caught his breath finally and stood up. "Wow. I…had…no idea…it would be so big. It's a whole huge wall. So, what do you hope to find on it?"

"Any reference to the Balance, the Book, or the Child. Or to Aton in the west. I don't know. It could be anything."

"It's not going to be easy. Look how the writing has worn away. You'd think they would protect it. With glass or something."

"They do protect it with glass. At least in the tombs. And sometimes in the temples. But not way out here."

He shaded his eyes and looked up at the stela. "Look, there's an illustration at the top. This is the sun disk, obviously, with all its rays ending in little cartoony hands. But whoa! Look at these people here. Long heads, skinny arms, and waay too fat asses."

"Show some respect. That's Akhnaton and Queen Nefertiti, worshipping the Aton." Tilting her fedora forward to shade her eyes, she read the inscription. "'On this day…His Majesty ascended, great in sovereignty…like Aton when he rises…every heart in gladness'… blank blank blank. There's a lot missing, but it still appears to be the usual lauding and praising. Let me skip down a little."

She knelt before the lower register of the inscription and blew sand from the incised figures. "'His captains fell down before him on their faces before his majesty, tasting the ground before his will.'"

Derek laughed softly. "This king had a power thing, didn't he?"

She went on. "Here it says, 'Through me liveth the Good God, Unique Bringer of the Light, Destroyer of Apophis'…blank blank. 'The Aton desires me to make unto him His city, presenting the earth to Him that put him on the throne. I uphold Him, magnifying His name. I smite His enemies. I cause the earth to fall down before the One, in whom liveth all things.'"

Derek wiped his handkerchief across a dry forehead. "Sounds to me pretty much like the same-old same-old. There is no god but Aton, and Akhnaton is his prophet!"

She got to her feet again. "Yes, you're right. Basic militant monotheism. But otherwise there's nothing here to suggest Rekemheb's prophecy. Or us."

"Except for the fact that Mr. Big Tush Akhnaton looks just like your friend Vanderschmitt." He fanned himself with the folded cloth.

Valerie took a step back. "Hey, you're right. Long face, skinny chest, plump hips. Bizarre. It's got to be a coincidence, though."

"After Rekemheb, do you think anything that happens to us now is a coincidence?" His speech blurred on the word "coincidence," and he rubbed the side of his face. "Can we leave now? I'm not feeling very good. Got to lie down someplace. What about that little white house over there by the village? The one with the dome."

"In the *koubba*? That's a shrine, Derek. If there are any local people there, they won't like it."

"I'll chance it. Just get me out of this sun before I stroke."

Half supporting him, she led him stumbling back down the slope to the white brick cube that sat squat and simple on rocky ground. On the north side she found a doorway open to an interior no larger than a tool shed. At its front, a step up from the floor, was a long granite box. Objects were arranged along the step as if left in offering: prayer beads, palm leaves, shards of pottery with words scratched on them.

While he leaned against the outer wall, his face pressed against his forearm, she went in to look for scorpions lurking in the shade. He staggered in afterward, collapsing to his knees.

She sat down on the ground next to him. "Here, lay your head on my lap. It's better than the stone."

Groaning softly, he curled up into the fetal position with the side of his head on her thigh.

"Give me your water bottle," she said. She poured the lukewarm liquid onto his folded handkerchief and smoothed the dripping cloth over his forehead.

"I'm sorry. I should have made you wear a hat. We'll stop at the next village and find a turban for you, like Yussif has. Even better, a *khaffia*. You'll look fabulous."

He laid his long, smooth hand over hers. "Fashion, style, and a good-looking corpse. Oh, you know me so well. Valerie, if I die, promise to make me look dignified."

"Die? Don't be such a drama queen. You've just got heat exhaustion. You'll be fine in a few minutes." She trickled more water over his forehead.

"I've got a killer headache." He winced. "What is this place, anyhow?"

"A mausoleum to some saint. That stone box with the calligraphy will be a sarcophagus."

"A saint, huh? Do you think he can cure my headache? I'll even pray to him if you tell me what to say."

"Why would you pray to a Muslim saint? You don't believe in Islam."

"I believe in everything. Don't you remember? Rekemheb said there was more than one hereafter. If there are Kas, there can be saints."

"Yes, and fairies and werewolves and elves." She trickled more water on the rag.

"Don't be such a cynic, Valerie. You know 'more things in heaven and earth, Horatio…'"

"'…than are dreamt of in my philosophy.' Well, I can't argue with Shakespeare." She lifted his head and shoulders from her thigh. "So, go on. Pray. You can start by praising his god. They like that."

Holding the wet rag over his forehead and eyes, Derek rolled over onto his knees and pressed his face into his hands. "*Allahuakbar. Allahuakbar.* Whoever you are, take pity on me who means no harm to anyone."

Valerie backed away from him toward the entrance. "Tell him… uh!"

Strong arms seized her. Before she could cry out, they yanked her roughly from the shade of the shrine and threw her onto the hot ground outside. She looked up at two men standing over her. "We mean no disrespect," Valerie said in Arabic. Wiry, ferocious in their short, dark beards, they were unarmed. One of them had a long camel face; the other was round, apoplectic. Breathless with rage, neither one replied.

Two other men, shouting, reached through the entrance and jerked Derek up from his crouching position. He did not resist, although their combined weight was scarcely more than his, and allowed himself to be dragged from the shrine. Without stopping, the two men held him by his upper arms and pulled him toward the village.

"Tell them we didn't mean any harm," he called back over his shoulder.

The two other men prodded Valerie from both sides, urging her to follow the first group. "They're not going to listen," she called back to him. A few minutes later she added, "It looks like they're taking us to the mosque."

"Oh, great. They're fundamentalists, right? And the penalty for trespassing on a shrine is what?"

Valerie tried to reassure him. "Don't worry," she said feebly. "I will explain to the imam—"

The camel-faced one seized her by the shoulder of her shirt and spat in her face.

CHAPTER XXI:
LA ILAHA ILL ALLA

The mosque stood at the edge of the village. The simple domed structure was flanked on one side by a concrete wall and on the other by an arcade forming a shaded walkway. Under the arcade, a man poured water into an ablutions urn. The captors prodded their two prisoners into the courtyard, and a crowd of spectators followed them, men at the forefront and some half dozen black-shrouded women at the rear. Valerie could make no sense of their angry murmurs but for the word *agaanib*. Foreigners.

The rumbling of the crowd stopped suddenly as a door opened within the arcade and a man stepped out into the sunlight. Tall, white-bearded, in dark blue galabaya and turban, he projected a somber authority. He stood for a dramatic moment in front of the captives, studying them.

"The imam, right?" Derek muttered.

"Uh-huh."

The four guards backed away from the prisoners, leaving them at the center of a silent, hostile crescent of onlookers. The white-beard turned toward the captors, awaiting explanation. The camel-faced one stepped forward again and began his tirade, gesticulating emphatically. When he paused, the crowd murmured agreement, like a Greek chorus.

The imam listened without expression to the accusation, then turned to Derek. "What were you doing in a Muslim shrine?" His Arabic was surprisingly polished, his speech magisterial, as of a man used to public speaking.

"Val, what's he saying to me? Tell him I don't speak Arabic."

She addressed the cleric, who declined to look at her but stared sullenly at some spot on the ground while she spoke. "Effendi, this man asks me to tell you that he was taken ill and sought relief. He did not mean to give offense."

The imam lifted his eyes suddenly—hard, bright stones. "But you *gave* offense, both of you. Entering a holy shrine for your comfort is a desecration."

She persisted. "My friend was praying for deliverance from an affliction, as do many pilgrims. A saint hears all languages, doesn't he?"

The cleric looked down at Valerie's boots and trousers. "You speak out of place, woman. The prayer of an unbeliever is a blasphemy on the mercy of Allah, in whom all things liveth."

In whom all things liveth. Valerie hesitated, taken aback at the familiar phrase. "My friend's supplication was sincere and respectful. His father is a preacher, an imam in his own church, and this believer kneels before the One. Isn't the god of the Muslims also the god of Jews and Christians?"

The cleric turned to the accuser who still stood with his hands on his hips. "Did you witness this man praying?"

The long face tightened. "He was not praying. He…he was bent over his knees with his face in his hands. He spoke in his own language, but first he said, '*Allah Uakbar*,' to mock us." The witness stepped back, suddenly uncertain, and the crowd murmured again.

The cleric faced his captives. "You come all this way to pray in a foreign language at the shrine of a saint whose name you do not even know."

"You can question our knowledge, Effendi, but not our intentions. This man prayed as a believer, and I am his witness."

"A woman bears weak witness and a foreigner none at all. These men would stone you if I allowed them to, and it would be a just thing, for your desecration. God is not mocked." He paused, touching his beard as if to draw wisdom from it. "But Allah is also merciful, and it is not for me to say what is in a man's heart." He looked down once again at the boots she wore and glanced away.

"By whichever way you came here, you must leave again. Quickly, or these people will do you great harm."

Relieved, Valerie translated the cleric's remarks to Derek and reached out to him.

He withdrew his arm from her grasp. "Ask him why he hates us so much, Valerie. What have we ever done to them? Go ahead. Ask him that for me."

The imam listened, pressing his lips together while she interpreted. Then he looked directly at the American. "Do you know how foreigners appear to us? Everything about you is display, of wealth and power and lasciviousness. Your dress and behavior is a corruption to the eyes of our young, for the foolish among them try to emulate you. You are the people of Satan, and where you go, you bring licentiousness, your idle freedoms, and the disorder of your culture."

He paused, allowing her to translate, and then took up his vituperation once again.

"You disdain the iron law of God and urge our own government to reject it, bending to the will of the West. We feel your contempt for us as you destroy our traditions, and we despise you in return."

Valerie turned to her friend. "He said—"

A gunshot sounded suddenly and the crowd broke apart. From the confines of the courtyard, there was no place to flee but through the gate, and a security truck suddenly blocked it. Armed men jogged in through the gate and laid about them with rifle butts in the crowd of villagers. In a few short moments the compound was littered with the battered and wounded. Two of the soldiers stepped before the imam and took hold of him, dragging him without explanation toward the police truck. A third soldier, an officer, approached and presented himself with a quick military bow. "No need to worry. You are safe now," he said in English.

"Wow. What a coincidence that you were here when we needed you." Derek's eyes darted from the officer to the villagers who were fleeing, some injured and staggering, through the gate into the street.

"No coincidence. Security patrols the historical sites every day to protect the tourists. We are also looking for someone. A Sudanese. Even more dangerous than these people." He turned to Derek. "If you would be so kind to show me your passport, just to be sure, then you can be on your way."

Valerie watched as the soldiers pushed the somber cleric into the rear of the police vehicle and closed the door. "It was just a misunderstanding. We were straightening it all out."

"Well, it was getting a little scary for my taste, and I'm glad you guys showed up. Here's my passport. See? American boy."

The officer took an indifferent look at the document and handed it back. "These fundamentalists are a big problem, especially the imams. We have to teach them a lesson. It would be good for you to go now and let us do our job." The officer bowed once again and returned to his vehicle.

In a moment, the truck and its prisoner pulled away and rumbled out over the desert road, leaving a gray-brown cloud hanging in the street behind it. The onlookers standing on both sides of the street fell back a few paces and covered their mouths from the dust. Their eyes watched, smoldering.

Derek spoke under his breath. "What do we do now?"

"We walk down the street quietly, toward the center where the well should be and, hopefully, our truck. Like this." Eyes straight ahead, she walked unhurried through the gate into the street.

Derek came alongside of her, and they set out through the gauntlet of sullen, bitter faces. No one called out to them, or moved or spoke. The only sound was the gravel crunching under their heavy shoes as they walked. No one followed.

At the end of the street with the crowd far behind them they stopped, uncertain. Several alleys spiraled off from the intersection where they stood, and none gave any indication of leading to a center.

"*Merde*," Valerie muttered. "I do *not* want to wander around in this place any longer. If one more person lays a hand on me, I'm going to finally use this." She patted the hard object in her belt under her jacket.

"What? I was wetting my pants thinking they were going to kill us, and the whole time you had a gun?"

"Do you think one little .22 revolver would have held off the whole crowd? Besides, we're fugitives, dear. The last thing we need is to shoot up a village in Middle Egypt."

"Well, you might have to still, unless we can find our way back to the truck. After all this time you'd think they'd come looking for us."

"Looks like they did, Derek." She pointed up to a terrace that projected over one of the streets, where something birdlike fluttered its wings. Only its head was all wrong.

"Hello, cousin." Derek waved to the Ba of Rekemheb. "It's about time you showed up."

The Ba flew ahead and disappeared, but the truck stood, as agreed, near the village well. Two spindly palm trees cast thin, useless shadows over it. While they waited, Yussif and Auset had put up the tarpaulin over the truck bed, mercifully shading it from the deadly sun. A small crowd of children had gathered around it, eating what appeared to be Auset's pomegranates.

She came toward them. "We were beginning to worry. What did you find out?"

"Nothing, really." Valerie took a long drink from her water bottle. "Akhnaton's monotheism is pretty much like any other. Same pattern: one deity and one spokesman. I've decided I don't like this Aton *or* his chief promoter."

Derek fanned himself with his hat. "Valerie is no doubt soured by the fact that Akhnaton was the spitting image of Volker Vanderschmitt. But geez, Valerie, tell them what happened afterward."

She took another drink. "The politics of religion happened. Derek got a little sunstroke and we took shelter inside a shrine. Some of the villagers saw us and hauled us up before the village imam. You were right, Yussif. It was reckless of us to attract attention in this part of Egypt."

"Val, honey, you're leaving out the best part! There we were, about to be stoned or crucified or something, and suddenly these security guys arrived. Police truck, rifles. They were in full force and they hauled the imam guy away, just like that! It was weird. Here we are on the run from the authorities, and they end up kicking around their own people for us!"

"That's what the imam was complaining about, though, wasn't it? That the government favors foreigners over its own people."

"Right. I didn't think about that."

"In any case, the patrol didn't know who we were, but that won't help us for long. Now we've drawn attention to ourselves. When the report of the whole episode gets back to Cairo, someone will be looking for us. I suggest we get the hell away from this place."

Yussif opened the door to the truck cab. "Maybe is better to go in desert."

Valerie considered. "What about the military? Aren't they always out there on maneuvers? I'm not keen on explaining us to the nozzle of a tank."

Yussif shook his head. "Not so much tanks in desert. Most of time I see trucks. Army is not police. They bring water when wells are dry. They look for terrorist sometimes, but not for little thief like us."

Unconvinced, Derek looked up at the truck canopy. "But are we equipped for the desert?"

Yussif shrugged. "We carry plenty water and some food. Truck is good."

Valerie gnawed her lip. "We've had one close call last night, and I'm sure word that we're down here will get back eventually. I think I'd rather risk the desert."

"I agree," Yussif confirmed. "I know this place. I think is okay." He stepped up into the cab.

Valerie held her hand out to Derek, who had already climbed up onto the truck bed. With a single tug he hauled her up next to him. They sat down on either side of the coffin, waiting for the breeze of motion to blow off the cooking heat of the steel.

Yussif turned the wheel sharply and the vehicle veered west toward the Nile. After a moment Valerie took off her fedora, letting her sweat-damp hair finally cool.

Across from her, Derek stared into the middle distance. "I have a bad feeling about this, Valerie. We're going out into wasteland. People die out there."

She leaned back against her mat, found a comfortable position, and closed her eyes. "No one is going to die, I promise. Trust me."

He did not reply.

People die out there. The phrase echoed in her mind as she awoke, parched. It was late afternoon, and they were already far out in the western desert. All that remained of the cultivated land along the river was a faint gray-green strip in the hazy distance. Derek was staring at the tracks that trailed off endlessly behind them.

"Any idea where we are?" she asked him across the wooden crate.

"Somewhere between hell and oblivion, I think." Derek pointed sideways with his thumb. "And over there is East Nothing. How's your cheek?"

She touched the spot in front of her ear. "Fine. Itches a little. How's your head?"

"Fine. Still don't have a hat, though."

"Are you sorry you got into this, Derek? Do you wish sometimes that you had gone back to your hotel after your opera and been spared this?"

"What? And miss this fabulous trip? No. Besides, I had to come. The prophecy said so. And now I know my ancestor, Rekemheb." He looked down dreamily through long lashes. "It's only been five days since we found him, and already he's like family."

"That's great for you, to have a lineage now. I confess I'm a little jealous. You have the kind of supernatural family I used to fantasize about as a child. Between six and eight, I imagined I was the secret Daughter of Isis. I was a little strange, I guess."

"How did you even know names like that as a child? I was only into comic-book heroes."

"My mother was an archaeologist, or would have been. Our house was filled with Egyptian antiques from my father and souvenirs from my mother's student excavation days: painted papyrus, pottery shards, even little statues of the gods she bought in the souq."

"Why did she quit? What happened?"

"I happened. In those days you couldn't have a baby and a career. Maybe she planned to go back later, but there was no later, only the car crash." She brooded for a moment.

"I wanted to keep my mother's statues with me at the boarding school where I was sent, but the nuns wouldn't let me. You know. Idolatry. So I kept them in my head."

"Poor Valerie." He caressed her hand.

She smiled and ran her hand lightly along the wood of the temporary casket between them. "Can you imagine what it must have been like?"

"Imagine what?" Derek leaned his head back over the side of the truck, trying to catch some of the wind.

"Rekemheb's entombment." She closed her eyes. "The droning of the priests chanting their spells, the smell of the oil burning in the lamps all along the way, the sound of the coffin as it would have been dragged down the ramp: shish…shish….shish. Pharaoh himself might have entered the tomb to offer the precious objects to the gods." She leaned her cheek back on her hand, feeling the faint soreness and the new scab.

"I would give a lot to have been one of the offering bearers, kneeling at the bottom of the ramp, my head on the ground as the gold-sandaled foot of Pharaoh stepped past me."

"You are *such* a romantic, Valerie Foret," he murmured, drowsing again.

"Yes, I suppose you're right. A romantic scientist. It's an oxymoron, isn't it?" She slid another folded mat under her bottom. Sleep was perhaps the best way after all to endure the heat. She laid her head down on her forearm and felt consciousness slowly swim away.

The bang woke them both instantly.

CHAPTER XXII:
DESHERET

The truck shuddered to a halt, and Valerie stood up to peer over the cab. The driver's door flew open, and Yussif jumped to the ground, wrapping a rag around his hand. He twisted open the latch on the truck hood and threw it open, recoiling from the blast of heat and the smell of scorched metal. "*Kharah!*" he swore into the smoking ruin that had been the engine.

Valerie and Derek leapt from the truck bed and came around to join him at the front. Derek winced and waved uselessly into the shimmering waves of heat. "The engine's damaged, isn't it?"

Yussif nodded bleakly. "I put full of water this morning. I was so careful. Maybe oil leaked. I don't know. It was no warning. *Kharah*," he repeated softly.

Valerie fanned the air with her hat. "Yeah, oil leak will do it, all right. The rod gets loose and bangs around until it goes right through the cylinder."

"Yes. Perhaps." Yussif looked defeated.

Auset struggled out of the truck cab and lumbered toward the others. The four of them stood in a baleful semicircle around the yawning engine compartment fathoming the disaster. Yussif wrapped and unwrapped his hand with the rag.

"Well, come on!" Auset spoke with such abruptness they all looked up. "We can't just stand around in the sun feeling sorry for ourselves, and we can't sit on all that hot metal. We've got to make some shade. Why don't you two men take down the truck canopy and set it up on the sand? Then we can do an inventory of the food and water we have left. Come on, get a move on!"

Derek climbed back onto the truck bed and began to undo the ropes holding the canvas. He stopped suddenly and looked up. "Wait a minute. We're forgetting about Rekemheb!"

Auset returned with another bag of pomegranates. "I don't think we have to worry about him. He's already dead."

"No, I mean his Ba. He came for us at Al Amarna, remember? Maybe he can fly out and get help."

"You mean like Lassie?" Auset was inexplicably cheerful.

Valerie climbed up next to Derek on the truck and began to roll up the canvas roof. "Who would he take a message to? The police? And besides, wouldn't your cell phone be more efficient?"

"Oh, right!" He snatched it out of his pocket and began dialing with this thumb. "Uh, except that it looks like the battery's dead. Damn!"

Auset shrugged. "Dead motor. Dead phone. So much for technology in the desert. But Valerie's right. Who do outlaws call when they need help, anyhow?"

"Well, maybe someone should try to walk to the last village. As opposed to staying here and dying of thirst, I mean. I'm willing to go. What do you think, Yussif?"

The driver shook his head. "Too far for those feet." He glanced down at Derek's oxfords. "And not necessary. Trucks come. Sometimes military. Better to wait."

"Just sit here, huh? How long have we got food for?"

Auset opened and closed various grocery bags. "Two days, if we ration. There's water for drinking, but none for washing. Now let's stop wasting time."

Relieved to be occupied, the group unloaded the truck and dragged their little household up a nearby slope. Yussif dismantled the canopy poles and carried them up the incline as well. It took only a few minutes to dig four holes in the soft sand where he could insert them. Valerie carried over the canvas cover, and together they draped it over the poles, creating a serviceable bivouac.

Derek helped Auset get comfortable among her sacks of food and then settled in next to her. "If you all don't mind, I'll stay in the shade." He rummaged in his pack. "I had one sunstroke already today. Doesn't the heat bother you, Yussif?"

"No, I am Arab, remember?" Standing in full sunlight, he unrolled a length of blue gauze longer than he was tall. "I always keep turban in truck." He wrapped the long swath around his head with sweeping hand motions, encircled his mouth with the last meter, and tucked the loose end into the folds in the top. Intense dark eyes peered out from between two layers of indigo cloth.

"My, don't you look fierce! Myself, I'm going for something a little more…Old Kingdom. One of those pharaoh head-scarf things that Rekemheb told me about. From my other shirt." He held up his sewing kit. "He said it's called a *nemes*."

Valerie looked at the useless truck, which shimmered in the late afternoon heat, and listened to the others talk about fashion. Nothing, it seemed, could faze them. Derek had obviously forgotten his earlier fear—that people die out there. She had not.

❖

"Look at them down there, poking at the motor like surgeons." As the sun set and the sky drained of its harsh light, Derek leaned back on his elbow. "But that patient is dead, I'm afraid."

Auset leaned back as well, there being no more household to organize. "Yussif is like that. Responsible down to the bone. If he can't drive the truck back to my father, he will carry it, piece by piece." She watched the dark forms hunched over the engine cavity and the spot of light that flashed intermittently from Yussif's hand. "He's the most honorable man I've ever known."

"Ouch, that hurt. But I guess I deserved it." Derek chewed his lip. "I'm sorry, Auset. I've gotten you into deep trouble. Twice. I'm the worst thing that's ever happened to you, aren't I?"

"Well, I did think that for a while, when I had to tell my parents I was pregnant. But then I remembered that night. It was so strange, like we were in a drunken haze…but we hadn't drunk anything!"

"Yeah. You're right. I was a little dizzy the whole time. I thought it was jet lag."

"No, it was something else that made us both a little crazy. Maybe Rekemheb's gods after all. I don't know. But I can feel the baby now, and that's all that's important." She took his hand and laid it on the side of her swelling. "This is your son, Derek."

He closed his eyes for a moment, then whispered, "This is the best of us, getting another chance." He pressed gently, and the swelling pressed back.

"Auset, I will support this child, from wherever I am. I swear it, on Rekemheb's gods and on mine. I will never let you down."

"I believe you, dear." She patted his hand and smiled wanly.

The metallic crash of the trunk hood falling into place caused the two of them to jump slightly and look below. Obviously defeated, Valerie and Yussif trudged up the slope through the transparent darkness.

"And speaking of Rekemheb..." Auset pointed toward the blue-green luminescence that wafted up behind them from the abandoned truck. "If I had seen that a week ago, I would have thought I was insane. But now..."

Valerie and Yussif sat down, and the arriving Ka stood by them, his feet not quite touching the ground. After a moment, he sat down too. He looked around at the faces that stared at him, and the expression on his face seemed to say, "What?"

"The 'roaring chariot' is useless," Valerie said to him in Egyptian. "Any chance one of your gods can give us a little assistance? Food? Firewood?"

The Ka shook his head. "The gods watch us everywhere, but they have no power or voice. Only in their temples can they reveal their wonder."

Valerie explained and Auset sighed. "What a pity. Here we are— Christian, Jew, Muslim, and scientist—all waiting to meet your gods. If they can't dazzle us with a few miracles, they're not going to catch on." She tossed a dark pebble into the center of the circle. "People sort of expect that from a god."

Derek stretched out lengthwise, resting his head on his palm. "Something I don't understand, Rekemheb. Egypt had so many gods. How did you know which one to serve?"

"The gods come each in their season or their hour, but it was Hathor who chose me." He looked up to the dark sky. "I served her joyously, for she is Isis and the mother of Horus. She is music and the warmth of love, and in her wrath she is the lioness Sekhmet. She has many temperaments, and each temperament has a name."

Yussif bent and picked up the pebble that Auset had thrown down. He twirled it between his fingers and rubbed it absentmindedly on his cheek. "The God of Islam also reveals himself in many ways. He is the Merciful, the Forgiving, the Almighty. But these are all One."

Rekemheb frowned. "Is this One-god also in the wind and sky, in birds and beasts, in sunlight and the moon?"

The Arab paused for a moment. "The pious man feels the presence of God everywhere. But always it is the One God, Allah, the Absolute. He has no forms or face."

"It's kind of the same for Christians," Derek added. "At least that's what my preacher stepfather says. For most of us, He seems to wait outside of things, until we face Him after death. But it may be different for Catholics. Didn't you go to Catholic school, Val?"

Valerie grimaced. "Yes, L'école Sacre Coeur. But Sister Marie-Henriette pretty much ruined God for me. When someone says 'God's will,' I think of the punishment closet. I have never sensed God and never expect to," she grumbled.

The Ka said softly, "I will show you one right now." He raised his open hand over his head, as if offering something to the night sky.

All four heads looked up where he pointed. The air was unusually clear, Valerie noted, and the dense stars did seem to her drowsy eyes to cluster into distinct shapes stretching across the sky. Yes, she could definitely see forms. Long arms reached down to the western horizon, and farther up, she noticed a roundness that could be taken for a head. Directly overhead the stars were dense, and toward the east they seemed to bifurcate again. She looked along the shape several times, her eyes sweeping back and forth, and each time it seemed more to be looking back. A wave of infantile comfort came over her. She could see it now, the sheltering curve of gray light. "The Sky Goddess Nuut," she said out loud.

"Yes," Rekemheb affirmed. "Nuut, daughter of Shu, the air, mother of the Sun God Ra, whom she swallows each evening and gives birth to anew each morning."

"Wow," murmured Derek. "I can actually see it."

Yussif covered his eyes and murmured to himself, "'Consider Lat and Uzza, and Manat, the third, the exalted birds'…No!" His hand closed to a fist. "I do not see it. I see only stars in the heaven which Allah has given to us."

"I have to agree with Yussif," Auset added. "I admit, it sort of has a human shape, but that's just me interpreting the random dots. I don't see any gods."

Valerie passed along the comments to the Ka, who shrugged. "You will see them soon enough, all of you."

Auset yawned, covering her mouth. "I look forward to it. But for now I'd like to see only a nice soft cushion. The seat in the truck cabin will do for now. As the only one among you who's pregnant, I claim it. I assume no one objects?"

"I'll go with you." Valerie got to her feet, gathering up one of the packing mats. "I'll sleep in the back. You boys can have the tent to yourselves."

The two women walked down to the disabled vehicle. With her flashlight, Valerie did a quick insect inspection of the truck seat for Auset and repeated the ritual for herself on the flat bed of the truck. Then she rolled out her mat alongside the casket and lay down. She was still restless and a bit feverish. The quiet throbbing in the side of her head persisted, like a stranger knocking, politely, but determined to be admitted. Weary, she looked again for the woman-shape in the night sky.

She saw only stars. But they were breathtaking. Stars beyond counting and beyond comprehension formed a bowl that covered the earth; stars sparkled even beneath her feet. The same stars that the priests of Ramses and Meremptah had used to measure the turning of the year. Did they once lie as she did now, on the roofs of their temples, discerning patterns, reading messages of both religion and science?

And one of those priests—she imagined him looking like Rekemheb—keeping bravely to his post one summer night, noticed that the appearance of the star Sirius on the horizon just before dawn coincided with the inundation of the Nile. What pleasure he must have felt at the discovery—that the sky and the earth were in synchrony. And from that discovery, at the beginning of human history, came the 360-day annual calendar.

And yet it was deficient, for the twelve thirty-day months did not bring the stars back to their starting point. They had to wait five more perilous days before Sirius rose and the orderly year could begin anew. When was the New Year, after all? Ah, yes, July 19.

She realized with a shock that it was already the night of July 15. The Egyptian timeless days had just begun, and there were four more days before the world could begin its orderly count again. She turned her head slightly to the right, to touch the mummy's casket with her forehead. She whispered through the casket wall, "I guess that explains why we're homeless tonight, Rekemheb, living and dead alike. How much worse can it get, do you think, in the next four?"

The silence of the mummy spoke volumes.

❖

The two men were stretched out on their mats on unforgiving ground. Derek made a little tent with his hands over his chest and tapped his fingertips softly against each other. "You must really hate me for getting us into this." He turned his ring around his finger. "If it helps, I feel really rotten about it."

Yussif scratched his chest. "I have not time for hate anybody. I must to fix all problems. How to take care of Auset and all of us."

"Yes, I want to take care of her too. I told her that. But tell me the truth, Yussif. Are we really in danger out here? Could we…like… die?"

"No. I do not think so. Desert looks empty but is busy place. Tomorrow or next day we see army, probably. Then only problem is to explain everything. You must to explain Rekemheb. And I must to bring truck back to Cairo. Somehow."

Derek sat up. "I don't know what a truck costs, Yussif, but I'll pay for it. I mean it. Here, to show you I'm serious, I want you to take this." He drew the heavy silver ring over his knuckle and rolled it once between thumb and finger, feeling the sapphires embedded all around it. "It should cover some of the cost. I'll make up the rest later."

Yussif closed his hand over the object and hefted it. "A rich man's ring. Are you sure?"

"Yes. It was a foolish extravagance, and now it can do some good. Put it on so you don't lose it." Derek patted the other man briefly on the shoulder and then turned away, dropping down onto his mat. "Now I have one less guilt to carry around."

They let a comfortable silence fall again between them. With the burdens of fear and guilt lifted from him, Derek fell into an easy sleep.

Yussif studied the ring, feeling the precious stones, and then slipped it on his little finger. He brushed sand from his mat and then lay down as well, troubled by a surfeit of thought. The truck: how to bring it back to Cairo or surely lose his job? The goddess in the stars: was that not the very thing the Qur'an warned against? The Ka: what, in the name of Allah, was it?

Auset.

He savored inwardly the sound of her strange name: Auset. The son of a village mechanic, he had hungered all his life to win the attention of a woman like her, and when she walked into her father's Cairo office after finishing university in New York, he was a doomed man. The sight of her long uncovered hair and the sound of her sharp words seized his interest and never let it go. He gave no outward sign of his obsession, but every day of his employment was a day of willing fealty to her.

The shock of learning that the spoiled woman was pregnant—a scandal which in another age or place might have meant her death—rocked his devotion only slightly. He searched his heart and found only anger that she had given a precious gift so lightly. But it seemed she had more time for him now. It seemed he had a chance.

Why look at a woman who had soiled herself, his father had demanded. How could he explain? He could not face the thought of marrying one of the dull, barely literate girls of his own class, who had not a thought in their heads and no desire other than motherhood. The foreign women were perhaps immoral. Yes, one had to accept that. Nor were they obedient. But for all that, they were…interesting. It was the happiest day of his life when Auset, swollen with her sin and unrepentant, had asked him to drive her to the Giza camel barn. Without a second thought he had joined her foreign friends in their crime. With Auset at his side, needing him, he would have driven into hell.

Now, here he was, lying half a meter away from the one who had defiled her. And yet, the man had every other virtue; he was generous with money and with gifts, and pious toward his elder. He had shown Auset every brotherly affection, while making no claim on her. Yussif touched his new ring with the tip of his thumb. How could a man know what was the right way? If Auset had broken *Shari'a* by giving herself before marriage, so he himself had broken it by stealing a dead man from his grave, by giving credence to polytheists, by considering Satanic verses.

She carried the fruit of her sin and could not go back. But neither could he. He was the same pious man as before, but perhaps Allah had other names after all.

CHAPTER XXIII:
BÁDAWI

Valerie awoke to the clanking of copper bells and the penetrating smell of goat. She sat up and found the truck an island in a sluggish stream of livestock. Out on the periphery, a dozen men sat on camels; their robes and thick turbans identified them.

Bedouin herdsmen, driving their flocks from one sparse grazing ground to another. She looked around her, fascinated. To the left, grayish brown sheep flowed past, driven by women, an oozing mass of newly shorn backs. Young men carried the new lambs draped over their shoulders or led donkeys carrying immense loads. The nearest one bore a mountain of kindling high over its haunches and goatskins of water on both sides of its forelegs.

The smell of fleece was overpowered by the stronger, viler smell of the goats that jostled by, bleating, on the right. Children walked among them, urging them on with sticks until they stopped to gawk at the spectacle of a woman standing in a pickup truck.

The men on camels seemed in no hurry to talk, although one of them had come close and studied the truck as she studied him. A gray-bearded man in a tan kaftan sat with his right leg hooked around the high horn of the saddle, the toes of his other foot gripping the camel's neck. His beast carried no baggage, but behind him, attached by a cord to the saddle, a wicker cage held a bird much too large for it. The way in which the man barked commands suggested he was the sheikh, or at least someone of authority. Valerie waved at him and called out, "*As salaamu 'alaykum.*"

He ignored her, although he had gotten close enough to the truck to hold a conversation.

"*As salaamu 'alaykum,*" a male voice repeated cheerfully, and Yussif waded through the flood of goats toward the rider. Derek followed close behind him. A few of the shepherds edged closer to the sheikh. They looked wild, biblical, in their wide desert robes that spread over their saddles. Yet several, she noted, had wristwatches, and one of the boys on foot wore a baseball cap.

Uninvited to the male discussion which was about to take place, she climbed down to join Auset, who was already making her way toward their little tent. It looked suddenly pathetic before the glance of real Bedouins. Auset glanced back over her shoulder and laughed. "Yeah, come on over here to the harem and let the menfolk take care of business."

Sheikh and driver spoke for a while and, although they were too far away to hear, it seemed that Yussif explained their situation and negotiated for something. Valerie wondered if the custom of desert hospitality applied to reckless foreigners as well. Finally the men returned to the tiny campsite.

"They are tribe of Mahamid who take flocks to Dakhla Oasis," Yussif reported. "Sheikh's name is Janazil. Sheikh says they know nothing of trucks, but will give us food and water. If we want, they will let us walk with them to oasis."

"Well, that beats dying of thirst. How far is it?" Valerie asked.

"Two days' walk, he says."

"Two days on foot in the desert?" Derek looked down at his oxfords, where powdery sand was already embedded in every seam and hole. "What about Auset? Did you mention that one of us is eight months pregnant?"

Yussif's thick beard parted in a smile. "Yes, of course. And I ask to buy camel. Sheikh agree. One camel for one thousand Egypt pounds."

"That sounds like a lot. And besides, one isn't enough." Derek rubbed his back, obviously anticipating the discomfort.

"Yes, I know. So I say two camels for fifteen hundred pounds."

Valerie was beginning to admire the taciturn Arab. "Did he agree?"

"He says fifteen hundred pounds and black man's watch. Then we agree."

"My watch? Oh, great." Derek turned to the two women. "Do we even have fifteen hundred Egyptian pounds between us? All I have are credit cards."

Auset shrugged. "I have about four hundred."

Valerie calculated on her fingers. "I've got eight hundred and change. The rest of my money is in Euros."

Yussif patted his shirt pocket, as if he could count by feeling his wallet. "I have three hundred, for food and gasoline."

Valerie pulled out a wad of bills and added it to the pile in Yussif's hand. "That should be fifteen hundred. And Derek has the watch. I think we have a deal."

The bleating of the goats seemed a comment on the transaction.

Derek sighed as he drew the metal expansion band over his hand. "I hope you appreciate that I'm giving up a fine Bulova, worth about two hundred dollars."

"I will tell him that," Yussif said, patting him on the shoulder. "But is not so bad for you. You will have best camel. Someone must to carry Grandfather."

"You mean like before?"

"No. Is possible to tie box to camel on one side, food, water bottles on other. But I explain about mummy to sheikh and he does not like it. He says you must to ride behind the tribe. Is not allowed to carry dead man near the people. Very bad luck."

"So it would seem," Valerie said.

❖

"*Y'alla bina!*" The sheikh called for the march to continue, and the tribe of Mahamid resumed its amoebic flow southwestward. At its rear, keeping a discreet distance, the fugitives took their place. The unencumbered ones walked between the two who rode, burdened with coming or departed life. Auset rode the smaller camel cushioned by several packing quilts. Derek sat astride the larger camel which, with stoic dignity, bore the casket tied to its left side and camp supplies dangling on its right.

Valerie marched purposefully, modern muscles slowly learning the ancient rhythmic stride of migration. She glanced at Yussif, who walked alongside of her, and matched her step to his. He had untucked his shirt so that it hung over his trousers to his knees. Turbaned and rough-bearded as he was, he seemed at home among the nomads.

"Strange where fate takes us, isn't it?" Yussif said suddenly in Arabic. "You think you've got an idea of where you're going, and some hand comes along and sets you down someplace else. The only thing that is constant is the kind of person you are— strong or weak, pious or…" He paused, apparently trying to decide what the opposite of piety would be. "Or lost."

Valerie was taken aback for a moment, for this was the first time he had spoken to her alone and did not need to use English. She was surprised at how intelligent he sounded, at how much he had to say. Language, it seemed, was everything.

"I know what you mean," she said. "But I still resist the idea that some supernatural hand of fate plays with my life. I insist that I have a will. As for the sort of person I am, I'm afraid I stopped being pious as a schoolgirl."

"Did your teachers really lock you in a closet?"

"Yes, all of us, when we were disobedient. And I was disobedient a lot. It was terrifying. We were little children, and they thrashed us first. Then they locked us for the night in a small, dark place. Some of the young ones went in screaming and came out silent, broken. The nuns said it would teach us humility before God." She stared into the distance. "Whatever Rekemheb has to show us, it better have more to offer than brutal authority."

"Rekemheb is the mystery, isn't he? We thought we were carrying him, but I think now he's leading us, or at least his gods are." He scratched his beard. "To what end, I wonder?"

She had no answer to give and strode silently, trying to find a pace that she could maintain for eight hours.

Yussif began again. "The images in the stars we saw last night—"

"The Goddess Nuut?"

He chuckled bitterly. "Muslims called them Lat and Uzza, the goddesses of the moon and stars. The Prophet once recited their names to the people of Mecca, but he was under the influence of Satan. You must realize that from a Muslim standpoint, Rekemheb was revealing something that was long ago refuted." He shook his head. "And yet I saw them both with my own eyes."

"Oh, yes. The Verses of Satan. Sura 53, isn't it? About accepting the goddesses as intermediaries with God? Mohammed named them to win over the polytheists, but later he recanted. Is that what you're afraid of? That Rekemheb is Satan?"

"When you put it that way it sounds foolish."

She blew sand particles from between her lips. "'Sinner' is the name that believers give to those who have the courage to doubt."

"And you are not afraid of doubt?"

"No, not at all. In science, doubt is an excellent beginning. It lets the mind travel to places that are new…" She looked up at Derek on his camel, discovering himself both as father and as scion in an ancient lineage. He was on her eastern side, and his image was blurred by the corona around him from the morning sun. The *nemes* he had devised sat handsomely on his head, and it seemed as if the Falcon-god perched at the back of his neck and hung its wings down, protecting him as in the temple icons it once protected Pharaoh.

"Or very, very old."

❖

Enveloped in the cloud of dust stirred up by the flocks, Valerie wrapped another layer of cloth around her face. Muffled and dry-mouthed, she wandered silently from one end of the shapeless flowing mass to the other as the hours passed, watching the nomads through squinted, sand-scraped eyes.

She found herself at the periphery where the camels, like moving guard towers, formed the outer line. The beasts were lean, even the camel of the sheikh, although its trappings, as befitted a tribal leader, were striking. The red camel bag hanging down on both sides of his saddle was extravagantly tasseled, and the leather harness was studded in brass. Behind the saddle, the tiny wicker cage once again caught her attention. The bird it held was a hawk. Something to be sold at market in El Dakhla, she supposed. Its wings were tied back cruelly, and the cage itself was so constricting that the poor creature could not move. As she drew closer the hawk twisted its head toward her, wild-eyed and panting through its small curved beak.

She remembered another hawk and knew suddenly why she felt such horror. It was the hawk at Sacre Coeur, one of the family that flew daily over the school grounds, that had become lodged one night in the chimney of her dormitory. Lying in her bed, she had heard its desperate fluttering. It seemed to come from directly behind the crucifix that hung above the mantle. Shivering below it on the hearth, she prayed to the Virgin to set it free or end its suffering. But still it fluttered, hour after hour.

Finally she had fled, sobbing and hysterical in the middle of the night, to the Mother Superior, waking her by pounding on the door, demanding that the creature be freed before the morning fire was lit. But the furious nun had called her insolent and consigned her to the punishment cabinet for the rest of the night. After she was released the next morning and thrashed for her offense, a fire burned indifferently in the dormitory hearth. No one would tell her what had happened to the hawk. She was sick with dread for weeks afterward, tormented by visions of the creature being roasted alive.

"*Shuf! Akhiran, il bi'r.*" A man's voice startled her.

The sheikh pointed forward, toward a depression in the land. Of course, Valerie thought. If there's water around, it will be there. And a few hundred meters farther on, she saw it at the center of the dry riverbed, the stone lid of a desert well.

The sheikh dismounted first and strode to the well hole, where he prostrated himself and recited some brief prayers. In a moment other men joined him, and together they removed the covering of rocks and slid aside the heavy stone well cover. Valerie watched as they retrieved the goatskin sack from within. After examining it, they lowered it down the shaft and drew it back with obvious satisfaction. The well was high and contained enough water for both shepherd and flock. The men drank their fill, seemingly in order of age, for the graybeards went first and the young men after. Then the women clustered about the well with their children, wetting the small faces as they drank. Finally, a row of camel skins was laid out in a shallow trough, and the flocks were watered.

Derek blew powder from parched lips. "Man, I haven't even got enough saliva to spit out sand."

As if she had heard him, a Bedouin covered from head to toe in black cloth, with only her eyes visible, stepped away from the goats and beckoned the two women toward the well. Auset tapped her camel to kneel and heaved herself from the saddle to join Valerie. Together they walked to where the shepherd stood, a dark apparition on the bright sand. The blackness of her clothing was broken only by a string of gold and silver coins that hung from the left side of her head scarf. Henna-painted hands appeared from under black cloth and offered the dripping goatskin.

"*Shukran.*" Auset tipped her head back, letting the water pour into her mouth in a long thin stream that caught the sunlight. She passed the skin on to Valerie, who drank less skillfully, splashing water on her chin and shirt. Against the heated air the underground water cooled deliciously.

"May I share the water with the others?" Auset asked, and the veiled Bedouin nodded, refilling the skin from the well before handing it over. "Thank you. I will bring it back in a moment," she said, and lumbered back up the slope to the men.

Valerie waited awkwardly by the well, wondering if conversation was in order. It was difficult to chat with someone so anonymous.

"How goes your journey?" the Bedouin asked unexpectedly, in the pleasant, soft voice of a mature woman. "The red land is harsh to those who do not know it."

Desheret, she had said. The red land. In Egyptian, not Arabic.

"We thought we had prepared well for our trip, but the desert surprised us. We are grateful for your help."

The woman did not reply, but unhooked the embroidered panel that covered the lower half of her face, and Valerie startled. Once again, eyes looked back at her that were so black they revealed no character, only endless depth.

"Nira!" Valerie's heart leapt. She stepped forward to touch the other woman on the arm.

"My name is Nekhbet," the Bedouin said coolly.

Valerie stepped back again, confused. Could she be mistaken? It had been dark in the necropolis, after all. On both sides of her, goats bleated. "I'm sorry. It's just that—"

As if she had not heard, the woman pointed toward the slope above the wadi. "You should make your camp over there, above the slope. Someone will bring you fuel for your fire." Her voice was without warmth, disinterested. And yet she stared unashamedly for a long moment, as if studying a curiosity. Then, bowing her head so that the coins on her veil tinkled, she walked away.

Valerie watched her disappear among the other black-clad women in the camp, and for the first time in years, she felt like crying.

CHAPTER XXIV:
THE BARGAIN

B oy, it gets cold fast out here." Above the Bedouin camp,
Derek sat down next to Valerie and Auset, who leaned against
the casket of Rekemheb. Shivering, he drew his knees up to his chest
and wrapped his long arms around them. "Makes me wish I had one of
those long robe things."

Together they watched the Bedouin women, silhouetted against
the flamboyant orange sky, setting up the goat-hair tents. Young boys
drove the flocks into a natural pocket in the rocks below them. Toward
the west, the men couched their camels, tying up one of the animals'
legs so that they could not rise. At the center of the camp, girls prepared
the cooking fire, their high voices carrying over to the strangers in the
warm sound of lifelong custom.

"These people are so much friendlier than those in that village
yesterday," he added. "I wonder why."

"We're not desecrating their shrine, for one thing," Valerie said.
"And the Bedouins have a tradition of hospitality. But we shouldn't
push it."

Auset shook sand out of her hair. "What did that woman at the
well say to you? Will they invite us down to eat with them?"

Derek cocked his head. "We'll soon find out. There's someone
coming now."

A small figure, with features impossible to make out in the twilight,
clambered up the slope and stopped a short distance from the group.
Yussif shone the flashlight on it, and in the light column an adolescent
boy with wild hair shaded his eyes with his hand. Yussif turned the
harsh beam down to the ground, and in the half-light, the boy carried
out his recitation. It was a dialect Valerie could scarcely follow.

Yussif answered the boy and turned to the two foreigners. "His father Sheikh Janazil bin Mahamed invites us to receive from his hand things to carry away for our comfort this night."

"Carry away for our comfort." Valerie chuckled. "Sounds like we aren't invited in for dinner, but only for uh…take-away."

Auset pulled her scarf up against the evening chill. "I kind of expected that. We're carrying a corpse, after all. And the sheikh knows our guy is way past his expiration date."

Derek clutched his blanket around him. "That's fine with me. If we had to socialize, I wouldn't understand a word anyway. How about just you two go and leave Auset and me here. Uh…and the flashlight too, if that's okay."

Yussif spoke again and laid his hand on the boy's shoulder. The child nodded and led the two emissaries down the slope.

As they came into the Bedouin camp, the young men greeted Yussif familiarly. The sense of tribe in the camp was palpable, as each person was engaged in a long-familiar task. Women prepared food or tended the fire with infants in slings behind them, while older children carried bundles from tent to tent. None but the youngest babies was idle. In the course of an hour, a sort of village had sprung up.

Valerie glanced around at the clusters of women, searching for the shepherd from the well. It was impossible to distinguish one from another.

The boy stopped suddenly before a tent slightly larger than the others. A camel saddle, sacks of grain, and the hawk's cage were piled up at its front. As the guests arrived, a male figure bent low through the opening and came toward them. "*As salaamu'alaykum.*"

"*Wa 'alaykum as salaam,*" the guests replied in unison.

Deprived of his camel and its trappings, Janazil bin Mahamed was an unimposing sheikh. The kaftan that had draped so regally around him on his saddle was soiled and shabby. His mottled beard was sparse, and one of his two front teeth was broken in half. His manner was nonetheless authoritative, and he had grown sons—or kinsmen—to lend him presence. But it was obvious that he was poor. They all were poor. Valerie realized she was looking at what was probably the last generation of desert nomads in Egypt.

Janazil bin Mahamed registered the briefest surprise at the presence of the foreign woman and then addressed himself to Yussif. "I regret I cannot serve you coffee. You understand." Both guests nodded politely.

"But no man shall say that the Mahamed are inhospitable."

He snapped his fingers, and two girls who had obviously been watching came from the women's section in the rear of the tent. One handed a goatskin and a pile of pita bread to Valerie without raising her eyes, and the other laid a burlap sack of what appeared to be kindling at Yussif's feet. "Milk from our camels, bread from our fire, and fuel for your own. You are our guests, even on your hillside. Is there anything else you are lacking?"

"No, *Sayyid*. And we thank you for your kindness." Yussif took up the bundle and made the formal courtesies to depart.

Valerie held him by his arm and addressed the sheikh. "The Mahamed are well known for their generosity and for their skill in hunting."

The sheikh's brow wrinkled slightly. He had obviously not heard about the hunting part.

"We are grateful to benefit from it." She gestured toward the cage. "However, the hawk that your hunters have captured—surely it is an inconvenience. Would it not be more profitable to exchange it for some useful object?"

The Bedouin half closed his eyes. "Exchange? For what sort of object?"

"Well, I would take him. For my wristwatch. Worth as much as the one which bought our camel." She pulled back her sleeve to display the timepiece. The worn leather band, she realized, weakened her argument considerably.

The sheikh raised open hands. "Alas, I already have a watch, as you can see, and not much need to observe the hour. But you have something of value that I do not have." He pointed to the object tucked—discreetly, she had thought—in her belt behind her hip.

She patted the side of her jacket, feeling the rigid form beneath. "My pistol? Ah, no, that is not possible."

Yussif cleared his throat. "Perhaps something else. Our blankets. Jewelry. We have other objects of value, I am sure."

Janazil bin Mahamed clasped his hands together behind his back. "I am afraid I would only consider the pistol."

Valerie looked over at the cage where the captive hawk cocked its head, seeming to attend to every word. It no longer panted, but its small eyes caught the light from the nearby fire and glowed like tiny distant suns. Though its wings were tied back, inside the cage, she seemed to hear the sound of desperate fluttering. Her stomach tightened. "All right. One thing of value for another."

She unhooked the holster from her belt, avoiding Yussif's eyes, and handed it over. One of the sheikh's men lifted the cage and set it into her hands. It was surprisingly heavy.

The two paid their respects again and walked unguided back through the camp. Valerie shifted the cage to her hip. "Do you think I have done something foolish? Or that I have insulted the sheikh?"

"No, he was not insulted, I am sure. Only surprised. I doubt that he has ever seen a woman with a gun."

"Well, now I am a woman with a bird."

"It suits you better than a gun."

A slight movement caught Valerie's attention, and she turned her head. Yussif continued a few paces before stopping.

A single dark figure stood at the edge of the camp, watching. A woman, veiled and somber. A string of gold and silver coins hung from the left side of her veil. She stood, immobile. The breeze of the cooling desert blew around her, pressing her black abaya against her, revealing the faint outline of legs and hips. As if she had caught sight of something she should not have seen, Valerie looked away. The two of them continued on their way up the slope, the hawk rocking back and forth within its cage.

❖

Derek opened the sack and shone the flashlight inside. "Okay, this is kindling, but what are these? Looks like big oatmeal cookies." He pulled out a large crumbly disk, brought it to his nose for a fraction of a second, dropped it again. "Eeewww! That's disgusting!"

"Of course they're disgusting. They're camel chips. Good desert fuel, though. Give it here." Valerie took the sack of twigs and camel dung from him. "I've done this a few times on excavation." She made a pit in the sand and placed a handful of fine straw at the center, covering it with a teepee of the coarser straw. Over it she erected another cone of twigs and surrounded it with walls of camel chips. She clicked open the lid of her Zippo and held the flame under the tiny structure. The straw caught first, then the twigs, and finally the dung ignited into a satisfying pyre of yellow and blue flames.

"What's this? Dinner?" Auset had discovered the caged bird.

"Nothing of the sort." She opened the cage, and the hawk fluttered out with bound wings and tumbled across the ground. "Hold him, Derek, while I untie him."

He grasped the creature gently under its feathery breast. Miraculously, it did not thrash or bite while Valerie cut the crippling cord. Then it shot forward, tumbled again once over its own outspread wings, and lifted off the ground.

Auset watched it disappear into the night sky. "I bet it would have tasted just like chicken."

Exhaling, as if a great weight had been lifted from her back, Valerie sat down by the fire and poked the bluish flames with a piece of kindling. "You'd better not let Rekemheb hear you talk that way. I'm sure he considers the hawk to be a god."

At the mention of his name, the Ka of the priest appeared without speaking and sat down, as always, next to his descendant. The tiny fire gave out a hemisphere of light that illuminated Derek's face from below, casting eerie shadows above his cheeks. Rekemheb, insubstantial and with his own luminescence, looked as he did in daylight—waxen and shadowless. Valerie wondered if he could see himself in the mirror or if, like the vampires of legend, he cast no reflection.

Auset shifted restlessly, obviously searching for the position that would accommodate her aching limbs and the protuberance of her passenger. "I wonder how the Bedouin women manage this," she muttered. "I feel like such a cow."

The Ka's face seemed to brighten. "My own wife was two times cow-blessed, with son and daughter."

Valerie laughed. "Listen to you, Rekemheb. Your English is really getting good!"

"I listen even when you do not see me, and I learn much from my grandchild."

Derek seemed pleased. "It's true! We talk all the time now. What else have we got to do out here all day?"

"Cow-blessed?" Auset repeated. "What is that supposed to mean?"

"The cow is Hathor, the mother of Horus, the mother of a god. She is…" He struggled for a word. "…your Ka."

Auset rubbed the small of her back with her free hand. "That's good to know, Rekemheb. Please put in a good word for me with Hathor, when I am in labor."

Yussif, who had been silent, suddenly raised a hand. "Forgive me, but I have walked many miles today and I must sleep." He gathered up his mat and withdrew a few paces from the fire where he lay down again, his wide back turned toward the group.

Auset watched him for a moment. "He doesn't want to hear about the gods. I don't think he's ready for all this paganism."

Valerie brushed sand from her mat. "And you are?"

Auset shrugged. "If Hathor can make having a baby any easier, then I want to hear about her."

"This little Christian boy does too, as long as I can stay awake." Derek turned his head toward the spectre. "For starters, I'd like to know how you worshipped Hathor. I mean, did you pray, like we do?"

The Ka lifted his hands, as if to present a sermon. "In the daily service, I sang the hymn during the food offerings. In the great New Year festivals, when she was carried in procession, I went before her singing the anthems."

Derek took off his shoes and set them upside down on the sand. "Sounds just like the processions I've seen in Italy when they carry the statue of the Madonna through the streets."

"You sing to the Mother Goddess too." Rekemheb beamed.

Derek puzzled for a moment. "Mother? No, not really. In my…uh temple, we sing mostly about Christ."

Valerie explained to the priest, "Jesus Christ is the Son of God who is murdered and then resurrected. The Christian Osiris."

"Really?" Derek massaged his feet. "I never realized I was singing to Osiris, but I guess it's all the same thing. He's still our Savior."

The Ka looked perplexed. "Save your? From what enemy are you saved?"

"No, not from an enemy." Derek frowned. "More like from our own sin."

Valerie searched for a translation. "You can't say 'sin' in Egyptian. It's a Judeo-Christian concept."

"Really? The gods didn't tell men how not to be evil? Then what do they do?"

The Ka continued. "Osiris gives life. From his own body he sends the inundation and the divine Horus."

"Guiltless procreation." Auset had finally found a suitable position and curled up on her side. Closing her eyes, she gave her final opinion. "I think I like Rekemheb's Son of God more than I like yours, Derek."

He stretched out on his blanket, crooking his arm back to support his head. "No original sin. No forgiveness. Mmm. Gonna have to think about that." His voice was already blurring with drowsiness. "So much to figure out. So much…changing…" As he fell asleep, his closed hand slid from his chest to the ground and the fingers curled gently outward. The Ka moved over to sit next to him, laying his insubstantial hand in the solid palm of his kinsman.

"Yes, so much," Valerie repeated, leaning toward the ashes of the fire that no longer gave light but still a bit of warmth. While the others fell asleep, she looked out in the direction the hawk had flown, studying the panorama of plain and black hills under the star-peppered sky. On the one side, where the Bedouin fire still flickered, the land around it muted to obscurity. But on the other, where no spark broke the sleeping landscape, the plain of sand captured starlight and gave it back in gentle luminescence. Something caught her eye.

Clearly delineated, like a bird, with black wings spread over the sand, one tent stood apart from all the others. As she watched, a single figure emerged from it. Valerie stared awhile, bemused, and then realized what she saw.

"Someone waits for you, Valerie," the Ka said softly.

She looked at him, confused. He had never spoken her name before.

"She waits," he repeated. "Go on."

She stood up, her heart pounding. Pebbles rolled in front of her as she descended the slope, stepping gingerly over blurry obstacles. At the bottom she stopped, suddenly in doubt. Then she started forward again, step by step, until she stood at last before the sinister shape.

"Nekhbet."

CHAPTER XXV:
THE KISS

The dark form lifted the tent flap and motioned her inside. Crouching, Valerie took a step into the interior and sat down, drawing up her knees.

The other woman came in with a tinkling of coins and earrings and sat down across from her on the carpet. A brass lamp hung on a chain from a tent pole near her shoulder but gave scant light, its wick too deep in oil.

Suddenly reticent, Valerie looked around. Some five meters square, the room was simplicity itself. Six tent poles, the tallest in the center, supported woven goat-hair roof and walls. The only furnishings were a camel saddle that functioned as a backrest and a brass-studded wooden chest. A tasseled woven bag hanging from the center pole held household articles. A smaller one on the floor held grain.

To the side, embers still smoldered in a shallow pit. The woman added charcoal with brass tongs, pressed a tiny bellows several times, and set a battered kettle on the glowing coals.

"It is very peaceful here," Valerie said. "I sometimes think I could live as the Bádawi do, uncorrupted."

"Nature is broken here too, and full of sorrow, but it can be made whole again." Nekhbet shook something dark and gritty into a spouted copper pot. The scent of ground coffee and cardamom filled the tent. "That is why you came, isn't it?"

Valerie watched the other woman's hands, dark fingers with milky white nails. "To save the environment? That needs to be done, of course. But no, I'm afraid I was more selfish. I came simply to uncover a bit of Egyptian history, to add a piece to the puzzle. What I found was not a piece, though. It was, in a way, the whole thing." She stared into the gray-brown circle under the veil, trying in the dim light to make out the woman's features. "Some great drama is happening and the piece, as it turns out, is me."

Nekhbet set out a tray with glasses and a dish of rock sugar. She poured heated water into the serving pot and closed the domed lid. Fragrant steam curled up from the long, curved spout. "The drama is the old one. The battles are the same ones your ancestors fought." Her glance fell on the new scar on Valerie's cheek. "They have left their marks on you." She poured the steaming liquid into the glasses and handed one to her guest, along with the rock sugar.

Valerie took a piece of it in her mouth and sipped the hot coffee over it. The caffeine and the sugar together brought a sudden euphoria. "My ancestors? No, that's another part of the problem." She sipped her coffee again. She felt foolish, reciting her doubts to a stranger in a tent, as if in a confessional. "The ancestors that have shown up are not mine, but those of my friend." Valerie sighed. "I am wandering in the desert, acting out some sort of prophecy that doesn't even concern me. I have sacrificed a career for someone else's drama."

The Bedouin seemed to measure her words. "It may be that there is still much that you do not know about this drama. Perhaps when you have seen more."

"I have already been seeing more than I can handle. I came to Egypt as a scientist, but what I have seen so far contradicts that science and, worse, has made criminal my entire life's work." She shrugged weakly. "I don't know what to do."

The Bedouin held up her glass on the tips of slender fingers, the pale nails stark against the black coffee. "What did you do before?"

"Before?" Valerie drank slowly, reflecting. "Excavated, studied, wrote. My whole life was writing about Egypt."

The woman drew her knees up and leaned her arms on them. Her bare feet came out from under her abaya. "Those who write are as gods, for they name the things and make them live."

"Is that what we do?" Valerie glanced down at the well-formed brown feet, at the dusty soles and the rings of silver around both ankles. "Well, I can't write anything at all until this ordeal is over." She set her glass down on the tray and turned it nervously with her fingers.

"It will never be over," Nekhbet said softly.

Valerie looked up again. The Bedouin woman had drawn back her head scarf. Silken black hair that had been hidden hung in a curve over her shoulder. It had a faint sheen from the light of the oil lamp and, astonishingly, the fragrance of cedar.

Cedar. That was it. Impulsively, Valerie reached up to the oil lamp and turned the tiny wheel on its side, lengthening the wick. Suddenly the flame flared up, illuminating the unveiled face.

Valerie heard her own inhalation. The same solemnity, the same dark eyes, deep as history, that had mesmerized her in the souq and in the necropolis looked into her now. The same soft channel descended from between the nostrils to the bow of the lips. There was the same suggestive upward curving at the corners of the mouth. The mouth that had kissed her.

A silver earring poked through strands of hair. A bird of prey of some sort, with wings that hung down like arms. The ornament swayed tantalizingly, catching the light for a moment and glowing dully. Valerie watched it, hypnotized. Both seemed to hold her, the woman and the bird, hinting at protection and gratification. "It's you, isn't it?" she said. "You have followed me after all."

Nekhbet blinked slowly in the faintest hint of confirmation.

Valerie felt her hand lift from the carpet. With a separate will her fingers reached out, crossing a vast distance before they touched, at the very limit of sensation, the tiny earring. With half-closed eyes and pounding heart she saw her hand move down slowly along the forbidden hair and come to rest, lightly, on the shoulder.

In the appalling silence, the wick sputtered once in its oil, and Valerie leaned forward toward the slightly opened lips.

"Do not..."

Valerie's hand sprang back, as if from a flame, hung for an awkward moment in the air, and then dropped onto the coffee tray. Her empty glass fell sideways and clattered across the metal tray to the edge.

"Do not falter, as your mother did," the Bedouin continued, unperturbed, and rose up on her knees.

"My mother? What are you—"

Then warm lips were on her mouth. Astonished, Valerie opened her eyes. The woman was slightly above her, for she knelt while Valerie still sat, paralyzed. One slender, strong hand held her behind her head; the other lay along her fevered cheek, soothing it. She tasted bitter coffee, cardamom, felt the hint of moist flesh behind the dry lips. Breathless and aroused, she clutched at black cloth to pull the other woman closer.

It began as all other amorous kisses she had known, touching and withdrawing, teasing between breaths with tongue and teeth, each light touch increasing desire. Craving contact through so much cloth, Valerie slid her hand upward along the folds of the abaya, searching for form and flesh.

Then the Bedouin grasped her by the shoulders and urged her down onto the rug beneath her.

Surprised, Valerie gave way and felt the woman's form spread over her and the black-draped leg slide between her thighs. Heat rushed through her, beginning in her sex and moving down her legs. Then something happened in the center of her brain. Ardor gave way to confusion as something alien and vast broke over her like a wave. She thrashed for a moment, moaned through lips still locked in the predatory kiss, and slipped into unconsciousness.

Her dream mind soared on wide wings, over the Giza Plateau. Below, the pyramids of Khufu, Khefren, and Menkaur stood majestic, their faces gleaming with white limestone from the desert floor. At their tops, the tiny golden pyramidions caught the sun and sparkled. Before them the Sphinx crouched, its haunches toward the great tombs, its Khefren face, unbroken, brooding toward the Nile. Then all began to crumble. Her hovering spirit watched in wonderment as they were violated, despoiled, abandoned, and finally swept over by shifting dunes.

Gliding south, she saw the swelling and contracting of the Nile, as if it pulsed, through countless inundations. Millennia of storms blew over the landscape, interspersed with droughts, and through them came an endless ebb and flow of migrations and invasions. Towns sprang up, flourished, and disintegrated; were in turn Persian, Greek, Roman, Byzantine, and finally Arab. And as each conquest came, she saw it also reached up to the gods.

She was over Thebes. At the end of an alley of ram-sphinxes, majestic Karnak rose to meet her. She saw the scores of temples simultaneously in their glory and in their decay, heard phantom priests drone incantations while invaders, soldiers, and chattering tourists flickered among them like locusts, and centuries of sand flowed in and out. Then time halted and she cringed at what she saw. Amun, Mut, Khonsu, Ptah, Hathor. Through the pylons and columns of their precincts and from their graven images on the walls, she heard them shrieking as Coptic zealots chiseled away their faces and smashed their hands and feet. Mutilated, blinded, effaced from the eyes and minds of men, the gods of Egypt finally fell silent.

Overhead the ferocious sun disk hovered, and nature withered beneath its desiccating wrath. Standing guard before the light, the silhouette of a man with a camel's head raised its arm and loosed a spear at her. It struck her but did not pierce, shattering instead to sparks that swarmed around her head. Her mouth filled with their fire, and she spat them out, crying, "*Khetet! Rekhi renusen. Djedi medjatsen.*"

She fled, wheeling in a circle westward over the desert toward a high ridge marked by a familiar pattern of shadows. She lit upon it for a moment, her oath echoing in her mind, and then she plummeted to its foot. There, behind a wall of dry brush, she found herself at the entrance to a cave, and in the depth of the cave, she knew, something waited.

CHAPTER XXVI:
DREAM MAP

"Oh, finally you're awake. Are you okay?"

Valerie lifted her head from her blanket and stared blankly for a moment toward the source of a familiar sound. She closed her eyes and then opened them again, as if to give them a second chance to make sense. Then she sat up abruptly. "What am I doing back here?"

On the other side of the campfire ashes, Derek shook sand out of his ruined shoes. "Back? I didn't know you went anyplace. But just before dawn I saw you staggering around with your hand over your face. When I asked what was wrong, you mumbled something and curled up on the ground and fell back asleep. I covered you up."

"I was with Nekhbet—the Bedouin woman who gave us water. I...I fell asleep in her tent."

"Oh?" Derek's eyebrows went up.

"It wasn't like that. I mean...I don't know what I mean," she muttered, rubbing her face. "This is all getting far too weird."

He laughed. "There's something *more* weird now than what's been happening all along?" He rubbed sand out of his cap of tight curls.

She shook her head. "I mean what just happened to me. I was in the Bedouin tent. That woman kissed me—well, it started as a kiss, a pretty forceful one. But then I passed out and had a strange dream. Really vivid. I was flying along the Nile watching...it seemed like all of history. But it ended with a kind of slaughter and me shouting something in Egyptian. I think it was the words from the amulet, the ones I don't understand. And then I woke up here."

"Yeah, tell me about it! I've been having dreams like that ever since I spent that night with Rekemheb. Scenes like out of a Hollywood spectacular." He finished tying neat double bows in his battered shoes.

"They always end in some disaster."

She looked around, puzzled again. "Where are the others?"

"At the well, getting water for today's march." He tied on his *nemes* again and smoothed the wings down over his shoulder. "So what do you think? Of the dreams, I mean? It almost seems like they're coming from someplace." He looked heavenward. "Like a message that we're just not getting."

"You mean like Pharaoh's dream of the fat and lean cows?" She ran her fingers through tangled brown hair. Impatiently she pulled it back with both hands, resnapped the clip around it, and covered it with her fedora. She felt the usual strands pull loose immediately and fall in spirals over her ears. "I don't think so."

Derek had stood up and was folding his blanket. He stopped. "Yes, exactly like that. You don't think there can be messages in dreams? Why don't you get off your 'I'm-a-scientist' high horse and accept that there's a world out there you know nothing about?"

She bit her lip. "I've been off that high horse for a while now, Derek. And you're right. These dreams were definitely different from any I've had before."

"Mine too. Now we just need a Joseph to interpret them."

Valerie got to her feet and began to roll up her sleeves. A faint and agreeable smell came from them—the smell of cedar.

"I think we have one."

Valerie looked toward the spot where the Bedouin woman's tent had stood the night before. It was gone. Of course. Hit and run seemed to be the pattern. Valerie went down to the center of the wadi, where the tribe was far along in its preparations for the day's march. Women were rolling up the tent panels into tight cylinders and loading them onto camels. They nodded in greeting but did not stop working. Several very young girls, no more than six or seven, tied pots together on a cord. She marveled again at their intense bright faces under wild hair.

Bemused, Valerie climbed a rocky elevation and looked below to where the tribe's flocks were being driven together into a tight circle. Shading her eyes with her hand, she gazed back eastward the way the tribe had come. It looked rather much the same as the way they had still to go. "*Plus ça change*," she thought. No progress or purpose.

"Do you still fear the red land now?"

She spun around toward the familiar voice. Blood rushed to her face.

The mysterious Bedouin stood a meter away, unveiled. The severe and stunning face held her glance again. Valerie felt a wave of affection, desire, anger. "Last night. What did you do to me?"

"I did what you wanted."

"What? To be knocked unconscious?" Valerie frowned. "It was the coffee, wasn't it? You put something in the coffee."

"You needed to sleep. You were troubled, exhausted."

"I was expecting something else. I mean, you did kiss me." Valerie heard a whine creep into her voice and was annoyed with herself. She was not going to grovel.

An expression flickered over Nekhbet's face, concern perhaps, or even affection. Valerie could not tell. Then it passed and the air between them grew cold. Nothing more embarrassing than the morning after, Valerie thought.

"You dreamt, didn't you?" Nekhbet stepped closer. "Strong, violent dreams, and now you want to know what they mean."

Valerie would have preferred to talk about their embrace, but the subject was dreams. "Yes, I guess so. But I don't like it that someone is playing with my mind."

"No one plays. The dreams are your own, from all the old memories. You dream the things you know, what your ancestors knew." Warmth had crept into her voice again.

"But I spoke words I don't know. How could I do that?" She touched the cloth of the abaya that fluttered in the slight morning breeze.

Nekhbet looked down at the hand. "You also dreamt of a cave."

"Yes, how did you know?" Valerie closed her eyes, trying to visualize the scene again. "It was at the base of a cliff. The ridge over the cave had odd markings. Like this."

She knelt down on one knee, and with her penknife she scratched a simple drawing in the sand. "There were three long vertical fissures, like so, and odd curves on both sides."

Nekhbet knelt beside her. "Yes, the cave is close by, in that direction." She pointed westward. "But you remember the image crudely." She rubbed away the lines that Valerie had cut in the sand and redrew it with her finger. "At midday, when the sun is highest, it looks like this."

She drew three descending lines connected by a bar across the top. The two outer lines dropped three-quarters of the way and ended in narrow isosceles triangles with concave bases. The archaeologist recognized the image in an instant. "A balance."

"You must see it at midday, for these lines are shadows, and they reveal themselves only then."

They got to their feet. Valerie looked in the direction of the ridge. "How do you know all of this? What I dreamt, where the cave is? Who are you? Did Rekemheb send you?"

Nekhbet laughed, a strange sound that seemed foreign to her. "You ask small questions when the great ones wait to be answered." She touched Valerie's face lightly, letting her fingers linger for a moment over the fresh scar. "It is half a day's walk, and you must hurry. If you arrive after midday, the shadows will be gone."

Valerie looked back toward the Bedouin tribe. The families were beginning to flow westward. "Will you continue on to El Dakhla? I mean, when I come back."

"The shepherds stay at El Dakhla for the summer. But you have your own concerns. See?" She raised her hand to the side. "Your friends are also already on their camels and wait for you."

"I will come to El Dakhla," Valerie said with finality. She embraced the shepherd woman and closed her eyes for a moment. Then she kissed the dark cheek near the lips, ambiguously, as Jameela had kissed her. "I will look for you."

Nekhbet nodded wordlessly and gently pushed Valerie away, her tattooed hands lingering for the briefest moment on her forearms.

Valerie turned and walked away, feeling the dark eyes on her back like a protective cloak.

Four mortals and a spectre stopped before the cliff wall. Derek cupped one hand over his eyebrows. "There are cracks all along this ridge, Valerie. Big ones, little ones. How are we supposed to know what to look for?"

Perched on her camel, Auset made a little tent over her head with her scarf. "I don't know about this, Valerie. Shadows pointing to a hidden tomb. This sounds much riskier than Yussif's farm at Al Dahkla. This may be a wild-goose chase."

"If it is, it's my fault," Derek said. "I'm the one who's been hammering at Valerie to give the supernatural a chance. Let's just go as far with this as we can."

Valerie fanned herself with her fedora and looked at her watch. "This *is* as far as we can go. It's noon. More or less. If we don't find it fast, we'll have to go back to El Dakhla after all."

"Look!" Yussif pointed toward two horizontal lines that slowly sharpened as the sun reached its zenith. As they crossed the three vertical cracks, the image of a huge balance came into view.

Valerie exhaled as if she had been holding her breath and set her hat back on. "She was right. Now let's go see if there's a cave under there." She hurried the remaining distance, pulling Auset's camel after her.

Yussif stayed beside her, with the reins of Derek's camel. The two riders dismounted at the foot of the cliff, and Yussif staked the camels.

Valerie pulled aside the desiccated brush that had once sprouted and then withered at the base of the ridge. "There's something here, all right, but hardly big enough for a lizard." She gripped a small boulder at the side and it fell away suddenly, causing a small rock slide. The dust settled gradually, revealing an opening to a tunnel. "It looks good. I think we have our cave."

"Gods, I hope so," Derek answered and began to untie the battered casket from its high perch. As he carried it on one shoulder toward his friends, the Ka appeared. "Hey, Rek. It looks like we've got something. Can you go in ahead and see what's in there? I mean, nothing bad can happen to you, right?"

"Let us see if it pleases the gods to give me a new resting place." Rekemheb appraised the cliff face like a new home owner and floated into the tunnel.

Behind him, Valerie took the first step into the darkness. She stood for a moment, letting her eyes adapt, and then clicked on the flashlight.

Yussif helped Auset into the tunnel, then stopped behind her. "Is very quiet here. I do not like this place."

"You're right." Valerie directed the light beam at their feet. "No echoes. It must be the silt we're walking on. Absorbs the sound."

Derek hefted the crate onto his shoulder and came in behind them. "Less talk and more walk, please. This thing is cutting into my neck."

The four crept down the tunnel, by the light of the single flashlight. Valerie's boot shattered something with a muffled snap, and she shone the light downward. "Pottery shards."

"Grave robbers, you think?"

"Only if it's a grave."

The tunnel ended suddenly. A stone lintel showed where a doorway had stood, but the space below was filled with dirt and rocks to within a few centimeters of the ceiling. From the other side came the sound of a voice, unintelligible.

"A shovel would be good right now, wouldn't it?" Valerie kicked the pile. "It seems to be soft. Maybe we can move it away with our hands."

The four of them covered their faces against the dust and set to work. In a short while they opened a channel. Valerie shone the light into a chamber and stepped into it. She stopped short.

In the midst of broken pottery and splintered wooden chests, Rekemheb knelt over a low sarcophagus, his forehead pressed against its rim and his arms stretched over the lid. In the quiet tomb all could hear that he wept.

CHAPTER XXVII:
RECKONING

Derek hurried to the priest's side. "What is it? Have we done something wrong?"

The Ka raised his head. His eyes glistened in the flashlight beam, the only part of him that reflected light. "Not wrong, dear child. Rather a great right. Look where you have brought us." He lifted his hand from the lid of the stone sarcophagus. An inscription ran down the center of it in two lines, lacking only a single hieroglyph where the stone had been broken in two.

"It is the *Hotep di nesu* invocation," Valerie said. "'The King has given an offering to Osiris, lord of Abydos, and to Hathor, Lady of Dendara, that they may bestow such offerings of bread and beer, oxen and fowl, alabaster and raiment to the Ka of the revered, the justified servant and priest of Hathor...Hator-em-heb.'"

She looked again at the Ka, who had stood up. "Why do you weep for a priest of Hathor?"

"This priest of Hathor...Hator-em-heb...was my son."

"Omigod!" Derek bent over the sarcophagus. "Another ancestor. But why isn't his Ka here? Or is it?" He looked up at the dark ceiling.

Rekemheb shook his head. "He was only a child when I was taken, a boy of gentle nature, his sister only a year older. I waited for them in the afterlife, Hator-em-heb and my daughter Merut-tot, but the Kas of my children never came to the Duat. It can only be because their mummies were destroyed."

Valerie nodded toward the broken stone, the unmistakable sign of pillaging.

"This tomb held him once." The Ka raised his hand. "There is our story."

Valerie directed the light where he pointed high on the wall behind the sarcophagus. Cut in low relief and painted in still-bright pigments, the Barque of the Sun seemed suspended over the chamber. Ten gods, faceless but elaborately clothed and ornamented, stood decorously in two lines along the sides, attending the orb of Ra. Before the barque two figures knelt, one behind the other, their hands raised in adoration.

"The gods in glory circling the world," Valerie confirmed. "The icon of perfect harmony. Even Apophis is harmless here at the bottom." She pointed beneath the boat where a snake curled, distinguishable only by its color from the river itself.

"But the gods are ruined," Yussif said somberly.

"Yes, every face but one is hacked away." Valerie moved the light beam along the barque to the prow. "All but Seth."

"Who would do such a thing?" Derek asked.

"Coptic Christians, maybe. Or some other sect that hated the old religion. They did it in the temples too, to 'kill' the gods." Valerie walked around the sarcophagus to the wall. "Look at what they did to Seth standing there next to Horus. Whoever smashed the gods and spared Seth also erased his original arm. See? Someone painted in the new one hurling a spear, not at Apophis, but at the men."

Auset shifted her weight impatiently. "I don't get it."

"It is our story," Rekemheb repeated. "See, the cartouches hold our names." The Ka pointed toward the newly painted spear that plunged into the first kneeling figure. "It was thus that I was murdered by Sethnakht. As for my son, and my daughter too, I do not know their fates."

"Isn't he here, in this grave?" Derek set his shoulder against the lid at the corner of the stone. Yussif leaned against the opposite corner, and together they slid the stone slab diagonally, opening the sarcophagus. Valerie pointed the light beam down inside.

"Oh no," Derek whispered.

The Ka stepped toward the opening and looked down at the disintegrated wrappings, the smashed skull, and the tatters of brown leathery flesh stretched over shattered bones.

"I have known for centuries that I was the last of my line to reach the Duat," he murmured. "My children's souls were destroyed, but the line of their offspring was not."

He laid a hand on the shoulder of his descendant. "It seems that was the bargain."

"I am so sorry, Rekemheb."

"Do not be. The gods have let me share his resting place. This is a great comfort. Entomb me here over the mummy of my son in his sarcophagus."

Derek carried the wooden casket into the last chamber and pried open the lid. He lifted the covering blanket from the cadaver and folded it in three, making a sort of pallet. Then he rolled the second blanket up into a loose cylinder and laid both pallet and pillow into the sarcophagus over the ruins of the son. He paused. "Hator-em-heb. Tell me about him."

The Ka assumed a softness of expression Valerie had not seen in him before. "He was much in your likeness, Ayemderak. He spoke with your same sweet voice, and to make a point, he always set his fist upon his hip."

"So that's where he gets it from." Auset laughed softly. "I thought it was acting class."

"And your daughter?" Valerie asked.

"Merut-tot was my eldest. She was not given to temple service, but to words. It was her wish to be a scribe. Of her life and fate I also know nothing."

Derek lifted the mummy from its flimsy casket and placed it gently in the stone sarcophagus. Elevated upon the makeshift pillow, the gauze-wrapped Hathor-priest lay with ecclesiastical dignity.

Valerie drew out the golden amulet from her knapsack and set it gently on the gauze wrappings of the mummy's chest. "Rekemheb, this should stay with you."

"No, it should not." The Ka reached past her with a translucent arm to retrieve the plaque by its chain and then laid it with solemnity over Derek's head. "This is the prophecy, the scribe said, and you must hold fast to it, Ayemderak, just as I did."

He turned to the others with a wan smile. "You who have brought me to this place with such great labor, you are my family and my friends. Even in the underworld, I wait with you for the gods to reveal themselves."

His speech ended, the Ka's form disintegrated. His blue-green light seemed to glow for a moment under the gauze wrappings of his mummy before fading out.

Derek's eyebrows made a little chevron. "They always say they'll call."

"He'll call," Auset said. "He'll come back for the birth of our baby. It's part of the prophecy, isn't it? So can we go now? I'm not so fond of being in a tomb."

"She's right," Valerie said. "We've been here long enough, and we haven't even talked about where to go now. I think El Dakhla. We can get some road transportation back to Cairo."

"That's right. We're safe now, aren't we? Without the mummy, the corpus delicti, so to speak, they can't charge us with anything." Derek grunted as he helped the others slide the stone cover of the sarcophagus back in place. "I can't believe we've actually pulled this off."

The shuffling feet caused them to turn around. Valerie's flashlight sliced along the stone wall and stopped. A cold Akhnaton face leered back at them.

"No, Miss Foret, you have not 'pulled it off,'" the velvety voice said.

"Volker Vanderschmitt," Valerie said wearily. "You just won't leave us alone."

Something moved behind him in the dark, and she shifted the light beam to the side. A figure swathed in black stood there; its fathomless dark eyes looked back at her without expression. Valerie inhaled sharply and whispered. "Nekhbet."

It was then that she saw he held a gun in one hand. With the other he drew a flashlight from his belt and clicked it on. The two light beams confronted each other. "Is that her name? I never bothered to ask. Well, even with my ten words of Arabic, it was easy enough to convince her I was part of your team and get her to bring me here. You must thank her for me."

"I don't understand."

"How I was able to track you down? Oh, Miss Foret. You are as poor a thief as you are an archaeologist. You left a very vivid trail— in Amarna and with the Bedouins. Everyone remembered you, of course."

Her eyes fell on the gun in his hand, and the realization struck her like a stone. It was her own.

He waved it, taunting her. "You made quite an impression on the Bedouins particularly, Miss Foret. The headman was very proud of his new acquisition, but not so proud that he wouldn't part with it for a good price."

Derek interrupted. "There's no need to threaten us with a gun, Dr. Vanderschmitt. Things are going on here you don't understand. If you knew—"

"I know all I need to know, Mr. Ragin. I know that the four of you have committed a very serious crime, and you will do what I say or I will hand you over to the authorities. I cannot imagine that an Egyptian jail would be a very nice place to live in." He glanced over at Auset. "Or give birth in."

Valerie darted glances back and forth between the gunman and Nekhbet, still silent in the semidarkness. What was going on? How had the woman who seemed to know so much fallen into the hands of this demented man? Was she after all just a clever Bedouin who had made some lucky guesses? Or were Rekemheb's mysterious friends so inept that they could be thwarted by one revenge-obsessed academic? None of it made any sense. "Just what do you want, then?"

Vanderschmitt's thick lips formed a slight pucker as he tilted his head back slightly, and he spoke deliberately, as if he had rehearsed his speech beforehand. "Here is the way I see the story unfolding. You will go quietly back to Brussels and resign from the department. You can explain your resignation with some womanly weakness: physical exhaustion, emotional breakdown. You'll think of something. For my part, I will return the mummy to its original location and, more importantly, refrain from reporting this theft. I suggest you accept my offer and thus avoid imprisonment."

Derek stepped into the light. "We have a counteroffer, Dr. Vanderschmitt," he said, unfazed by the muzzle of the pistol a few inches from his chest. He drew the gold chain over his head and held it out. The jeweled pectoral sparkled in the light beam. "We will give you the amulet if you simply leave us—and the mummy—alone. Valerie returns to her position at the university, and all returns to normal. Except of course for the fame the entire university will enjoy for the discovery. I am sure you will see your face often enough in the papers to satisfy you."

Vanderschmitt chuckled. "Ah, yes. The amulet of Meremptah. You see, I also read the tomb texts and discovered its existence. And I noticed that you omitted it from your official list of artifacts, Miss Foret." He took the golden plaque and appraised it in the light. "Magnificent. I can see why you were willing to risk your career for it."

He hefted the amulet, then dropped it into his shirt pocket. His mouth tightened into a triumphant smile for a moment and then sagged into astonishment.

"What…is that?"

Valerie glanced over her right shoulder to see the ghostly Ka of Rekemheb, his otherwise serene visage darkened by anger. In two paces he was before Vanderschmitt, reaching toward the necklace. The otherworldly voice spoke in a deadly monotone, and Valerie recognized the ancient curses.

Vanderschmitt backed away from the spectre. "No…no. Impossible." He shook his head. "No such thing."

The shimmering finger touched him and he flinched. At that moment, the Bedouin hurled herself sideways against her captor. In the same instant, both men lunged toward him, knocking the light from Valerie's hand. Both flashlights crashed on the ground, plunging the tomb into pitch blackness.

The gunshots were deafening.

CHAPTER XXVIII:
SLOUCHING TOWARD THEBES

"G od *damn* it!" Volker Vanderschmitt threw the jeep into gear and the vehicle lurched forward. The heat radiating from the steel hood blew across him in waves.

He looked down at the pistol on the passenger seat where he had tossed it. What the hell had gone wrong? He had been so careful, so diligent, even after the fools from Antiquities had dropped the case. Even the Arab woman had proven surprisingly easy to single out from the tribe and to bribe, with minimal communication, to lead him to the fugitives. It should have been a nice clean confrontation, with him, however it turned out, as the hero of the day.

And what was that thing he saw? An impossibility. Already he was certain it was a hallucination. Or a half-naked guide he had not seen riding with the fugitives. Yes, that was probably it. And together with that native woman, they had attacked him. Three times he tried to knock them away with the pistol, and three times it had gone off. If anyone had been injured in the scuffle, they were to blame for it.

He patted the object in his shirt pocket. It was just too bad that he would have to hand over the amulet. But maybe not. There was no mention of it in the report, no photograph, only her word against his. And she was a thief. In a way, you could see it as a just reward for a long and difficult job that no one else was willing to do.

He had been a good detective after all, tracking them down, and without help from the damned Egyptians. Sometimes he wondered why he bothered with them; they were so corrupt. One couldn't tell the authorities from the thieves. "The people that dwelleth in the darkness." The words of Isaiah came to him with a sudden clarity. There had always been that kind of darkness, and it was men like him who brought the light. Stalwart men who were willing to set aside ambition and comfort to fight in a righteous cause.

And that was it, when you got down to it, was it not? One was either of the party of God or the party of evil, a crusader or a heathen. That was surely what was behind the dreams he kept having—of standing guard and sensing the great light at his back.

He took the amulet out of his pocket and pulled the chain with one hand over his head. The golden image slid heavily down inside his shirt and dangled between the soft swellings over his pectoral muscles.

A calm came over him, and he relaxed his foot on the gas pedal. The jeep slowed perceptibly, and he found himself nodding as he reflected. It all made sense now. That was why he had been named chairman at precisely the time the splendid tomb was discovered. He had been chosen to prevent the theft, to set things right. It had been exhausting, dangerous even, but he accepted the sacrifice because that was the kind of man he was. A crusader. Yes. He liked that.

❖

The three fugitives struggled eastward. Two of them, wounded, held on to the swaying camel seat while the third one walked. Footprints of man and beast stretched out for kilometers behind them.

Derek shook himself out of his stupor and brushed away the insect that adhered to the sticky crust on his neck. The bleeding had stopped finally, and the *nemes* that he had pulled down over the top of his ear at least covered the open flesh. The wound, it turned out, was slight, but the pain persisted. "Are you sure this is the shortest way?"

"Yes. Yes." Plodding forward and holding the camel's rein, Yussif checked Valerie's compass again. "Luxor is over there, east, always east. We are maybe halfway now. It will be okay."

"Of course." Derek tightened his grip on Auset, riding in front of him. With hands pressed together over the emergency bandage on her swollen abdomen, she leaned, feverish, against him. He held the water bottle in front of her mouth, and she drank from it obediently, without saying anything. He could sense her fear; it was his fear too. That the baby was already dead and the rest of them would die in the desert.

"You hear that, sweetie? It's not far. Yussif knows the way to Luxor. Just hold on a little longer." For the first time in the journey, Auset was silent.

Derek wanted to talk, to be reassured. Things looked very bad, and he hadn't even told them his passport was gone. Left in the tomb, probably, or at the Bedouin camp; he had no idea. But now that was the least of their worries. "I can't believe he pulled the trigger," he rambled. "He already had everything he wanted—his damned tomb and the amulet too. And now he's killed someone."

No one responded. Hot wind ruffled the wings of his *nemes* and seemed to sharpen the sound of Yussif's shoes crunching on sand. "Where are they, those gods? You'd think they'd look after us a little better."

Derek squinted toward the direction they traveled, where the harsh sunlight was less piercing. Too difficult to look elsewhere, least of all behind them toward the afternoon sun. High overhead vultures made a wide arc and seemed to circle back toward them. "Oh, great," he muttered. "Death by cliché."

"How much longer?" Auset rasped.

She still held her hands over the baby's mound, and Derek saw with alarm the bright red moisture seeping through her fingers. "Not much," he lied. "Just a few hours. Try to sleep. Yussif and I will take care of you. What more could a girl ask for, right?"

His eyes were so tired, his damaged ear rang endlessly, and the torn ear lobe throbbed. He closed his eyes and concentrated on the sounds, grateful not to be the one walking. Insects still buzzed, and the plodding footfall of both Yussif and the camel in different rhythms made a curious kind of syncopation. In the background he heard a soft rumbling.

Auset moaned again, and he jerked out of his trance. "Yussif, can we go any faster?"

The Arab looked back over his shoulder. "I am sorry, my friend. We cannot run. Maybe you ask your ancestor's gods to give us nice truck."

Derek moved his head around, stretching the muscles in his neck. He blinked in disbelief. "Uh…you mean like those over there?" He pointed off behind them where the harsh sun had kept them from looking. A small convoy of armored vehicles rumbled toward them.

Yussif stopped in his tracks, tugging downward on the reins. The camel honked furiously. "Egyptian army, Frontier Corps, I think."

The convoy spotted the wanderers at the same time, and one of the covered jeeps veered away from the line. In a few moments it pulled up next to the group. The passenger, an officer, set one foot on the ground, but before he could stand, Yussif ran toward the jeep. He spoke rapidly, but it was clear from his gestures that he was asking for help. The one officer nodded and spoke into a handheld radio.

"What did he say?" Derek asked anxiously.

"Is good news. This convoy has medical officer. They are on way to Dakhla, but we are closer to Luxor so they will take Auset to hospital there."

"Thank God!" Derek said softly, and then spoke into Auset's ear. "You see? Everything's going to be all right."

In a few moments a personnel carrier pulled up alongside the jeep. The wide red crescent painted on its roof identified it as a medical vehicle. A tall, angular man got out of it, and the crescent insignia at the top of his sleeve identified him as well. Yussif tapped the camel on the flank, and it kneeled for the dismount. The officer leaned over and did a cursory exam of the feverish woman while two men came directly behind him with a canvas stretcher.

"She has a gunshot wound," Derek said to the officer in English, and Yussif translated. "You'll be all right now," Derek repeated to Auset, releasing her.

She said something unintelligible and fell limply into the arms of the medics. They laid her out efficiently, if not gently, on the narrow military stretcher and set off at a brisk walk.

Derek slid off the camel and stood uncertain as soldiers carried the mother of his child away from him. He could not even appeal to Yussif, who stood outside the vehicle in conversation with the medical officer.

The officer climbed into the van next to the stretcher and looked out, obviously waiting for something to be clarified or settled. Outside, Yussif argued with another man who had just arrived, also apparently an officer. This one seemed angry, and he kept his hand resting on his sidearm.

Finally, Yussif threw up his hands, and the two men walked back to where Derek stood bewildered. Yussif was agitated. He kept looking back at the van where, in the open door, the medical officer still called out to him. Something was going wrong. Very wrong.

The officer stopped in front of him. Shorter and beefier than the medic, he had sagging pockmarked cheeks that accentuated his scowl. His desert camouflage uniform was ill-fitting, and the shirt strained at its buttons over his midsection. Derek braced himself.

Yussif said, "He asks who you are and why you are in the desert. I tell him you are tourist traveling with us, but he does not believe. Or does not want to. He looks for Sudanese assassin."

"The assassin again? Did you tell him I'm an American?"

"Of course. But you are not dressed like American, so he wants to see identification. Show him your passport, quickly, so we can go."

"I…I don't have it. It's lost. Explain to them, Yussif. You know what to say."

The driver of the medical vehicle started his motor, and Yussif began backing toward it. He raised both hands and called out to Derek, "Please, my friend. Auset is in great danger and maybe die. Someone must to take care of her on the way. We have to go and you must to explain yourself."

Then he seemed to change his mind and came back again, unwrapping the long blue turban from around his head. He draped it around Derek's neck and clasped his hands in front of him, as if in prayer. "Forgive me, my friend. I *must* go. You will explain to these men and come later to Luxor. Everything to be okay. *Inshaa' allah.*"

Yussif turned again and ran toward the medical truck. Without looking back, he climbed into the passenger side and pulled the door closed. In a moment it drove off eastward, spreading a low wake of dust behind and to the side.

Derek still stood before the pockmarked officer, who in the meantime had waved two soldiers over to join him. "Do you speak English?" he asked anxiously. "Does anyone speak English?"

"I speak English." The officer drew his pistol. "You are under arrest."

CHAPTER XXIX:
PYRRHIC DEFEAT

The failing flashlight on the lid of the sarcophagus sent a weak cone of light across the chamber. Beneath it, crouching against the stone side, Valerie held the limp form of Nekhbet in her arms. The satiny hair, still smelling of cedar, brushed against her chin.

The yellow light grew smaller, browner, and finally faded out, and she was once again in the black punishment closet, in stifling punitive darkness. She gave herself to it, remembering the strange violent kiss and the delirium afterward. What had happened?

She pressed her lips to the cooling flesh of the woman's forehead. She had been puzzling so long that her reason had collapsed, like a muscle worked to the point of failure. Now the many questions that crowded in on one another cancelled each other out and left her with only emotion. Regret, longing, and an overwhelming sense of guilt.

She buried her face again in the thick hair. Whoever the strange woman was, she had lain in Valerie's arms and had been mortal after all.

"You must not linger here. There is a prophecy to fulfill."

She opened her eyes to the dull luminescence hovering in the darkness. She was no longer impressed. "Get the hell away from me," she hissed. "Take your damned prophecy elsewhere."

"No, you must take your mourning elsewhere." He folded himself up next to her, illuminating her from the side in a dull blue-green light. "You cannot weaken in this fashion. You are chosen to accomplish a great thing."

"No, you've got it wrong. I don't belong to this 'chosen' lineage, although I threw away my career for it for some myth of the gods."

"No myth. The gods were real and will be real again."

"I can't tell anymore what's real or unreal, what's my world or your world. I only know that this woman seemed to care for me. Now, because of us, she's dead. If she was working for you, it didn't do her much good. Now I've got to take her back to her people and try to explain why she's dead. I don't even know why myself."

"You foolish child. You have given up after only a few days and a single death, when I lost everything and yet waited thousands of years." His tone became gentle. "Did you think there would be no sacrifice to save the world?"

"Save the world? Is that what we're trying to do? Well, we aren't doing very well, are we?"

The Ka dimmed and brightened again, as if with faltering current. "No. We are not doing well. And that is why you must confront this murderer before you give in to personal sorrow. He is important. If you will not pursue him for my amulet, you must bring him to justice for this woman's death. It is better for your heart to do this than to carry her back to the shepherds, who will not thank you for it."

"Pursue Vanderschmitt? Perhaps you haven't noticed that he's in a jeep while I have a camel?"

"Many things will stop a machine that will not stop a camel. Are you afraid?"

She felt the dead woman's breast pressed against her own in the intimate embrace that death allowed and was ashamed. Infatuation did not cease as abruptly as life did. "Yes. Of course I'm afraid. He has my gun, after all. You know what a gun is, don't you? That's the thing that killed her and hurt Auset and Derek. My gun." She closed her eyes at the irony, which was unbearable.

"You have a weapon he does not have—the desert gods."

"Desert gods? They've been pretty useless so far, haven't they?"

"Do not speak disrespectfully of these gods which one day may speak for you."

"I'm sorry." She sighed. "But what's the point? I can't catch up with him."

"My Ba has seen him. He travels confidently, with your weapon far from his hand. Shu will delay him. And when you face this man, you will flatter him. He has a high opinion of himself, but he is not strong. This is a thing you cannot let pass."

She again pressed her forehead against the face of the dead woman. Then she laid the body gently down beside the sarcophagus. For a moment she knelt, studying the dark form, and then she kissed the cold, slightly open lips. "No, it will not pass."

❖

The ferocious afternoon sun beat down on her back, baking away precious moisture, and she took another drink of water from the goatskin. When she recorked it she saw the lines of red-brown stain around her nails. She had blood on her hands. As much as he did.

His wheel tracks in the sand were clear and led in the direction they had come a few hours before. But he was way ahead of her, increasing the distance every minute. How in hell was she going to catch up with him on a camel?

She looked northeastward and saw the creeping ridge of gray. Wind, stirring up sand. "Shu, God of Wind," she said into the air. "Do you know a Ka named Rekemheb? He seems to know you. Or a Bedouin woman named Nekhbet? I am doing this for them. For an amulet and for justice. So if you can help me out somehow…"

The sandstorm was still far away, could go in any direction. She drew a checkered scarf from her pack to cover her face and urged the camel into a trot.

Then she saw them, spots in the distance. Was it a mirage? Her weary eyes burned from staring at lines in the sand. No. She recognized the objects—and the location. It was the wadi that held the Bedouin well, and the larger spot was a jeep. She rode closer, eyes riveted on the second moving spot until she could make it out clearly.

A man in trousers with something white around his hips knelt facing away from her. Her camel padded closer, and she gradually made sense of the scene. Tools lay on the ground near the rear wheel; he must have had to change the tire. It would have been an awful job in the heat. His kneeling made sense; he had tied his shirt around his waist and was washing himself at the well. Then he stood up, still facing away, his back bare to the waist.

He must have finally heard her, for he turned around and she saw the glitter on his chest. Of course. His trophy. Well, she had something better to offer, but she would have to make her proposal quickly. She took the ivory case out of her knapsack and hung it on her shoulder by the leather strap.

"Stop right there," he called out when she was a dozen meters away.

She did not reply and let the camel drift closer, puzzled. She had never seen him shirtless, and she guessed he took pains never to be seen that way. His upper body was almost womanly; his arms were soft, unmuscled, and his pectorals swelled like breasts. Below his waist, his torso widened into plump hips. The belt of his trousers had dropped below his swollen belly, and the shirt tied around his hips rendered them even more pronounced. There was something distastefully familiar in his long face and his pear-shaped body wrapped in white cloth.

She stared for a moment, as if he were a puzzle piece she held, until it came to her. He was the image, complete with white kilt and royal ornament, of the monotheist Akhnaton. Derek had been right.

"You are persistent, Miss Foret. I will grant you that. Not unlike myself."

She was above him, still mounted, and on the slope above the wadi. He had to look up, and he tilted his head a fraction, grudging respect. "But what do you hope to achieve by pursuing me? Whatever happened back in that cave is on your head." He untied the twisted sleeves from around his waist and drew his shirt on again, but the amulet chain was still visible, and the Akhnaton image still spooked from him.

She lowered the camel for the awkward dismount. "You needn't have run away, you know. Nothing much happened in the cave but a lot of noise," she lied. "Well, you did take a nasty slice out of Derek's ear. They're all on their way to El Dakhla now. You scared the hell out of us."

"You deserved scaring." He rolled up his right sleeve in precise turns of each cuff, over and over, to his elbow.

She kept her tone bright. "You know, if you hadn't escalated our little disagreement so quickly, you would have seen there are things we can agree on. I found the tomb and the world knows it, but my resignation will not help you nearly as much as my cooperation. You can be another Howard Carter, if I go along with it. And I would…for the mummy."

"Why this obsession with a mummy? What's so special about it? If it's the jewels you wanted, you could have simply taken the necklace out of its coffin and left."

His question took her off guard. Should she tell him? "You think this whole thing was about the amulet?" She shook her head. "It's nothing like that." She paused again while he rolled up the second sleeve. "You know what a Ka is, don't you? Well, this mummy has a Ka—that's what you saw in the tomb."

"What are you talking about?" He squinted at her for a long moment, as if studying her face for clues. "You mean to tell me you have been carrying around a corpse because you think it has a ghost? The heat has gotten to you, Miss Foret."

"I thought I was crazy too, at first." She sauntered closer to the jeep. Out of the corner of her eye she saw the pistol on the passenger seat. "But he's real, I can assure you. If you talked to him, he would tell you amazing things. Things that would change everything you ever believed in."

"Oh, really." He snorted. "You call yourself a scientist, but you stand there with a straight face and propose a myth that twenty centuries of Christianity has laid to rest." He shook his head. "The ever-hysterical female. I should have expected that."

"Well, perhaps you will let me keep my illusions," she said, changing tack. She stood between him and the jeep. "But I'm willing to give you another artifact in exchange for the amulet." She laid her hand on the ivory and gold case that hung on her shoulder. "A scribe kit, in ivory and gold, from the court of Meremptah." She held the scroll case up for him to see.

He stared at the artifact without touching it, appraising its authenticity. She had his attention.

"You know, we're a lot alike, Dr. Vanderschmitt." She let go of the scroll case, letting it simply hang from her shoulder where he could see it. "We're both good archaeologists, and I think at the end of the day, we want the same thing."

"You have no idea what I want, and we are not at all alike." His eyes moved to her face. "But you *are* just like a woman I once knew. I saw through her, however, just as I see through you."

She was in front of him then, and when he lifted his right hand to take the scroll case from her shoulder, she reached behind her into the jeep and snatched the pistol from the seat.

He reacted instantly, seizing her hand and forcing it skyward. In defense she pounded upward with her other fist against his nose. Something seemed to give with a faint snap. He grunted in sudden pain, and his thick lips went white. Bubbles of blood appeared at his nostrils as he exhaled, and when they burst, blood streamed over his lips and dripped onto his shirt. He leaned against her, forcing her up against the jeep and knocking her hat into the backseat. The pistol fired once into the air, causing them both to flinch.

The pain of his nose seemed to stun him, while the adrenaline of rage pumped through her, and she managed to force him a step backward. "Murderer," she snarled. "You are pathetic."

"What?" His eyes brightened at the word, and the skin of his face increased in color. His grip tightened on her wrist, and he twisted her hand back until the gun barrel pointed down at her.

"Corruption," he grunted, his breathing audible and wet. Panting, he forced his thumb into the space over her finger and pressed down. "An offense to men and God."

A white-hot bolt plunged through her. She gasped as agonizing nausea erupted upward to her lungs and downward to her groin. Dropping the pistol, she stood frozen in disbelief, pressing both hands over the spreading stain above her belt. She crumpled to her knees.

He watched her gasping, and for the briefest moment he understood her helpless outrage, recalled his own a lifetime ago. Before he had found God. Then lucidity returned and he realized he had finally made his point. He stepped back and pulled a folded handkerchief from his pocket. Pressing it to his throbbing, bloody nose, he bent over and retrieved the pistol from the ground. "You see what you've done?" he said almost ruefully. "If you had only left well enough alone."

Dust swirled around him as he turned away. Without looking back, he climbed back into the jeep, driving off northeastward, the wind-driven sand hissing against his windshield.

Valerie still knelt. Her viscera a glowing mass that swelled with every heartbeat, she watched him with dimming vision. The increasing wind tangled her long hair and coated her face with the light brown powder of the desert. Slowly, pain faded along with consciousness. As if in Muslim prayer, she curled forward onto the sand, and life seeped away through her limp hands.

❖

He drove as fast as he dared on the rough ground, careening around rocks that could puncture his remaining tires, trying to outrun the storm. All the while, thoughts pounded in his head like drums of every volume and pitch. All right. He had killed her, just like in the dream, but it was self-defense, that was clear. She had stolen the mummy and the amulet, had chased him into the desert. For God's sake, she had broken his nose and then drawn a gun on him. He dabbed again at the blood that still trickled from both nostrils.

That damned gun! He reached over his shoulder and tossed it onto the backseat. What would he tell the police? Would he have to even admit finding her? He should have buried her. Maybe the sandstorm would cover her. What about the others? What lies would they tell?

The prickling wind blew off his hat. He peered through nearly shut eyes to keep the powdery particles from blinding him as they spun in the back draft behind the windshield. Soon they filled the air, forming a crust over his bloody upper lip and searing his nose with every inhalation. Slowing the jeep enough to free both hands, he opened his blood-soaked handkerchief. Quickly, clumsily, he tied the handkerchief in a triangle over his mouth and grabbed hold of the wheel again.

He could hear the sand blowing into the radiator; the engine was overheating, and the thick brown air was like a wall in front of him. With a deafening bang, the engine seized up and the jeep rolled to a halt.

The searing wind tore at him, scouring his upper face and ears. He pressed his eyes shut against the agonizing sting but could not keep the sand from collecting in lumps in the moist corners. They burned unbearably and so he untied the handkerchief and, holding his breath, wiped them clear.

The relentless wind caused the handkerchief to flutter and twist in his hand, then snatched it and sent it flying away from him. He pulled his shirt up over his mouth and climbed over to the passenger side. If he could just get his face out of the wind. He curled up on the floor of the jeep, pressing his face between his knees and covering his head with his arms.

There was more sand than air now; he felt it filling his hair, trickling down inside of his shirt, lacerating his forehead. Powdery sand, tiny particles of the desert, crept along his nose and throat, minute soldiers breaching his defenses. He could not breathe slowly enough to keep them out. When the first tiny, sharp pieces entered his lungs he began to cough. Each wracking cough required an inhalation, and each inhalation brought more cutting sand to tear him from within.

The spasms became more violent, the burning in his chest more agonizing. The bloody mucus he began to expel trickled down his chin, hardening quickly into lumps of brownish grit. As the suffocation began, he thrashed in wild paroxysms in the steel chamber of his jeep, smashing his head on the underside of the dash. Harder and harder he thrashed, inhaling fire, coughing out pieces of his lungs, until the desert finally stilled him.

The sand continued hissing around the jeep, filling its interior, fixing him in place for the scavengers of the red land.

Chapter XXX:
Orpheus in the Desert

The officer planted himself in front of Derek, one hand resting on his holster. But his short slender body, his narrow belly swelling out over his gun belt like an early pregnancy, severely undermined his posture of authority.

"Arrest? This is insane. I'm an American. I don't even look Sudanese, and I don't speak…whatever they speak down there. That woman in the car is…my wife."

"Your wife?" The officer sucked air noisily through tobacco-brown teeth. "Your friend say is *his* wife. I think American guy does not dress like this." He reached over to pull off Derek's *nemes* and held it up in the air between them. "Maybe you want to change story." He let the cloth drop. "You go to Luxor, yes. You get passport to show you are okay, we let you go. To wife or anyplace."

He was joined by a second man, who was at once menacing and comical. His teeth protruded slightly, and when he did not press his lips together, the middle two slid out between them, rodent-like.

A third soldier joined them, moustached and scowling.

Derek replied to the first officer. "My friend told you. My passport is lost. We were attacked by a gunman. You can see I was wounded too." He tilted his head to show the scab-encrusted ear. "I must have lost it then."

"You explain this to Luxor police." The officer produced a length of cord and wrapped it around Derek's wrists in front of him. He barked orders in Arabic, and the other two soldiers walked their prisoner forcefully toward a military personnel carrier.

"What is it with you guys and foreigners?" Derek twisted in their grasp. "This is the second time in three days I've been yanked around this way."

Ignoring him, the two pressed him into the back of the vehicle. It smelled of old sweat and cigarette smoke. Tooth-man, who seemed to know no English, started the motor while moustache-man got in on the passenger side and lit up a cigarette.

The driver took the car around in a wide curve and drove eastward away from the convoy. From his seat in the rear Derek looked between the shoulders of the two soldiers onto the road, searching for the medical van, but it was already out of sight.

"You guys gonna tell me what's going on here? I mean you can't really think I'm Sudanese. Uh…do either of you speak English?"

Neither man replied, although moustache-man raised his open hand to signal "silence."

Derek stared sullenly down at the cord that tied his hands together. An amateurish job. Or maybe the officer had simply gone through the motions of securing him and didn't care. He clenched his fists, stretching the cord, and then relaxed them. Yes, that would do it. He flexed again.

The terrain had grown rougher. Boulders and rocky ridges rose on the landscape, and the straight desert road began to curve left and right around them. He could not be sure, but he reckoned they still headed eastward toward Luxor. Then the driver suddenly spun the wheel and took the car off the road.

"Where are you going? This can't be the way to Luxor."

The soldiers ignored him and began talking between themselves, glancing at him occasionally through the center mirror. He was certain he heard the words "*fuloos*" and "*agnabee.*" His vocabulary in Arabic was miniscule, but he had certainly learned the words for money and foreigner. If they were talking about his money, it was not a good sign.

Staring with feigned indifference out the side window, he worked more urgently on his bindings, clenching and relaxing, until he could force a thumb under one of the cords. With a minimum of movement, he unraveled the rope and then wrapped it back around loosely, grasping it so it looked the same as before.

Then he leaned forward again, studying the road for any indication of where they were taking him. Nothing but rock and sand. Moustache-man tapped another cigarette from a crumpled package and lit it with a slender Bic lighter.

Derek turned his head away as the man exhaled a long stream of smoke. Coughing, he stared sullenly through the side window. Something caught his eye—a band of gray dust on the horizon. It was the movement that made it ominous, for as he watched, the band wavered and swelled at the center. "Hey. I think there's a sandstorm over there. That's not good, right?"

"What you think, American boy?" The smoker laughed and picked a speck of tobacco from his tongue. "This is stupid tourist car? No. Egyptian army is good. Military motor is protect from sand."

American boy? Derek glanced down at his hands again. The alarm that had been buzzing softly at the back of his brain suddenly clanged. They knew he wasn't the Sudanese. It wasn't an arrest, at least not anymore; it was a kidnapping.

He forced calm on his face while he considered every possibility. It didn't look good. They had every advantage. What did he have other than free hands? They were armed soldiers and he was—an actor.

They were approaching a rocky outcropping. Flat, slightly bigger than a theater stage. And the sandstorm was getting closer. It was showtime. "Hey, guys. I have to go to the bathroom. You know. *Hammam. Toilette.*"

Moustache-man said something in Arabic, and the driver abruptly stopped the car. "Open door and piss."

"Uh, it's not that. It's the other. Really bad. Diarrhea." He rocked slightly, forward and back, suggesting urgency, dire consequences. "You know? Tourist's sickness."

"Okay. Go and make shit." The soldier winced disgust. "You have one minute."

Derek opened his door with bound hands and walked toward the rocky slope as far as he dared. The driver leaned through his window pointing his pistol at him.

"One minute, yeah, sure. Okay." Derek looked around. The sandstorm was almost upon them. It was his only chance.

"More fast!" The soldier got out of the passenger side and stood with his pistol aimed over the hood of the car. "Shit or come back to car!"

With his back turned, Derek hunched over, pretending to undo his trousers. The thickening air hissed around him. From a crouching position, he threw the cord from his wrists and broke into a run.

The soldier's gun roared, and the bullet zinged off the rock beside him. He spun around to the other side of the outcropping, heard two more gunshots. The air was suddenly dense and biting wherever it touched skin. As he ran, he wrapped Yussif's turban around his head and face, leaving only a tiny slit for vision. Over the slit he wrapped a single layer of the turban and tucked the ends of it deep under the folds so it would not unravel. With faint, gauzy vision he groped his way along the rocky formation. A fourth gunshot sounded; a bullet struck close to his foot.

The irregular rock table afforded narrow footholds, and desperation drove him like a spider up to the top of it. The wind was full of needles, and he shut his eyes as he scrabbled along on hands and knees. Finally he felt the opposite edge. His pursuers had goggles, he knew, but by now they too were useless, for the air was opaque with sand. The blind pursued the blind.

And sightless, he had an advantage. On the rock table that was his little stage, he knew exactly where he was. Fifteen years of singing with spotlights scorching his eyes had taught him spatial memory. After a moment's glimpse, his perfect inner compass could point to every object. He let himself slide down on the other side over the rough stones that tore his shirt and abraded his skin. He felt the desert floor again, then stood for a fraction of a second, his back pressed against the stone. Sand whirled around him, and he forced himself to breathe in shallow breaths through the four layers of cloth. The car he judged was…stage right…there, where the standing basses of the orchestra would have been. He groped his way sightlessly forward in the roiling dust.

"Oof!" He felt his knee bang into metal. He had misjudged slightly and hit the rear of the vehicle. He groped his way forward. In a moment he had found the door handle, and he threw himself into the car, ripping off his turban. Miraculously, the key was in the ignition, and at the first rush of the engine, he slammed the motor into gear and lurched forward.

He drove wildly into the gray and yellow maelstrom, praying there were no rocks in the way, but the desert floor stayed smooth. Finally, when the sound of gunfire seemed distant enough to be harmless, he stopped. His heart pounding, he pressed trembling fingers to the sides of his head.

Now what? How long did a sandstorm last, he wondered, and could he ever find the road again afterward? How long could he hold out sitting in the Land Rover? He looked around inside.

A walkie-talkie lay on the dashboard. He chuckled, imagining himself using it to inform the Egyptian army that he had hijacked one of their vehicles. He leaned over toward the passenger side. A wooden box on the floor held ammunition for the soldiers' sidearms. In the side pocket he found a manual in Arabic, metal tools whose purpose he could not guess, a map in Arabic, and a flashlight.

The air brightened in front of him. An avenue seemed to open, inviting him forward. At first he did not budge, fearing to wander aimlessly following a fickle wind until he ran out of gas. But the wind behind him became stronger, the crash of swirling sand more violent, piling up on the rear window. To avoid being engulfed, he drove forward, red-eyed, toward calmer air.

Urged forward in fits and starts, he had time to think. He agonized first about himself and then about the others. Auset, dangerously wounded, and the baby—his baby—in mortal danger. He clenched the steering wheel with dusty hands. And Valerie, who had insisted on staying with the dying Bedouin woman. Where was she now? Had the Bedouins thanked her for bringing back one of their own—murdered? It was unlikely.

He drove toward nothing but vague light, until finally the storm dissipated. When the air cleared he saw nothing but more desert and, in the distance, a spot of vibrating blackness. He drove toward it, apprehension turning to dread. When he grasped what he was seeing, his stomach lurched.

❖

He stopped next to the jeep. "Oh, my God," he whispered as the roiling mass of black feathers and bobbing leathery heads broke apart and the smaller scavengers fluttered away. The larger birds, fearless, hulked close by, waiting. He forced himself out of his vehicle.

There he was, or the grotesque remains of him, crouching on the passenger side half packed in sand. The vultures had eaten all they could reach, from the face and neck and downward into the chest; only the shirt had slowed their penetration. Below the rolled-up sleeves, the forearms were picked meatless and one of the hands was torn off. The shredded shirt was still buttoned over the half-devoured chest. On the car seat, near his knee, its chain obviously broken, was the amulet. It confirmed the identity of the faceless carcass which that morning had been a man.

Derek snatched the object and then, leaning on the rear of the sand-scoured vehicle, he retched.

He wiped his face with his sleeve and tried to get his bearings. How much longer could he last before he died of thirst? Keeping his head turned away from the grisly corpse, he looked into the rear of the jeep for water, for anything. Then he saw it and whispered, "Oh Jesus."

Her fedora lay on the backseat. He plunged his arm into the piles of sand feeling for anything solid, dreading to find a part of her. His hand struck something hard, and he pulled it out. Her revolver. He blew off the gritty powder, opened the chamber, and emptied the cylinder into his hand. Five empty shells and a loaded one.

He thought back; it had fired only three times in the cave. The other two must have been in the desert. But who had shot whom?

He turned slowly, his eyes sweeping the barren land. There was something in the distance. Vultures...no...a single large vulture lighted on something and fluttered its wings. Another carcass? He got behind the wheel again and rumbled toward it, the word "carcass" tightening his stomach again. "Please, Jesus, Hathor, Mary," he murmured, "please let it be a dead animal."

When he saw the familiar boot protruding from the sand, he burst into tears. He dropped to his knees, pushed away the sand that half covered her, and lifted her up into his arms. He held her against him and pressed his cheek against her cold forehead.

The scavenger had not flown away, but watched him from a short distance. He threw sand at it, cursing.

Bereft, he stood up and carried the limp form to the car, setting it gently in the passenger seat. He went around to the other side and got in beside her, gently brushing the sand away from her hair. He let his hand rest awhile on her cheek and cried again. It was like a part of him at the end of his arm had been rendered dead.

Something thumped and he jumped violently. The vulture had leapt to the hood of the vehicle and stared at him through the windshield. The long neck was covered with a soft down, and a ring of white feathers formed a sort of collar at the base. The ferocious beak that could penetrate leather and rip out organs was slightly open as the bird panted. Its eyes, ageless and black, peered at him. Then the creature turned, extended vast wings with foot-long black plumes at the end. The wings wafted once, twice, and the heavy body lifted on feather-trousered legs from the car.

Derek followed it with his eyes as it rose from the desert floor into the air and swept gracefully toward a ridge. A high ridge with three vertical fissures. It was too late in the day to see the shadows that would identify the cave entrance, but he would find it again, damn it, no matter how long it took. He would take her to Rekemheb, who traveled between the worlds, who knew both the living and the dead. He started the car.

❖

He puzzled for a moment about how he could hold the flashlight while carrying her body with both arms. Then it occurred to him that he could wrap the long cloth of the turban around him diagonally and anchor the light with it on his shoulder. It wobbled with every step but stayed in place.

Thus equipped, he lifted her limp body again and carried it down the silt-softened tunnel. In the burial chamber the body of the Bedouin woman still lay near the sarcophagus, and he knelt down to carefully place Valerie alongside of her. Two innocent women dead. And in Luxor maybe a third. It was more than he could bear.

He pounded with both fists on the stone. "Rekemheb! Come back. Come up. Come from wherever the hell you are and help me!"

The Ka appeared over the two women as if he had been present all along, startling him.

"Look what we've done to her," Derek sobbed. "You never said this would happen."

"Be comforted, grandchild. The amulet has already shown it to you."

"This thing?" Derek yanked the object from his shirt pocket. "If this is what she died for, I don't want it any longer," he said, and threw it onto the lid of the sarcophagus. The chain clattered as it slid over the stone.

"All this time you had this and you never looked at it." The Ka took up the pectoral from where it lay and tilted it before the face of the flashlight. "You see? This is her own Ka that stands before the Balance. I have witnessed this. Thus the prophecy begins."

"Don't tell me that!" Derek leaned toward the priest, both hands on the sarcophagus. "Nothing in the prophecy said anyone had to die. If I had known that, I wouldn't have gone along with this. I want her back, Rekemheb. You can do that. I'm sure you can. You can go into the underworld."

"No one can bring her back. She has been summoned to carry out her part, just as you have. The gods have chosen you both."

"You're telling me Valerie was 'chosen' to die, and I was 'chosen' to abandon her body to go and play husband to a woman I don't love? Or has Auset been 'chosen' to die too?"

"No. She is well. She will be called to the temple of Hathor when her time comes, and you will too."

"Oh, will I? Commanded to appear? And what if I refuse?" Derek paced the short width of the chamber. "You never mentioned that we could get killed doing this. What sort of gods are these who can't protect their 'chosen ones' from one petty tyrant with a gun?"

"There are those who would seize power among the gods too." Rekemheb frowned. "It is the same conflict, both here and there. That is why your friend has been called to the Duat." The Ka laid gentle hands on his descendant's shoulders. "But your role is given here, as father of the child. Go to Dendara."

"The child is dead, and for all I know, Auset is too!" Derek knocked the spectre's hand from his shoulder and leaned his forehead against the stone wall of the cave. "Besides, if the gods were trying to make a 'holy family,' they got it all wrong. Yussif is the one who loves Auset. He should have been the father. Valerie is…was…a scientist who didn't believe in God at all. And me?" He fingered the turban that was still draped across his chest. "I just liked the costumes."

"Auset lives and needs you. The gods of Egypt need you too." Rekemheb pressed his palms together as if in prayer. "Do not weaken, son of my sons. It is a great advent, whose hour has come. Do not fail it."

Derek turned his back to the Ka and knelt down between the bodies of the two women. He adjusted the cloth covering the Bedouin's face and murmured, "If your spirit still hears me, forgive us for causing your death." Then he bent over the body of his friend, taking her cold hand in his. Tears streamed down his face again.

"Valerie Marie Ghislaine. Who would have thought we would find ourselves here in a tomb together, Radames and Aida, in the middle of the grandest opera of all? You can almost hear the orchestra getting ready for the final act." He entwined his fingers with hers, while with the other hand he drew her pistol from his belt. He closed his eyes. "Forgive me, Jesus," he said weakly, and fired into his own heart.

CHAPTER **XXXI**:
DUAT

Valerie Foret awoke in terror. Armless, legless, incorporeal, she sensed suffocating confinement. Her whole mind a single wail of fear, she labored, writhed, twisted upward from some dark narrow place and at last broke free.

Tendrils of thought curled outward to sensation of something that was self. Appendages. She urged her will into them like blood and felt them open awkwardly. She fluttered, tumbled, fluttered again, and felt herself lift up. Exultant, she ascended, higher and higher, then turned to circle over the fearsome place that had just released her. "Oh, gods."

The body of Valerie Foret lay below her on the desert floor; the mortal lips from which she had broken free were still open.

The Ba shot upward, fleeing her cadaver. High overhead she hovered, panting, sensing the roundness that was her chest swell and contract painfully.

Below her she saw the riverbank and the familiar crossing barque; a slender ferryman in a linen kilt stood at its stern. She spiraled downward again to water and saw the bird form reflected. She recoiled at the confirmation and then, exhausted, let the wind carry her to shore.

The ferryman turned slowly toward her and beckoned. She wondered if there were other passengers, and then she saw what lay on a bier along the ferry's center. Black and without dimension, it was the shadow of herself. Behind it, another figure crouched, and as she approached, it too turned and smiled at her with her own face. Understanding leapt into all the entities at once.

Suddenly she could see herself perched on a stone. She studied the parrot-like creature that had no beak but only her face in miniature and felt the reciprocal perceptions of her several selves. Her thoughts came in disparate tones from three directions: timorous and hysterical in the Ba, thick and plodding in the shade, and finally focused into words within her Ka. Her Ka-self said to the ferryman, "Take me across."

The man leaned on his oar, pushing the ferry from the shore and urging it in gentle surges toward the other side.

She shifted perspective and studied her Ka form, translucent and yet familiar. Even the ivory scroll case she had with her at the moment of her death still hung on her shoulder, not quite substantial. Questions rushed uselessly into her mind, like clowns crowding in a doorway. What waited, in what form, and who else would be there? What were the gods like in their own kingdom?

Something bumped the boat suddenly, and the ferryman stopped his rowing.

"What's that?" she asked, alarmed, but she already knew.

"Apophis," he replied somberly, hunching over his oar.

She stared over the side and saw a dark mass slide by just below the surface of the water. Like a whale, it curved downward, as if to dive, but no fluke broke the surface; only a seemingly endless length of mottled gray slid past. He must have been enormous.

The tomb portrayals had been correct. The monster lurked within the water of the underworld, ever threatening the barque that crossed.

"Does he ever…succeed?" she whispered as the dark creature thumped again against the craft. "I mean, what happens then?"

"He consumes the Ka, undoing its creation. All the Duat must stand guard against him."

The monster seemed to lose interest and remained below. The ferryman, seeming relieved, rowed more vigorously toward the opposite shore.

She noted that, while the departure side was flat, with gentle palm-studded banks, the side toward which they sailed was more uneven. It rose in places to rocky elevations and descended again to beach and marsh.

Then she saw him, a figure waiting on the other shore. He was unmistakable. Anubis, the Opener of the Way, stood stiffly, his arms hanging motionless at his side. Valerie's momentary fright gave way to the scientist's amazement at how perfectly his man's body was joined with the long jackal head and high pointed ears. He stepped toward the water as the ferry neared in pulses. Finally, they beached on the dark bank, and the three parts of her gathered before the Jackal-god.

She waited for his pronouncements, but the Jackal-god's greeting was only a silent nod and a sweep of the hand to indicate direction. "Hurry," he said, and turned away.

"This way to customs, eh?" she muttered as she followed him, trying to dispel the persistent fear. What was the rush, she wondered. The canine deity led her several selves at a rapid pace along a rising path. On both sides, fields of reeds dropped to marshes with pools of silvery water. Rising above the lowland, the winding path approached a great edifice fronted by pylons. A palace, right at the waterfront, as splendid a structure as she had ever seen, surpassing even Karnak. A row of guards stood before it, each man holding a spear taller than himself.

"What do they guard against?" she asked the ferryman.

He spoke brusquely, glancing over his shoulder at her. "Against Apophis, the undoer, eater of words." He raised his hand in signal. The line of guards broke in half and, between them, great bronze doors swung open to the vast chamber.

Awestruck, she started to follow him through the portal, but at that moment, she saw the flinch of one of the guards behind her. She looked back in time to see the great snake, with a diameter the size of a train, rise up above the surface of the water. It swayed for a moment, terrifying to behold, before it sank again. Valerie hurried after the Jackal-god, relieved to hear the sound of the great doors closing behind her.

The Hall of Judgment was breathtaking. How little justice was done to it in the tomb paintings and on papyri, for it was vast. Its stone pillars reached high overhead, dwarfing those at Karnak and disappearing into mist. On each side of the Hall, the judges sat in rows. She did not need to count to know there were twenty-one on each side. The Messengers of Osiris.

At the center of the Hall, brass scales the size of a house caught the light of the torches in the Hall. She had not expected it to be so beautiful. Yet, crouching below the scales, waiting to consume her if her heart was found wanting, the Devourer drooled menacingly from crocodile jaws.

Osiris sat mummy-wrapped before the scales on a simple block throne of gold. Green hands protruded from the wrappings, holding a king's crook and flail. On his unwrapped boyish face were the false beard and the kohled eyes of a king, and on his head the crown of Upper Egypt.

Anubis drew her Ka forward and she bowed. "Lord Osiris," she said.

The mummy did not move, but the god's eyes sparkled recognition.

Anubis motioned her toward the center of the Great Balance. In the one scale she saw her heart, bloodless and quiescent. In the other scale, the Ma'at feather of truth and justice stood upright.

Her Ba flew to its place at the top of the scales, and she stood for a moment, awaiting instructions. None came. Forty-two pairs of eyes looked down on her from galleries around the Hall. Then she realized what they waited for: the Negative Confessions. Fragments of them came to her, bits and pieces of the more lyrical oaths. But she had no hope of reciting them all from memory.

She clapped her hand to her side. Yes! She smiled into the air. The ivory case had passed with her into the afterworld, and it held the list of invocations.

She raised both her hands to the galleries. "Hail to you, Great God, and to you, Lords of Justice. I know you and I know your names. You live on truth and gulp down truth. Behold, I have brought you truth as well." She turned around the room, sweeping with a grand open-armed gesture past the faces of all forty-two judges. "I have come to you without falsehood, and no one testifies against me."

An approving murmur arose from the judges. So far so good, she thought, and drew the papyrus from the scroll case. There they were, in formal temple hieroglyphs, as bright as the day they were painted.

She made another respectful rotation with uplifted hand and then began to read. "'O Far-Strider of Heliopolis, I have committed no falsehood against men. O Fire-Embracer, I have not robbed. O Swallower of Shades, I have not stolen. O Twofold Lion, I have not destroyed food. O Green of Flame, I have not stolen the god's offerings. I have not impoverished my neighbors. I have done no wrong in the Place of Truth. I have not encroached on cultivated land or deprived the orphan of his property.'"

She stopped for a breath. The eyes of Osiris sparkled as before. Anubis nodded encouragement.

Valerie continued, addressing each judge with a declamation. "'I have not driven animals from their pasturage. I have not diverted the water in its season or built a dam against its free flow. I have not tampered with the balance-plumb. I have not caused any to labor in excess of what was due. I have not made hungry or to weep. I have not betrayed the servant to his master. I—'"

"Abomination!"

She stopped in her recitation. A figure came from behind the Great Balance, unlike the other gods. A narrow camel-like skull curved downward to a snout. Rectangular ears that stood upright atop his head recalled no animal at all. But she knew this god.

"Seth, Great of Strength, speak your thoughts," the God of the Underworld said.

The feral lips opened over clenched teeth. "These confessions carry no weight, for this mortal is a nonbeliever. She has desecrated tombs, exposed their mummies, and extinguished the light of the justified." He turned to face her, his eyes bright with rectitude.

She knew what he said was true. With every mummy she had excavated and sent to a museum or—worse—to a laboratory, she had severed the ties between spirit and flesh. One by one, year after year, she had murdered the dead.

At that moment the heart scale on the Balance sank with a crash. On the other side, the delicate Ma'at feather flew upward and wafted to the floor.

The voice of Osiris, God of the Dead, sounded throughout the Hall. "If this is so, and none speak for her, she must be condemned."

The Devourer beast padded forward panting and with fetid breath clamped its wide jaws around her leg. She felt the pressure of its teeth and wondered if the dead could still feel pain.

CHAPTER XXXII:
THE STORY THAT YOU TELL

At the back of the Hall a door thundered open, and the heads of the judges turned. Down the center aisle of the Hall a male figure strode—virile, rapacious, hawk-headed. He stopped halfway to the Balance, but his piercing voice carried the length of the chamber. "Horus speaks for her." His eyes darted around the Hall, defying contradiction.

"This mortal came upon me in captivity among the wandering people, and she bought me free. Even as a child, she heard my suffering and wept for me. My brother Seth misspeaks. This Ka is true of voice."

Around the Hall, the judges murmured acknowledgment.

From the side, a female form drifted in, her very substance twinkling stars. "She has lain beneath me in the wilderness and spoken my name when others saw me not." Sparks effervesced from her hand as she gestured toward the accused. "Let her heart be light, for the Goddess Nuut speaks for her."

The judges murmured again.

From across the Great Hall a robust figure stood up. A single plume grew upright from his head and fluttered in the tiny tempest that swirled around him. "This woman has called upon me in the desert. I have avenged her, and I have guided her companion back to her. Before the messengers of Osiris, the Wind-God Shu speaks for her."

"Ahh." The sound repeated itself all along the gallery of judges.

From the same great portal where the Falcon-god had stood, a goddess entered. Her cow's head held tall horns that curved around a ball of orange light. A melody of flutes followed her where she walked, and a familiar figure attended her carrying a golden stool. Rekemheb maintained the formal bearing of a priest in service, but he glanced to the side conspiratorially. A hint of smile played over his face, as if to say, "See? We are here together at the Balance, after all."

The goddess glanced contemptuously at Seth. "I have seen her taking refuge in a village mosque while she rescued my priest. I speak for her." The light between her horns seemed to increase in brightness.

The judges said together, "We hear the words of the Great Mother Hathor."

The sound of metal scraping on metal drew all eyes back to the Great Balance. The heart dish had risen slightly from the floor, but it still trembled below the other dish where the Ma'at feather once again lay.

Seth leaned toward the accused, his snout glistening. "These testimonies carry no weight, for she offends my father the Aton, in whom all things live. As His light shineth, so am I the thunder in the sky." He extended his whole arm toward the new Ka, nearly touching her. "I am His voice and His right hand, and I condemn her."

The heart dish dropped a millimeter and the Hall fell silent with uncertainty, rendering audible the tap of the goddess's golden stool as Rekemheb set it down. Valerie looked over toward the two, waiting for rescue, but neither had more to say.

Then Rekemheb's face brightened, and he inclined his head in deference as another figure appeared suddenly beside him.

The new god wore a simple snow-white kilt that hung to his knees and a wide collar of turquoise beads across his chest. At the top of the collar, a slender neck ended in the small white head and long curved beak of an ibis. Peering through round bird's eyes, the Scribe-god looked myopic and professorial. He held his stylus over what looked for all the world like a clipboard. In three small steps, the god walked toward the Balance and turned around.

At that moment the long beak evaporated upward, and the bird face metamorphosed into the face of a white-haired man. A man who had served her tea.

"Jehut!" Valerie exclaimed.

"I am called Jehuti here," he said, with the same John Gielgud voice he had used in the necropolis. He glanced at Seth, who stood wide-legged and hostile before the center of the Balance. "You overstate your complaint, Son of Aton." He looked up at the judges on the left and on the right. "The Son of Aton, who loves not his brother, nor any of us in this place, shall not accuse her. Do you not recognize this mortal? She is one of the chosen, and my palette and reed have been given to her."

The God of the Dead nodded stiffly in agreement, his greenish hand lifting his crook and bringing it down again on his knee.

The Scribe wrote on his tablet. "She is justified," he declared, and held the tablet up to display the all-important hieroglyphs: the platform and the oar.

The judges did not speak, but forty-two staffs began to tap, each one a heartbeat after the other, circling the Hall like distant thunder. At the final tap, the heart dish slowly rose, the feather dish sank, and the forty-two judges said in unison, "*Ma' heru!*"

"True of voice," Osiris repeated, before his eyes glazed over. At the same instant, the divine witnesses faded from sight, and the ring of judges froze to form a frieze of stone around the empty Hall.

"That's it?"

Fear had ebbed to annoyance, and the newly acquitted Valerie-Ka turned to her rescuer. The Scribe-god was already halfway through the portal. She hurried after him.

Outside the Hall it was twilight, though whether it was dawn or dusk she could not tell. Against a faintly orange sky the objects on the landscape were still black. A path descended to a field of reeds, and as she scurried along behind the god, she sensed herself as well among the Ba-birds gliding overhead. *Yes, here I am*, the two parts of her thought, surveying the green landscape from above and from below. She searched in her mind for a sensation of her shadow, which had not followed from the Hall. She detected it finally, somnambulant among others of its sort, soundless anchors among the dead.

The god had stopped before a river, not the dismal water that the ferry had crossed, she noted, but a stream so wide she could not see the other bank.

"That's all there is?" she repeated. "You've judged my immortal soul and that's the end of the story?"

"Ah, no. It is rather the beginning. Listen well, Valerie Foret. You are newborn to the afterlife and know as little as you did when you were newborn into the world." He swept his hand downward the length of her in the air. "Behold. Bereft of your earthly ties, this is the essence of yourself."

Her initial fears dispelled, she realized she had paid little attention to her new self. She looked down at her chest, examined her arms. In the twilight, she saw she was translucent as Rekemheb had been, though of a slightly bluer cast. She held her hand up to her face and found she could render it invisible. Like flexing a muscle, she willed her arms to fade but, horrified at the sight of her armless self, she brought them back again. She wondered whether the laws of physics were suspended in the afterlife, or if laws existed that science had simply overlooked. "And my Ba?" she felt her bird-soul think.

"Your Ba has the same ability, if less need to conceal herself from the living. But you should stop playing now and set yourself to the task the gods have given you." A low table, such as a scribe would use, appeared before them on the ground, and he motioned her toward it. "Sit down."

She hesitated for a second and then lowered herself to the sand. The god sat down across from her, as he had done under the calligraphed arcade of the Emir Sharif al Kitab. His face was still kind, avuncular, but it confused her to see the soft-spoken Arab she had met in rags now bare-chested and in the ornaments of a god.

"This is it, then? This is where all the world's souls come?" She looked around, making no effort to conceal her disappointment. "What happens to the billions of nonbelievers?"

Jehuti took his palette and scroll case from her shoulder and laid them across his lap, then leaned his elbows on his knees. "Every creature has its story, and at death, each one goes to its own hereafter."

She frowned. "Rekemheb told us that in the desert, but I never quite believed him. I still can't get my mind around it."

"No? Yet your Christian Book of the Dead proclaims, 'In the Beginning was the Word, and the Word was God.' You are surely familiar with that truth."

"You mean the Bible? Yes, I suppose so, but I always assumed those words were just mumbo jumbo. What have words got to do with life after death?"

"Do not doubt the spirit, which is everlasting, for it lives in you as understanding. Even the scientist must agree to that."

She nodded cautiously.

"And what else is understanding but words, the words you use to interpret the experience of life and to tell yourself all things. It is through words that you comprehend death as well as life."

She nodded again, frowning as she struggled to grasp what he said. He added, "It is in these selfsame words and images that the spirit lives on."

"The spirit lives in its own story, you mean. So that the hereafter we 'understand' is the one that we experience?"

"Yes. The story that you tell is the story that tells you."

The sky overhead seemed to lighten imperceptibly while they spoke, revealing that the half-light they sat in was in fact dawn.

"That is your creation story, then?"

"Before the Scribe there was no story, only the Light and the Darkness. But then the Light gave rise to me, and I spoke forth the rest." He laid a bony hand on his upper chest.

"You are the Creator, then?" Valerie asked, awestruck.

He shook his head. "I am the Words of Ra. I am that which spoke 'water' and it came to be. I told the names of things: 'papyrus,' 'lotus,' 'sparrow,' and they took form."

In the increasing light Valerie looked at the objects he pointed toward, and as he named them they seemed to take on sharper outline. It was as if he had spread form over some other formless thing, something vibrant and vast and yet that needed him.

"Then Ra is the Creator."

"As water is the creator of the wave. Ra is the force that enlivens the lion and the jackal, the river and the wind, and we are the forms of his divinity. This was understood by men until the Aton appeared."

"The Sun Disk? But how is the Aton different from the Sun God Ra?"

"He is an aberration of Ra, a demented form of him which claims all power."

"Then why is the Sun Disk guarded by Seth?"

"Seth does not guard the Aton so much as represent it and in his story is its herald. But he has his place in our story as well. The strength of Seth holds back Apophis, which is the enemy of all. Apophis is the emptiness which swallows up my words and so undoes them."

"Then Seth serves a good purpose. Chaos must not reign."

"Neither must the single will. For the light of the world is not one but many, and some of the light is darkness."

"Interesting way of putting it. But what has all that got to do with me?"

"It is you who must tell the world of the first crime, when the Aton silenced the gods and declared omnipotence."

"With Pharaoh Akhnaton, you mean?"

"Clever girl, to have puzzled that out. It was but the usurper's first appearance, and soon he came with other names, offering men an irresistible inducement. In exchange for obedience to his single voice, he freed men from service to nature and gave them dominion over it."

"What was he called?"

"In each nation he came forth with a different name but always with the same blandishment, that god's image mirrored that of men. Oh, excellent of flatteries. 'Inasmuch as you abjure nature and worship me, your God, so you shall be like me.' But the One-god has not done well by His believers. He has failed to keep them from each other's throats or from the despoilment of the earth." The god reached over and with a slender finger touched the small fresh scar between ear and cheekbone. "See how he chides the disobedient?"

Valerie listened, her lips pressed against her knuckles. He spoke of nature's silence and yet, as the light neared, she could sense nothing but its vitality. The wide river had begun to glisten, wrinkling under the morning breeze. Birds and insects crisscrossed in the air. Seed and blossom, worm and burrowing animal began to stir, and she felt their every wakening.

The god continued. "Ra reigns with the other gods here in the Duat, but the Aton reigns in the land of the living. Foreseeing this, I gave to Pharaoh Meremptah a dream of the crime and of the man whose lineage could one day undo it. I gave the dream to you as well."

"The dream of flying came from you? Then maybe you can explain it. It ended with sparks springing from my mouth and turning into words. Words that even as I said them I couldn't understand."

Jehuti chuckled softly. "They are older than the languages you know. For you, unfathomably old."

"The first word, '*Khetet*'? What is that?" At the moment that she asked, she sensed a vast benevolence approaching from the east, and her mind yearned toward it.

"The opposite of that which stirs in you now."

"What do you me—" Then all around her palm and lotus, bird and beetle began to give off melodies, and every object shimmered with color and perfume. Creatures under the water and in the ground, desert creatures in the vast distance called out to her in every hue and timbre, and each new voice seemed to increase her.

In the onrush of sensation, she could scarcely see or hear the god as he handed back the scroll case. "Tell our story, child of Rekemheb, as you see it with your heart. Write it with my reeds and ink which were given you. Do it quickly, for disaster hastens, and every word that floweth forth herefrom will live forever."

"Child of Rekemheb?" she murmured. She felt her own light increase as she joined the crescendo of greeting for the majestic light that neared. She beheld it through closed lids, euphoric, as if she stood within a vast chorus of rejoicing. Then the Barque of Ra was upon her, and she gave herself over to the rapture of its passage. Horus suffused her first in his taut virility, and she felt him in every fiber of herself. In a moment his aggressive maleness gave way to the voluptuous femaleness of Hathor and Isis. Then Ra itself ignited in her, in a single outburst. She soared on the hissing winds of Shu, rippling desert sand, and was cooled by the moisture of Tefnut. Ma'at enveloped her then with harmony for a moment before the sharp wit of Jehuti focused her inner vision. Finally she felt the ancient ladies course through her, the savage protection of Nekhbet and Wadjet.

The passing sun barque warmed her face, and she held her eyes shut, prolonging the joy and peace. Then, through closed lids, she sensed a shadow come across her face, and she heard the soft crunch of sandals stepping on sand.

Chapter XXXIII:
Che Farò Senza Euridice

"So, you have fallen for their little spectacle, then," she heard him snort. "You will tire of it soon enough."

Valerie opened her eyes to the figure that stood before her with the sun at his back. He remained motionless, except for his long upright ears, which twitched slightly. "You do not belong in this place," the figure added.

She tilted her head back. "Seth. Haven't you heard? I am justified. There is nothing you can do now." She shifted out of his shade and then, blinded by the light that radiated behind him, she shifted back. "If you were trying to keep me out of the Duat, then you have lost."

"If I have lost, then you might consider what you have won." He looked around, drawing her glance to the empty landscape. "It's quiet, isn't it? You haven't asked yet where the other Kas are."

She followed his glance, dread beginning to increase again.

The camel mouth widened in the hint of a smile. "They're all gone, all but a few tenacious ones, and they will pass soon enough. The mummies are all found, you see, or disintegrated." He looked around again. "As hereafters go, this one is a wasteland. Even the gods are barely hanging on."

"I don't believe you. The gods were in the Hall of Judgment, and I felt them passing in the sun barque. And you yourself are here."

"Oh, but I've gotten out. I serve the One God and live as He does, in your world. I've been through most of your history. It's a much better story than this one."

"I don't know what you are talking about." Hating to be on the ground looking up at him, she struggled to her feet and stood as if bracing for a physical attack.

He went on, lightly. "Oh yes. I've been all over your world. I've been looking out for you too. But you would have your way, wouldn't you, and it got you shot."

"What? That was you, who made Vanderschmitt pull the trigger?" Unconsciously she touched the spot just under her heart where her life's blood had poured out.

"No, it was you who made him shoot. What possessed you to pursue him when you knew he was desperate—and had a weapon?"

"I went because Rekemheb…" She stopped, appalled. "Are you saying that he engineered my death?"

This time the smile was unmistakable. "Yes, my dear. You have been tricked. Jehuti has brought you here to write his Book and resurrect a dead religion. Do you fancy yourself a Moses, or Mohammed, able to formulate the central gospel of a religion? What message do you have, anyhow?"

She could think of nothing to say and looked around. Where was Jehuti, to make his case?

Seth pressed his argument. "He has torn you away from life and your friends and set you working for them. If I were you, I would give thought to getting out of here."

Her hands went to her hips. "Why? I just went through an ordeal getting in here."

"But you died for nothing." He blinked slowly, and she saw for the first time that he had long, rather beautiful, eyelashes. "The Bedouin woman still lives."

"Nekhbet is not dead?"

"No, she is not. But you are, aren't you? And all for nothing. And your Ka will last only as long as your cadaver. Did you think they had changed the rules for you? Jehuti is gambling everything on you, on your writing his chronicle quickly, before your Ka dies its second death, and while you scribble, your mortal body is cooking in the sun."

She imagined herself lying on the desert floor and felt her Ka-light darken. "Then why did they kill me in the first place? I could have written their Book in life."

Seth glanced sideways, as if preparing his words. "You…are not like the sons of Rekemheb. You are…compromised, not altogether theirs, the gods would say, and in your own world most unpredictable. Only in the Duat can the gods control you."

Valerie stood speechless. Of their own accord her hands rolled up the blank papyrus. It fit smoothly inside the incantation scroll in the hollow ivory palette.

Seth added the final stroke. "Do you know what has happened to your loved ones?" He took a step forward. "They are wandering in the desert, bleeding and thirsty. Wouldn't you rather be there, helping them—than here?" He gestured once again toward the empty landscape. "Go back," he repeated. "Jehuti has overstepped himself in letting you die for his foolish project."

She chewed her lip for a moment, then met his cold eyes. "Even if I wanted to go back, I couldn't. You know that."

His camel mouth formed what might have been pursed lips. "It is true that none has gone back, but then, none like you has ever come here before. You must only reverse your path. The judges cannot stop you if you do not wake them. And once you have passed through the Hall of Judgment, you need only cross the river."

"The river, right. Will the ferryman take me back to the other shore? And what then? How can you reverse death?"

Seth raised his own hand, reassuringly. "Do not worry about these things that you do not understand. Flee this place. It is the darkness from which the one light has sprung." He stood with his feet spread apart, his unmuscled arms folded across his chest. His voice became almost kind. "Go back quickly. You may still be saved."

Uncertain, she walked back up the path, hanging the scroll case again on her shoulder. The two arguments warred in her mind. She was part of a great mystery of renewal. Or she was a fool. Why during the whole misadventure hadn't anyone asked her what she thought or wanted? What did she want anyhow? As she stood finally before the rear portal to the Hall of Judgment, she knew. She wanted life.

The great doors stood partly open, though guards stood before them, as they did at the front portal. She feared she knew why; the way back was forbidden. As she approached, her fears were confirmed, for the guards stepped forward and crossed their spears in front of her.

It was a small obstacle, one that she would have easily gotten around a few weeks earlier. But now, the sum of all the shocks, fears, and horrors came together in that one gesture, and it broke her. She threw herself against the guards, seizing their spears, one in each hand, and forced them back a step. But the other two joined them, and the four of them fought her off, throwing her to the ground.

Then something terrible occurred that had not happened to her since she was a child. The recollection of her losses accumulated in her like a floodwater, and she suddenly dissolved in tears. Clutching the front of her shirt, she wept incoherently for all that had been taken from her: for her career that had been ruined, for her friends who had been harmed on her behalf, and for herself, robbed of life for a mystery.

It seemed so unfair. She had asked for so little from life and had worked so hard. No family had supported her; no great love had sustained her. She had dragged herself up to success as if climbing from a pit and had been thrown back in, her sense of self and purpose shrunken to the mere urge to live. Broken, she covered her face with her hands.

Then she heard it. She was not sure at first; it seemed impossible. But then she made out the high delicious sound, the faint melody, and she recognized the words coming from inside the Hall.

"Che farò senza Euridice..."

She looked through the space between the great doors. Unbelievable. There he was, on the other side of the Balance, hands outstretched to the judges overhead. A long scarf—it looked like Yussif's *khaffia*—was draped over one shoulder and the other forearm. In the ranks overhead, the judges did not sit but stood at the balustrade, and they seemed agitated.

What was he doing? Singing in Italian to Egyptian judges? He was mad. And yet the bright sound rose up, plangent and compelling, and the judges seemed to listen.

"Dove andrò senza il mio ben."

He turned back and forth to both ranks of judges as she herself had done, sweeping the air with supplicant hands. The drapery wafted gently back and forth as he moved and postured, a black Apollo Belvedere.

"Euridice! Euridice! Oh Dio! Rispondi!"

The door guards too were affected, and they watched him, speechless. She had heard him a score of times in concert halls surrounded by an enraptured public, but this—there was never anything like this.

"Io son pure il tuo fedel!"

"Fedel." Oh, yes, he was faithful, following her into the underworld. More faithful than any lover.

"Più soccorso più speranza. Né dal mondo, né dal ciel!" He finished his aria on a delicate, high pianissimo. She waited, breathless, for the murmur of the judges.

For a moment there was no reaction at all. Then, quietly at first but with increasing volume, the tapping began, and the clattering of the judges' staffs made its stately way around the Hall.

Derek then simply walked around the Balance. The heart-dish and the feather-dish had never moved, neither up nor down, as if the rules of judgment had been suspended for him. The Devourer sat in his place panting like a housedog as the singer walked the length of the Hall. At the rear doors, he stepped out and, as if enchanted, the guards stepped back.

"Hello, you!" Valerie whispered as he came near, and she waited for his exuberant embrace, his reciting of all her names. But as he arrived in front of her, he closed his eyes. Behind him in the Hall, the judges hardened once again to stone.

"What's wrong?" Valerie laid her hand on his chest.

He did not reply, but with both eyes still tightly closed, he made an about-face and stepped back into the quiescent Hall.

"What are you doing?" She followed him, reaching out again to touch his shoulder.

He curled his fingers over hers without speaking. Leaning forward, he pulled her with him back through the Hall, looking nervously up at the frieze of rigid judges.

"Please tell me what's going on. You came all this way, sang your way into the Underworld, and now you refuse to even recognize me!"

Derek halted abruptly. Though she could not see his face, the sudden tilt of his head told her he rolled his eyes in exasperation.

"Oh." She nodded, finally getting it.

"Whew," he sighed, reaching back to pat her fingertips on his shoulder.

"Well, then. Let's get out of here," she whispered.

They tiptoed forward together down the center of the vast chamber, toward the front portal. They crept, step by soundless step, and there was no reaction.

Finally they came to the Balance, where the mummified Osiris sat staring vacantly and the Devourer beast slept. The Balance and the Book, Valerie thought, and felt Jehuti's scroll case brush against her hip. She began to have doubts. Jehuti had chosen her, thousands of years ago, and now she fled from him. A twinge of guilt arrived like a prod in her chest.

The Balance tipped with the squeaking of unoiled metal. One of the dishes suddenly held a heavy heart, and its weight drew the dish downward. A judge turned his head ominously. The Devourer beast stirred.

"*Merde!*" she thought, taking another step forward. The Balance creaked again.

"Be light of heart, light of heart," she whispered to herself. She called up happy memories—the rendezvous at the souq in Cairo, Derek's laughter, Nekhbet's kiss.

Nekhbet.

The heart-dish crashed to the marble floor, and Osiris's eyes flew open. The stony judges burst as one into color, and their indignation rumbled around the chamber. The Devourer huffed to its feet.

"So much for silence!" Derek seized Valerie's hand and propelled them both toward the front. At the portal, they threw their weight together against the huge doors. At the first opening, they squeezed through, one at a time, and broke again into a run. Behind them the great bronze doors thundered closed again, but the row of guards and the Devourer beast pursued them.

Concentrating on her footing as she descended the hill, Valerie dared not look back, but she sensed something in pursuit; through its eyes she could see herself fleeing. Then, smiling inwardly, she realized it was her own Ba, fleeing the underworld with her.

But all that stretched before them was the dark river. The ferry to the other side, to life, was gone. Seth had lied.

"What now?" Derek called out without turning.

"Don't know!" she called back breathlessly. She was so sick of running, of being manipulated, cheated. Would something always be at her heels? And now there was simply no place left to run. Nothing but the endless shore that rose over rocky promontories and descended again to beach. And they had blundered to a cliff. The guards were on them now; she felt a hand brush against her back, about to seize her.

Derek halted only for a second at the edge and flung himself with outspread arms into the rippling water. Valerie leapt after him, for a moment feeling herself suspended in the air. Then the icy water rushed through her Ka, chilling her. Instinctively she held her breath, although faintly aware that a spirit could not drown.

She saw Derek swimming awkwardly in front of her, his legs kicking froglike. She wondered if they could still make it to the other side. Then she saw it. Apophis, as big as a train, snaked toward him through the water.

He saw it too and stopped, thrashing to turn around, but the creature was on him in an instant. Vast jaws opened over him, and his eyes widened in horror looking up at them. She saw his mouth form a silent scream as the maw closed again, engulfing him.

Scarcely had she turned herself—uselessly, she knew—when the creature was upon her. Blackness surrounded her, but for the line of gray-white teeth that formed an ellipse in front of her. Then the creature's jaws snapped shut, and she was sucked into its gorge.

CHAPTER XXXIV:
HOUSE OF HATHOR

Yussif gave a slight wave through the window as the military vehicle pulled away from Luxor International Hospital. He owed the soldiers a lot. They had been surly at first, obviously annoyed at having been ordered to act as ambulance drivers for reckless civilians. He could tell by their accents that they were from the hinterlands, and he knew their kind: rough pragmatists whose "honor"—if they had any at all—was purely tribal, and who stayed in the military because they had no place else to go. But he had engaged them, and when it emerged that one of them was from El Dakhla, his own village, they became almost brotherly. Auset, who had slept feverishly, had no idea of the complex tale he had woven of truth and fantasy to keep their goodwill. He would tell her one day—when it was all over.

The buzzing monotony of television news drew his attention as he slouched against the window sill of the visitors' room. Anything to distract him from the agony of waiting. Another attack on Western business interests, this time by arsonists on an Esso fuel depot. The footage was dramatic. Fountains of flame rose in the air and billowed sideways like speckled orange froth, engulfing sheds and vehicles, which in turn exploded.

The blazing scene outside was followed by somber footage in a jail somewhere. The camera swept along a row of sullen bearded faces. The government had obviously been swift in its roundup of known Islamists. Terrorists, they called them now. Yes, if they blew up oil tanks, they were surely that, but it unnerved him to see their faces. They looked like all the men he knew, men from the villages, from the poorer streets of Cairo, the shops of the souq. Where would it all end?

"Mr. Nabil?"

Yussif smoothed his soiled shirt, self-conscious in the immaculately scrubbed room. "Dr. Bakar."

A man of his own age approached and held out his hand. The doctor's trim moustache and cleanly shaved chin stood in harsh contrast to his own rough beard peppered by sand.

He shook hands but did not ask the question for fear of the answer.

"Your wife is stable but weak, Mr. Nabil. We have given her antibiotics, but she requires surgery. The bullet that struck her lodged in the curve of the pelvis bone. It must be removed, of course, as soon as possible."

"But the baby…"

The doctor dropped his eyes. "The baby is dead. It appears the bullet passed directly through it. We will remove the dead fetus during the operation, of course. With your permission, I will schedule the surgery for early tomorrow morning."

"I must talk first to…my wife. Tonight, please."

"Yes, of course. Come this way." With a detached smile, the physician held open the door to the stairwell leading to the women's corridor.

❖

Auset lay half upright in the first of the two beds in the room, an IV tube running from her arm up to a pouch of some clear liquid suspended over her. She dozed, her head facing the other empty bed as Yussif came in. She had been bathed, he noted, and strands of her hair hung still damp over her cheeks.

He stood for a moment, uncertain, at the foot of the bed, then walked softly into the connecting washroom. It smelled of lemon and antiseptic cleanser. A bottle of liquid soap stood on the sink, and he helped himself, lathering his arms up to the elbows and washing his face and neck. A week before he would have washed that way for God in preparation for the evening prayer. But now the stranger he saw in the mirror washed for himself alone. The washing felt incomplete, futile.

"Yussif?"

He stepped out into the hospital room and walked toward the bed cautiously. "How are you feeling?"

"I'm all right. Drowsy from the painkillers. But the doctor won't tell me anything."

Her voice was weak and he came closer. He dared not take her hand, and so he set his fist on the mattress next to her arm. "I talked to him. He says they have to operate soon to take the bullet out. And…it seems the baby is dead."

She looked around the room for a long moment, biting her lips; then, as her mouth began to tremble, she lifted one hand to cover it. Her quiet weeping grew into sobs, and he cleared his own throat, which had suddenly grown tight. Finally, he reached out one hand and laid it on her shoulder. To his surprise, she grasped it and held it against her cheek. He felt the moisture of her tears under his palm and could find nothing to say.

"Oh, Yussif. We have been through so much. Running away from Cairo, wandering in the desert, never knowing what was ahead or behind us. But always I was certain I would finally come home and have this baby. I didn't care whether it had anything to do with Rekemheb's gods. It was *my* baby." She sobbed again. "And now it is all for nothing. This miracle that was supposed to happen, it's all gone."

A female voice said, "Jehuti's story is not gone."

Yussif spun around, annoyed, to a woman in a plain white dress. "We did not ask for a nurse."

"Who are you?" Auset's voice was hoarse.

"I am the one who can help you now. Your physicians know nothing of the Ka of things."

"Ka? You are a friend of Rekemheb?" Yussif asked.

The woman tilted her head back, and her soft laughter was like tinkling bells. Two horns curled slowly upward from her temples, and a ball of orange light began to glow between them. She continued in the same musical, soft voice. "I am, you might say, Rekemheb's employer."

"Hathor!" Yussif confirmed, blocking her from the injured woman. "Haven't you done enough?"

"We have not done this." She pointed past him. "And there will be time for explanations later. I can save the Child, but you must come to my temple at Dendara. Right now."

"Dendara? No, that is out of the question. Auset has been through a terrible ordeal. Because of you. First you caused her to carry this child, and then you caused her to lose it. What cruelty is this?"

Auset looked back and forth between goddess and man. "This is the first time in five days I've been safe," she said weakly. "Why didn't you come to help us in the desert, or even in the tomb before the gun went off? And what about our friends? What happened to Derek? And Valerie? Weren't they part of this? Why do you show up only now?"

The goddess took a step closer. "I have no power where men have forgotten me, not even the power to bring you away from here. Only in my temple can I assist you. But you must hurry."

Tears appeared again on Auset's face. "Why have you done this to me? I'm not religious, or political, or anything. Why me?"

The goddess wafted toward the sickbed, carrying with her a fragrance of fruit and flowers. Her face was somber with affectionate concern, and her voice was golden warm.

"Because you are my blood and bone, Auset. This is how the Egyptians today speak of Isis, which is my other face. Isis, whose son Horus was killed by his brother. You are myself, and we are the mother of a murdered child."

Auset sighed weakly. "What about Yussif? Who is he named after?" Her tone was bitter. "Have you chosen him for anything?"

"He has proven himself worthy and he will know us. Only come to Dendara. Come quickly."

Her voice faded, along with her image, gradually, from the feet up until only the warm orange sphere atop her head remained, and that too evaporated.

Unfazed by the epiphany, Yussif turned back to Auset. "You do not have to do this. We can go back to Cairo where you will be safe. I will take care of you."

Auset wiped the wetness from her cheeks. "You'd like that, wouldn't you, Yussif? For us to pretend that nothing ever happened. And my parents would pretend I was never pregnant with a foreigner's child." She looked up at the ceiling for a moment, then turned again to his face, which had become so gentle. "That's the choice, isn't it? Between respectability and this…this call of a strange heaven." She held her belly, swollen with the stilled fetus. "What should we do?"

Yussif laid his hand on top of hers. "You must decide. It is you who carried their child and who is in danger. So much has happened these five days, I am lost in wonder and know nothing. But a week ago

I was certain I knew everything and was as wood.

"Yes, I am changed too." He sighed softly. "There is some great mystery we do not yet understand, only that everything we thought before is…incomplete." He thought for a moment, looking into space. "The prophet Mohammed must have stood before a decision like this— to return to Medina and accept the ways of his people or to listen to the angel. It must have seemed like madness. I do not compare myself with the Prophet, peace be upon him. But…I too have seen an angel. And my heart wants to hear."

Auset curled her fingers in his. "I want to hear the angel too. We will listen to her together, *Habibi*."

❖

Alhamdulillah, he thought, there are always taxis in Luxor, day or night. Always poor men to drive them. He approached the nearest one and leaned over the driver's window. "Brother, I need a taxi tonight. It is an emergency."

"Emergency or not, I cost the same." The driver smiled with broken teeth and started his engine.

"I have no money."

"Ah, then. Not driving costs the same too." He turned off the motor.

"But I have this." He drew the heavy silver ring from his last finger and held it close to the splotchy-bearded face.

"See the stones all around it? Sapphires. With this you can buy yourself another taxi. Look, I bet it even fits your finger." He tapped the ring on the back of the driver's hand.

The driver took the ring and turned it between thumb and forefinger. "How far do you want to go?"

"Dendara."

"Dendara? That's forty-five kilometers!"

"My brother, you will only sit idle out here all night anyhow, and my wife is very sick. I must bring her to…her mother."

"You want to take a sick woman *from* a hospital?"

"Yes. To her mother." Yussif scooped the ring from the driver's palm. "Look, do you want the ring or not? There is another taxi right behind you."

The driver nodded and shook his head at the same time. "All right. But if the ring is not good, I will come again to your wife's mother and demand more money."

"Yes, that's fine. Wait here. I will be back in five minutes."

❖

"I have a car, *Habibti*. Are you ready?"

"Yes, I think so." She struggled to sit up, wincing. "If you can carry me."

"Of course I can." He slid one arm behind her back and the other under her knees. With a single powerful lurch, he lifted her from the bed and steadied himself, balancing the weight. She drew her knees up, trying to make herself small, and encircled his neck with her arms.

He closed his eyes for a moment at her first intimate touch and laid his cheek lightly against the top of her head. The smell of her hair sent a wave of resolve through him. He would carry her any distance and never weaken.

The corridor was empty, but as he turned the corner he confronted a female orderly who mopped the floor. She called out to him, but he passed without answering. She stood for a moment in consternation and then hurried away, sounding the alarm.

Yussif kicked open the double doors to the stairwell that led to the lobby. Two nurses confronted him, and a man called out to him from behind. He plunged past the women through the main doors of the hospital into the night.

The driver had waited in his battered black-and-white as agreed, and Yussif laid the feverish Auset in the back. He climbed in next to the driver just as half a dozen men poured shouting from the hospital entrance, and the car lurched forward.

"*Alhamdulillah*," the driver said.

"Yes," Yussif replied, not daring to bring the words over his lips.

❖

Inexplicably, in spite of the late-night hour, the gate at the forecourt of the Temple of Dendara was wide open. Yussif helped Auset from the taxi and held her for a moment on her feet as the car sped away. Then he swept her up in his arms once again and slow-marched across the wide court toward the vast temple façade.

The stones underfoot were irregular, and he paced cautiously, surveying the temple grounds. In the moonlight he could make out the main buildings, the majestic temple at the center, the secondary buildings and ruins in the forecourt. Glass panels formed a long facade against the low wall along the right side of the enclosure, silver in the reflected moonlight. "Glass?" he murmured. "Strange."

"To protect the reliefs." Auset laughed weakly. "Valerie was right."

"You are cheerful, *Habibti?* I am glad." Yussif quickened his pace past the wall of glass as small night creatures came out from the ruins and seemed to gather behind them. In a few moments they were at the entrance of the great hypostyle hall.

"Put me down, Yussif. I want...I think I can walk in here on my own."

He set her on her feet, his arm still around her waist. "I will not let go of you in the dark."

"Dark? No, look. Up there." Auset pointed to the rounded columns that rose high over their heads. At the top, wide triangular faces looked out to the four directions with Mona Lisa–like smiles. The outer columns disappeared upward into darkness, but the innermost columns, near the entrance to the naos, glowed softly around the face of the goddess. "I think they've left a light on for us."

In cautious, shuffling steps, they passed through the hypostyle hall, and she glanced at the hieroglyphic texts that ringed the columns. "I wonder what they say?"

"Prayers, songs." Yussif shrugged. "I don't know. Do not worry about them. Save your strength."

"There is so much to know." She took hold of his arm again and tilted her head back to study the strip of ceiling between the columns. Two rows of carved gods marched in single file, one toward and one away from the temple interior.

Yussif followed her glance. "Gods that are animals. Animals that are gods. I don't know."

"Strange," she mused, not hearing him. "I seem always to know what room we're in. This, I'm sure, is the Chamber of Offerings."

The last room, softly illuminated at all junctures where wall met ceiling and floor, emanated both mystery and welcome.

"Yes." He nodded. "And this is the sanctuary."

Auset gasped suddenly and stopped.

"What's wrong?" Yussif asked, alarmed.

"I think…oh!" She curled forward. "Oh!" she repeated, and broke into tears.

"What is it?" He put his arms around her.

She sobbed quietly for a moment, leaning against him, and then caught her breath. Her lips still trembled, and she pressed her fingertips against them.

"Oh, Yussif. Just now…as I entered the sanctuary…I felt it."

"What, *Habibti*?"

"The child moved."

CHAPTER XXXV:
LAZARUS

Valerie awoke lying on silty ground. She turned her head. A meter away, a parabola of yellow light spread dimly over the ground, its apex toward the lens of a flashlight. It lay, she saw, on the palm of her friend slumped against a stone wall, and its light shone on a gold and heavily jeweled object.

Fears assailed her like a gang of thugs. Derek. Why wasn't he moving? Auset and Yussif. Had they made it to Luxor or had Auset miscarried along the way? Jehuti. Her hand felt for the papyrus at her side, for the test that she had failed. She felt guilt like a burning coal somewhere in her chest. Her mouth was dry as paper. If this was resurrection, it was overrated.

Derek stirred and the flashlight rolled away from him. Valerie sat up as he opened his eyes. He rubbed his face. "What the hell was *that*?"

"Apophis." She shook her head. "Incredible. Jehuti said, 'He swallows up my words and thus undoes them.' I guess that's what happened. It was all undone. We aren't 'justified' anymore."

"Or dead!" Derek pressed his hand on his chest, feeling his heartbeat. "Yep. Definitely not dead."

"And I thought Seth had tricked us," she mused. She clenched and unclenched her hands, trying to get rid of the tingling.

Derek looked around in the semidarkness. "And this is Rekemheb's cave tomb, right? Yes, I remember now. I brought you here to Rekemheb. I asked him to take me into the underworld to get you back, but he said you were fulfilling your part of the prophecy."

"Yes, that was the plan, apparently."

"Yeah, and they don't like it when you try to change it. He refused to take me to the Duat, so I had to do it myself." He picked up the pistol that lay by the side of the sarcophagus.

"My God! You mean you killed yourself just to come and get me? Oh, you sweet, insane man. How could you be sure you'd find me or ever make it back?"

Derek massaged his ankles, trying to bring blood to his still-numb feet. "I figured one underworld was like the other, and I'd kind of 'been there, done that,' you know? Onstage, I mean."

"So that's what you were doing in the Hall, playing Orpheus to my Euridice."

"Yes, but that was just to get in. I hadn't much thought about getting out again."

"Who would have believed that the way back was through Apophis? There's certainly no mention of that in the mythology. I wonder if Jehuti knows…"

Derek's attention had wandered. "Uh…Val? Where's the Bedouin woman? She was right here. I put your body down right next to hers."

"Seth was right, then." Valerie touched the empty spot on the tomb floor. "He said she was alive." She shook her head. "I don't know who to believe anymore. I don't even trust Rekemheb now. He tried to keep you out of the Duat, but he sent me into it. And what about Auset and Yussif?"

"The army found us before we got to Luxor. They arrested me, but they promised to take Auset on to the hospital. Yussif went with her. But when I came back here, Rekemheb kept saying, 'Go to Dendara. She will be at Dendara.' What does that mean?"

Valerie looked at the scroll case that still hung from her shoulder. "It means the story's not over."

"What are you talking about?"

"Things have changed, Derek. We're not helpless pawns anymore. We've made it back from the underworld. We're important to the gods, and we can make demands. You are the chosen father of the child, and you have just defied the gods." She was on her feet finally. She brushed silt from her pants with several decisive slaps.

"And I am their storyteller."

CHAPTER XXXVI:
EPIPHANY

"Praise God," Yussif whispered. "The gods," he corrected himself and looked at Auset. "How can you be sure?"

She wiped her cheeks with her fingertips. "My water just broke. The baby's coming."

Yussif looked down in horror at the trickle of fluid that seeped down her ankle and onto the stone. "Hathor!" he called out. "Where are you?"

"Ohh." Auset bent over, clutching at the cloth of his shirt.

"Hathor!" Yussif shouted again, fearful for the first time.

Something behind them breathed noisily, and Yussif turned. A dwarf with a beard and a mane of wild hair stood in the doorway. Under one hairy arm he held a rolled-up object and in the other a clay urn nearly as tall as he was. He waddled into the sanctuary, throwing his weight from side to side with each laborious step. Pivoting around to stop before them, he pressed the rolled mat into Yussif's hands. Then he stepped away and with two hands tipped the urn toward the center of the stone floor.

A frothy, yellow-brown liquid flowed out in a widening pool, hissing softly as it spread. The smell of fresh beer was pleasant as the fluid covered the stones and rose in a dense vapor. In a moment the sanctuary floor was dry again, with a sheen of polish coating the stone.

Yussif looked down at the bundle he held, a linen mattress some three inches in thickness, filled with straw. Without speaking, the dwarf took it and spread it out on the floor next to the rear wall.

"I'm guessing that's for me, Yussif."

"Ah, yes, of course." He guided her to the wall and held her gently as she eased herself onto it. His hands shook slightly as he knelt beside her and unbuckled her sandals. A familiar voice sounded behind him.

"*Djed meddu,* Yussif." The glowing form of Rekemheb appeared, standing before the goddess Hathor and holding her golden stool. He repeated the formal declaration in strangely accented English. "The words are spoken. The prophecy is fulfilled." Then he smiled with an expression that seemed to say, "I told you so."

"Grandfather!" Yussif shuffled to one side on his knees, and Rekemheb set the stool down next to him.

The Mother Goddess seated herself regally, and when she had arranged her skirts, she bent toward him. "Yussif Nabil, you have brought my daughter to me in your arms. Thus is your faith strong."

"Faith?" He shook his head. "I don't know. I came here for Auset's sake. You promised to take care of her."

"And so I shall. But this hour is for you as well. Behold…"

Auset moaned with the onset of the next contraction. Yussif adjusted her cushion with inept tenderness until the pains subsided. She smiled weakly, but then her glance slid past him, consternation clouding her face. He turned to see what troubled her.

A monster stood in the doorway. His wide chest was half covered by a collar of gold and turquoise, but above it, on muscular shoulders, a wide feathered neck rose to an enormous falcon head.

"My son Horus." The Mother Goddess finished her introduction. The two mortals flinched as the god came near. He bent over them, half prince, half raptor, gray wrinkled eyelids blinking over predatory eyes the size of walnuts. Around them dark feathers showed the divine markings, the lines that fell like tears below the iris, one in a curve and the other straight down.

The rapine head came close, and the sharp hooked beak opened. "Horus greets the mother of the gods' child," he said, his high, shrill voice at odds with his ferocity. He bowed formally and was about to back away when he seemed to have an afterthought and pivoted around again. "The son of Ra does not taste like chicken."

They looked after him, speechless.

Another god entered the chamber. His step, as he approached, was light, as if he preferred not to be seen. And yet he was conspicuous, for his camel-like snout and long upright ears made him look both disdainful and slightly comical. He stared down at the birthing woman without comment.

"Seth," Hathor-the-hostess said. "I am surprised to see you here."

"Surprised? How so? I come like my brother Horus, to pay my respects. Am I not one of the sons of Ra?" He turned without waiting for a reply and went to join his brother at the door of the chamber.

Frowning, Hathor waved the two out into the vestibule and snapped her fingers. A young woman appeared in a simple linen dress, her hair covered by a cloth. She held folds of white cotton in one hand and in the other hand a glass bowl of what appeared to be wine. "The Lady Meskhenet will attend you," Hathor said.

The assisting divinity knelt down to spread one of her cloths over the laboring woman's knees, then sat back on her heels. Rekemheb appeared at Auset's side and placed a gold cup before her lips.

She drank in large gulps, then wiped her mouth with her hand. Her head rolled slightly as the liquid took effect, and her speech slurred. "Mmm." She licked her lips. "Is this the same stuff they clean the floor with?"

Yussif looked over at the goddess. "What about the bullet? The doctor said—"

Hathor raised her hand gently. "Put your mind at ease, Yussif. The gods of Egypt look after her now."

"Gods of Egypt, yes." He glanced around at the animal heads in conversation in the vestibule and then at the sanctuary walls covered with their images.

Seeing where his eyes went, the Ka of Rekemheb reached out to him and pulled him to his feet. "Come," the spectre said, turning his back, and strode before him out of the chamber.

Hesitant at first, Yussif sidled past the divinities at the door and then, relenting, let himself be led along the eastern corridor. As man and ghost turned the last corner to the foot of a long staircase, they stood in darkness but for the gray-green iridescence of the Ka himself.

Rekemheb stepped up on the first step and took hold of Yussif's right hand. "Read, and you will know us." He placed the Arab's palm against the staircase wall.

Under his fingers Yussif felt the outline of a face, the last of a long procession leading up the stairwell. "Ah," he said, as he recognized the being, not just the name-hieroglyph that burned in the darkness through his fingers, but its very essence as god and beast.

"Read," the priest repeated. "And by this touch you will know them." Then, gently tugging, himself walking backward, the Ka drew the man up the dark stairwell.

Yussif followed, sightless, step by step, his fingertips dancing over eyes and horns and beaks carved along the wall, and each god image drew him in. He swam through a kaleidoscope of minds that changed at each new step, and each one in a different way revealed the world to him. He looked down upon it from a barren crag, saw up to it from a moist burrow, recognized it from underwater, from the swamp, and from the searing sand. He heard the night wind breathing over sand dunes, the dung beetle clicking between the rocks, the raven's croak, the shriek of the baboon. He felt each god-beast's appetite and sense and knew nurture, patience, cunning, rut, and ravening hunger.

Drunken with revelation, he found he had reached the top of the staircase, and he staggered out onto the temple roof. The full moon shone down on him so brightly that he cast a shadow. Before him on the walls more hieroglyphics called out to him: incantations, blessings, hymns of praise, all in a solemn, stately language. What texts he could not read by moonlight, he could detect with his fingers. He laid his hands on them with the same reverence as he had once held the Koran and felt their truth.

"Recite, Yussif," Rekemheb said, and Yussif nodded.

"'I have spoken no falsehood against men. I have not robbed or stolen. I have slain neither man nor woman. I have not impoverished my neighbors or deprived the orphan of his property. I have not taken grain or encroached on cultivated land. I have not driven animals from the green land or diverted the water in its season. I have not tampered with the Balance weight or required anyone to labor unjustly for me. I have not made hungry or to weep.'"

He found himself laughing, as he read, at how little was expected—and how much. There were no commandments, laws, or admonitions, only the affirmation of a decent life. Countless gods had to be revered and appeased, but the way to appease them, after paying tribute, was simply to live righteously.

He turned around and leaned against the wall, feeling the lines and ridges of the confessions on his back. How rich he was now, knowing these things. How full the earth, how sheltering the sky with moon and stars.

"Mak! Sothis!" The glowing Ka stood at the edge of the roof, his arm extended toward the horizon. *"Mak,"* he repeated, and Yussif understood, "Behold."

Yes, there it was, at the rim of the predawn sky, like the call of a distant trumpet, the Dog Star, Sirius, the herald of the solar year.

"Dewa netchar!" Yussif responded joyfully, as if he had said it a thousand times before. It was the first day of the new season, *Opet Nefer Renepet*, the opening of the good new year, and beneath their feet in the sanctuary a child was being born.

Euphoric, the convert descended the staircase to take his place in the nativity.

CHAPTER XXXVII:
FOR UNTO US

Hands pressed over her eyes, as if to block out the pain, Auset rocked from side to side, knocking over the empty beer cup. Each contraction merged into the next one now, depleted muscles working automatically.

Panting, she seized hold of the two arms closest to her, of the Mother Goddess and of Rekemheb. She arched her back and moaned in a long exhalation through clenched teeth.

In the silence that followed, she suddenly heard a tiny bleating, a weak vibrating "Eeeeehhhh."

Meskhenet reached under the cloth with both hands. *"Djed meddu!* The Child is here."

Yussif watched from a cautious distance. He could not see under the cloth and resolutely did not want to, but he could tell by the motion of the midwife's hands that she washed the infant with wine between its mother's feet. In a few moments Meskhenet wrapped the pinkish gray creature in a cloth and presented it to the exhausted mother. Auset kissed its damp head and rocked it gently as she passed the afterbirth.

When the visceral aspects of the birth seemed over, Yussif ventured close again and knelt again beside the new mother. He touched the back of his index finger to the infant's cheek and whispered, "Welcome."

"Welcome indeed, child of Rekemheb," a voice said from the doorway. Horus and Seth stepped apart, and the angular figure walked between them into the chamber. Yussif recognized the long narrow beak that curved downward from the small head.

"Jehuti," Hathor said. "You come at the right moment."

The Scribe-god came forward and knelt on one knee before the nativity. The two brothers behind him remained standing.

"The prophecy is fulfilled," the Mother Goddess said, taking the baby from Auset's reluctant arms. Holding the head and narrow shoulders in one hand and its tiny bottom in the other, she rose from her stool. "*Djed meddu*. Behold the Child of the gods."

The newborn opened large dark eyes, and Rekemheb exclaimed, "Oh, how beautiful is his face!"

Seeming to sense its precarious position in midair, the baby inhaled deeply and emptied its lungs in a long vibrating wail.

Rekemheb exclaimed again, "How robust is his cry," and Horus murmured agreement.

The infant thrashed with tiny arms and legs, and the swaddling that had covered it fell back, exposing the tender torso.

Horus's hawk-eyes widened in shock. Jehuti stood up, his beak open. Seth snickered.

Hathor pivoted the tiny body around to see what problem there might be. "Oh," she said.

Seth stepped forward. "A girl child. Is this the best the gods can do?"

"Do not defile my temple with derision, Seth," Hathor snapped back. "You once were one of us."

The god retreated a pace. "Once, yes. But now?" He spat air. "You are a sorry sight, the three of you, in this filthy, ruined temple. A forgotten goddess with her darling son and a scribbler who cannot even convince a mortal to tell his story." He turned to the Ibis face. "Where is your new Book, Jehuti?"

The Scribe-god blinked, but had no reply.

"His Book is here," a voice said. Bats fluttered in the halls and all heads turned.

The two of them, dust covered, stood for a moment in the doorway like brother and sister. Derek once again wore the jeweled medallion, and Valerie stood with the Scribe's palette hanging from her shoulder. Holding it to her hip like a weapon, she announced, "And I will tell his story."

Jehuti nodded and repeated the ancient question. "Of the rebirth of the year?"

"Of the rebirth of the gods," she ritually replied and held up a single page of handwritten text.

Beaming, Rekemheb left the side of the Mother Goddess and strode toward them. "Then lo, I am witness to these things: the Balance and the Book—"

"And the Child too." Derek touched him briefly on the shoulder and hurried past him. "Auset. Are you all right?" He stopped before her, where Hathor still held the infant.

"Yes, I'm fine, and the baby's fine. But the gods seem to have an…issue."

Hathor laid the tiny creature in his arms. "You have a daughter, and she is strong and beautiful, but…"

Derek looked down at the squirming bundle. "Ohh, she's perfect!" He kissed the infant's forehead. "Look, Rekemheb. The next generation. And you're here to witness it, just like in the prophecy."

"No," Seth shook his head, contemptuously. "The prophecy has failed. This child, this paltry knot of flesh, is nothing to Aton, nothing to the gods. An irritant, merely." Then he seized the infant suddenly from Derek's arms and spun around.

Auset screamed *No!* Yussif sprang to his feet. Derek reached out uselessly with one arm. Seth ran a stride ahead of them toward the chamber door.

A dark form blocked his way.

The tattered black abaya still hung from her, and torn strips of it fluttered in the air like feathers as she entered. Seth backed away.

Her shrouded head still drooped forward as she extended rag-hung arms. They lengthened grotesquely as she rose in height. The torn abaya and the dark fingertips became feathers and extended outward until powerful wings wafted along both temple walls. Then, above the ruffling torso, the veil fell back, and the great terrifying head of the desert vulture looked out over the sanctuary.

Horus found his voice. "Mistress of the Desert, Protector of Pharaohs, Guardian of the Royal Blood, Ancient Mother of all Things, Nekhbet!"

"Nekhbet?" Valerie said softly. The woman who had twice kissed her, the woman she had fallen in love with and on whose behalf she had been killed was…

"The Vulture-goddess," Derek gasped behind her. "Wow. Sure didn't see that one coming."

"What kept you, sister?" Hathor looked up to the vulture head that towered over her and all the others.

"Complications," a woman's voice replied. But then the huge curved beak of the scavenger opened, and the Mistress of the Desert thundered, "Open the temple!"

The walls seemed to vibrate for a moment, and then, with the sound of cracking ice, all Dendara became as glass. Over the soft yellow ambience of the chamber, the night sky appeared with the sharp light of the full moon.

The goddess spoke again. "I call on every god that dwells in the Duat and in the Field of Reeds and in the Temples of Kemet." Her head swayed from side to side, addressing east and west. "All those whom this Child's advent shall rejoice, come hither and attend me." The solemn cry seemed to echo as it faded.

The night gave back its silence. Somewhere in the temple the scarab beetle rolled its dung ball across a stone, and in the dark recesses of the corridors bat wings rustled again, waiting.

Finally it came, barely discernible at first, then unmistakable, the thrumming of a distant multitude. Valerie and the other mortals drew together and watched, incredulous, as they came from the horizon.

In a long aurora borealis they snaked, in streams of luminescence, emptying the underworld. Majestically they curved first northward and then to the south, then headlong toward the temple, as if the procession itself were the celebration. Slowly they neared, joyous and solemn, delaying revelation, till finally the mortal eye could make out their individual forms. Macabre and stunning, they were a bewildering demon host of half-humans, birds, felines, canines, rams, and nameless creatures; they sported horns, feathers, flowers, moons, and spheres of heavenly light.

In proximity it was almost not to be endured, as in kaleidoscope they spiraled, forming rank after burning rank, an amphitheater of inconceivable color suspended over the soft gold of the sanctuary below. Rekemheb was prostrate, and Valerie stood enthralled, naming the deities to herself as they came in overhead: "Anubis, Knum, Sekhmet, Ptah, Amun…" until she too was overwhelmed by the sheer spectacle and dropped to her knees. "This is all the Duat," she murmured. "These are the very forces of the earth."

The Vulture-goddess reached out winged arms toward Seth, who had not dared to move, and with slender hands emerging from the wings' middle joints, she took hold of the silent infant. From the center of the temple, the Mistress of the Desert rose up to meet the waiting host and hovered over them in the crackling air. Sable feathers curled around the child, sheltering her as in a cradle against the wind that blew between the worlds beneath her magnificent wings.

"Hail to you, gods of Egypt! I know you and I know your names!" the vulture spoke, and the temple walls reverberated. "This is the hour. And this is the Child who shall be under my wing. Greet her as your own, for her name is *Nefer-renepet*, the Beautiful Year."

Murmurs of wonderment rippled through the Host of the Duat. A child of the modern age, a girl child no less, and from the lineage of a mere priest. Yet the oldest of their number, the protector of all things royal, had proclaimed it: This was the Child, the Messenger. Agreement spread throughout the ranks. Then jubilation, at every pitch in the myriad mouths and beaks and maws, accumulated like a gathering storm in an unbroken crescendo, until their collective acclamation rumbled like rolling thunder across the African sky, "*NE FER REN E PET.*"

Crouching still on the floor of the temple under the spectacle, Auset reached out to touch Rekemheb. "All right. I get it. Your prophecy is fulfilled. Now, please, let me have my baby back."

He took her hand in his. "She is the gods' child too, Auset, and she will need their care, for the governments will be upon her shoulder."

Auset fell silent. Drenched in the sweat of her labor and the heat of the sanctuary, she shivered.

CHAPTER XXXVIII:
ATON RISING

A faint line of color appeared on the horizon. A voice called from among the divine host, "The sky lightens!"

Jubilation ceased. Disorderly and flamboyant, the gods broke ranks, fretting like guilty party guests about the hour, and rose up from the temple precinct. In twos and threes they streamed toward the horizon, the golden lines of them threading into the pink and orange that secreted from the east. Horus and Seth trailed after them, two long comets.

The Vulture-goddess descended to the sanctuary, and its walls opaqued behind her. Folded black wings metamorphosed to slender bronze arms, her coat of feathers to the familiar sheath dress of tomb portraits, and the appalling scavenger head to the face of the shepherd at the well. As woman, Nekhbet knelt down and placed the curiously unperturbed infant in her mother's arms. "The gods will watch over her. See to her earthly welfare until she hears her calling."

Auset's eyes darted anxiously over the handsome head and shoulders of Nekhbet, as if fearing the vulture might reappear.

"Earthly welfare. Calling. Yes, of course." She wrapped another layer of swaddling around the infant's legs, her firm grip indicating that there would be no more baby-passing.

Nekhbet rose again, and as a woman she wafted from the sanctuary, glancing for an instant toward Valerie as she passed.

Derek knelt down over his daughter, who sucked with concentration on her fist. "You have your god-name now, a great big one, but I'll call you Nefi." He touched her other hand with his pinky, and miniscule fingers encircled it. "What a baptism. You got a whole circus, a carnival, and a visit of the heavenly host, all in one. Isn't that wonderful, my kitten?"

"More like a Bosch painting." Holding her infant in one arm, Auset raised herself up with difficulty. "And they're all our new in-laws."

"Yes, Nefi's in-laws." Unperturbed, Derek pressed his lips against the top of his daughter's warm head. "My cricket has all kinds of ghosts looking after her. Just like our great-great-great-grandfather, Rekemheb."

Rekemheb knelt on one knee over the newest of his line and took her tiny feet in his hands. At his touch, the infant opened her eyes wide and her mouth formed an *O* as she squirmed, raising both fists. Then she yawned and stared dreamily at him. "She much resembles my daughter Merut-tot," the Ka said tenderly. "What will her worldly name be?"

"I...I don't know. That's up to Auset, I guess. I promise this child everything I can give her from my own country, but I'm not ready for fatherhood." He rubbed his cheek against the infant's damp hair.

Hathor sat down again on her golden stool and adjusted her skirt. "No, you are not. In this, we seem to have miscalculated."

Derek looked pained. "I know what you're going to say. I abandoned Auset, didn't I, when I died for Valerie."

Auset looked up at him. "What? You died?"

Hathor continued. "The gods had not planned for mortal love. Its fevers led you astray from our prophecy, but it also brought us this good man." She raised her hand toward Yussif, who had sat in silent wonderment through the entire spectacle.

"Yussif Nabil, you have embraced the gods this last night of the old year, and your heart is full. Will you care for this woman and this child as man and father?"

"With all my heart." He looked tenderly toward the young mother. "If she will have me."

Auset still frowned. "Derek was dead? Like Nekhbet? Has anyone else here been dead that I don't know about?"

"Everyone, actually," Valerie said. "Except you and Yussif. We'll explain all that later. I think."

Hathor held out her arms, encompassing the group. "Now, my dears, you must be gone from here. Strangers will arrive in my temple soon, touching everything, understanding nothing. Go home now, all of you, and begin this our New Year. We will be watchful."

Without ceremony, she evaporated. Rekemheb remained a moment longer, holding the golden stool. Then, grinning in unpriestly fashion, he wiggled his fingertips at his descendants and disappeared after her.

Auset looked at the empty space where the goddess had stood. "Home. Right. Has anyone thought of how we're going to get there?" She took hold of Yussif's arm and struggled to her knees. "Oof. Amazing how everything you do requires stomach muscles."

"Don't worry. You'll rest for a day in Luxor, and we can train to Cairo tomorrow." Valerie reached under Auset's right elbow, which was curved around the baby, and found herself inches away from the infant's face. Clear eyes stared up at her, and she could smell the buttery scent of its newborn skin. Valerie let her hand linger a moment on the tiny, warm foot. "Can you walk?"

Yussif took hold on the other side, and together they pulled Auset to her feet. She winced. "I think so."

The new family shuffled toward the sanctuary doorway. Behind them, the dwarf reappeared and gathered up birthing cloths into the middle of the straw mat. He rolled it all together and, with the bundle curved over his shoulder, he waddled toward Valerie.

She smiled. "That was you in the Necropolis, wasn't it? I should have recognized you. Thank you, Bes, God of Birthing Women."

The panting dwarf reached out a plump fist as if to give her something. Puzzled, Valerie held her own hand under it. The stubby fingers opened, and something tiny and hard dropped into her palm. The misshapen god turned around and waddled away through the doorway.

Valerie stared, perplexed at the strange dark pellet in her hand. "Oh," she murmured, recognizing the lead slug from her own gun. Chagrined, she put it in her pocket.

Alone in the sanctuary, she turned in a circle, as she had done in the tomb of Rekemheb, sweeping her eyes over the reliefs and inscriptions. She had been right. They had spoken to her alone, telling the old story. And now she was called to tell the new one.

She drew out the folded pages that she had tucked into her shirt and thought of Seth. Telling the old mythology anew was insane, he'd said, and he was right. It was folly to attempt to resurrect a dead religion. But now she knew what had killed it.

She unfolded the paper and read the opening words to her manuscript:

Everywhere before his burning eyes the beasts, the winds and waters, and the hills cried out. Pitiless, the Sun Disk rose and smote them, rendering them dumb. Then Seth, iron-eyed guardian of the light, loosed his spear upon the vanquished. But lo, a humble priest stepped forward, an amulet in his hand, and the spear blade shattered into sparks upon it. Gathering the sparks with the power of his breath, he sucked them in—and spat them out again as words.

She had grasped, finally, the nature of the thing that had to be undone. Militant monotheism. The Bible had it backward, it seemed. The first crime was not disobedience to the absolute, but the absolute itself. Man had not sinned against God; Almighty God had sinned against life. And life—in all its forms—would not be whole, or safe, again until it once more had its names and voices.

Jehuti would be pleased, for she would tell the story that he told her, the one in which she lived and acted. The others—Derek, Auset, Yussif—all had their stories too, but she was the scribe. She would sit down with them in the coming days and months and weave in their accounts.

Only Vanderschmitt remained opaque. What drove him to pursue her with such zeal was still a mystery. How could a man who was merely irksome, who in his tenacity was not unlike her, become her murderer? And why had the gods not saved her?

And then there was Nekhbet, whom she had begun to love and who still stood among the columns of the great hypostyle hall. Valerie approached the goddess, hesitant, wondering if anything was left of the woman who had kissed her. Who had twice pressed warm human lips upon hers.

The hall was somber but the goddess seemed to contain her own light, for Valerie sensed every detail of her. How stunning she was, a woman's form harboring ferocious power. The simple sheath clung to her from midbreast to midcalf, and Valerie could see now that it was no dress but a coating of tiny feathers, iridescent black, like a crow's breast. The ageless eyes of Nekhbet turned toward her, then to the paper in her hand. "You have begun?"

"Yes. A few thoughts. But I'll have to talk to the others as well. There are so many questions." Valerie glanced toward the front of the hall. In the transparent darkness she could just make out the forms of her friends who waited. "A curious holy family, isn't it? One child with three parents."

"An adjustment to the original plan," the goddess replied coolly. "We had not reckoned with human emotions. Always so troublesome." She looked out at the dawn gray, which had sent a strip of dull light along the stone walk at the center of the hall. The morning breeze floated through the columns, lifting a few strands of her pitch-black hair. "But see, the New Year begins. You must leave now."

"I thought we would have more to talk about." Valerie tried to discern emotion in the majestic face but could not. "I mean…that night, in the Bedouin camp. You kissed me…"

The goddess looked away. Her voice was velvet, but toneless. "Enlightenment. Such was given to every Pharaoh."

Valerie's face grew warm. "The Kiss of the Gods, as on the tomb wall." She closed her eyes in disbelief. "Of course. How could I be so stupid? It just seemed so…personal."

"We meant it so, to win your devotion." Nekhbet still did not look at her.

"My devotion?" Valerie was aghast. "You mean so that I would go to my death for you? So that I would descend to the Duat and be given my assignment?"

The goddess shook her head. "It was not so simple as that. We were in a struggle with Seth. As he moved Vanderschmitt, so we had to move you. He had also to be taken out."

"Vanderschmitt was part of the scheme too?" Valerie laid her hand on her forehead. "Oh, this just gets better and better. You manipulated my affections, my fears. And you assumed that once I was in the Duat, I would forget all feelings."

Nekhbet looked out toward the courtyard at the waiting family. "Feelings. I have had quite enough of mortal feelings. They have been a plague on the great plan for centuries."

"Centuries? What are you talking about?"

"About your lineage, which we chose for Jehuti's noble story and yet has failed in one way or another in every generation. Your mother nearly ruined it, and now you might do it as well. Will you never control your desires?"

"My mother?" Valerie's voice became a whisper. "What has my mother got to do with this?" She searched her memory of a woman who no longer had face or voice, and found nothing.

The goddess gazed back at her, compelling black eyes holding her in place.

"Monique Foret was much like you. She was our chosen one, in her day, but she failed us. You provoked Seth, and we could manage that, but she surrendered to him."

"My mother 'surrendered' to the god Seth? What does that mean, exactly?"

"Not to the god. But to his chosen one, Vanderschmitt, from the lineage of his priest Sethnakht. He knew your mother and got her with child. But if you give the world our story, Seth can be defeated after all."

Valerie shook her head as if forcing herself to wakefulness. "Wait. You're telling me my mother knew Volker Vanderschmitt? That she… was pregnant by him?"

"That's what I am telling you. This man was your father."

Valerie staggered back as if struck. Leaning on her hand against the stone pillar, she shook her head again. "It's not possible. Jehuti himself said I was a child of Rekemheb."

"And so you are. By your lineage you are the child of Hathor's priest, but also, and more recently, of a man of Seth. The two bloods mingle in you. His visions of us were much like yours, but tainted by the zeal of a follower of the Aton. In your quiet hours you can witness the troubled workings of his soul. They will be familiar, for you live in the Aton world. But now you have seen our world as well, and you must choose between the two."

Valerie walked close again. "Look, you keep springing new information on me, revealing these mind-shattering secrets. But when will I know all the secrets? At what point will I know enough to make this choice, between my world and yours? All I can be sure of is what I knew before I met you, and that's quite a bit. I am not a blank slate that you can write on. I have a story too."

Impulsively, Valerie stepped across the distance between them and took the majestic head in her free hand. Surprise registered on the goddess's face, as it had once on Valerie's own. The divine lips of the Mistress of the Desert, Goddess of the White Crown, opened slightly in astonishment; then mortal lips covered them.

The goddess flinched and her empty hand rose in the air. Valerie pressed the kiss, warming with excitement, as if the body she leaned against could be excited in return, as if the nubile mouth, tasting still of cardamom, were not of unfathomable age.

Memory of their last kiss, when the Bedouin Nekhbet had thrown her down and answered her passion with pedagogy, returned to her. It angered her to have the kiss explained away, the passion nullified. This now was her response, and she was the one who threw the other woman down and answered smug instruction with unashamed desire.

She pressed the feather-clad goddess up against a pillar, felt a woman's thighs against her own thighs and the panting breath flow from human nostrils across her cheek. Her hand that had reached ardently for the Bedouin breast searched now again, with more insistence. And when she found it, firm and womanly, she caressed it once as she invaded the moist interior of the goddess's mouth.

A familiar vision ignited then between them like an explosion, and she soared again above the Nile. But now two entities, not one, spun together in the timeless air, and two wills contested. The ancient predator dominated first, pulling the young spirit back into murky memories of the beginning. Steaming swamps alive with prey appeared beneath them, reeking of nourishment and blood, of fecundation and decay.

Then youthful wings beat against the weight of centuries and forced the turning, so that the two of them rose upward. The land below them dropped away to savanna and then to desert fed by a single twisting vein of water flowing northward on the broken shoulder of a continent. The landmass shrank away, revealing dark blue waters on both sides and a gauze of white clouds that swirled across its center. Still the ground receded, the eastern and western horizons curving in to join at the north and south. Finally the earth appeared in its entirety, a frothy blue-beige-green sphere suspended in black space.

Their commingled being that hovered over it broke apart again; the youthful one gave forth the image while the ancient one beheld it, awestruck, dazzled.

"*Rekhi renusen. Djedi medjatsen*," reverberated throughout space and time, and the voice of the Vulture-goddess gave it back in the new language, laughing. "I know their names and I will tell their story."

"Val, honey, what's taking so long?" A familiar sound broke the vision. The euphoria ebbed away to the sense of solid ground, decayed stone columns, and the smell of mold from under the high temple ceiling.

Valerie opened her eyes to see she still held the goddess as a woman in her arms.

Nekhbet was quiescent, and for the briefest moment tenderness flickered across her face. Then she drew away. "Let me go." She twisted sideways, and the dark feather covering began to grow up over her shoulders.

"No, wait. Not yet," Valerie pleaded. "Look at me." She held the goddess a moment longer. "You do care for me. Say it, please, before you go."

Fathomless black eyes looked away. "You do not know what you do," she said, and twisted away again into empty air. Nothing remained of her but the flutter of invisible wings.

"Valerie, hurry. We've got to get out of here before the tourists come!" Derek's voice summoned her again, now *molto agitato*.

She hurried forward from the shadows of the hypostyle hall into the sacred court, where the new family waited. "Happy Egyptian New Year," Derek said and started forward.

"Happy New Year," she greeted back and followed a step behind him.

"So, is this prophecy done?" Auset looked back over her shoulder. "Can our lives go back to normal now?"

Derek draped his arm over Valerie's shoulders. "Well, my friend's got a book to write, and we still don't know what that sun-rising-in-the-west thing is all about."

Auset shifted the sleeping infant from the crook of her arm to her shoulder. "I wouldn't worry about that, after everything else we've been through. Whatever it means, I doubt it has anything to do with us."

Walking behind the family, Valerie took a long last look around the temple precinct, trying to memorize it. On the eastern side the ruined boundary opened to the plain, offering a long vista to the horizon. Directly ahead of them the entrance gate—amazingly—was still unguarded. Finally, to her left, a row of glass panels leaned against the western wall. Bathed in the comforting, hopeful light of dawn, every object seemed to warm with anticipation.

Overhead two military jets ripped northeastward across the modern sky. She wondered vaguely where they headed: Saudi Arabia? Israel? It did not bode well.

Then, with sudden violence, the sun itself burst up from the horizon. Its first bright light that scorched the eastern sky sparkled also in the glass panels leaning toward the west. Staring horrified at the glass, Valerie halted as if struck.

"The sun disk, rising in the west, in the hundredth generation."

Ahead of her, the family walked across the beam of warm reflected light. Valerie watched, appalled, as the ominous western sunrise illuminated first the sleeping infant's face and then the others, one by one.

About the Author

Justine Saracen was a college professor for fifteen years before leaving academic life for the arts. Her scholarly book, *Salvation in the Secular*, addressed themes that persisted into later fiction: the role of religion in history, the leitmotifs of fanaticism, and the power of language. Her second "career" in opera management provided another favorite theme: the power of music. In the 1990s she leapt onto the freight train of Internet fan fiction with "The Pappas Journals," "In the Reich," and "Lao Ma's Kiss." More important was a trip to Egypt with her Egyptologist partner to study the Ptolemaic temples. The experience gave rise to the Ibis Prophecy, a series that follows a lesbian archeologist through modern, medieval, and ancient Egypt. The first novel of the series, *The 100th Generation*, was a finalist in the Queerlit 2005 contest. Her upcoming work is the sequel, *The Vulture's Kiss* (2007). Justine is a member of the Publishing Triangle in New York City and is currently studying Arabic, Islamic history—and parrots.

You can visit her at her Web site at http://justine-saracen.tripod.com.

Books Available From Bold Strokes Books

Forever Found by JLee Meyer. Can time, tragedy, and shattered trust destroy a love that seemed destined? When chance reunites two childhood friends separated by tragedy, the past resurfaces to determine the shape of their future. (1-933110-37-6)

Sword of the Guardian by Merry Shannon. Princess Shasta's bold new bodyguard has a secret that could change both of their lives. *He* is actually a *she*. A passionate romance filled with courtly intrigue, chivalry, and devotion. (1-933110-36-8)

Wild Abandon by Ronica Black. From their first tumultuous meeting, Dr. Chandler Brogan and Officer Sarah Monroe are drawn together by their common obsessions—sex, speed, and danger. (1-933110-35-X)

Turn Back Time by Radclyffe. Pearce Rifkin and Wynter Thompson have nothing in common but a shared passion for surgery. They clash at every opportunity, especially when matters of the heart are suddenly at stake. (1-933110-34-1)

Chance by Grace Lennox. At twenty-six, Chance Delaney decides her life isn't working so she swaps it for a different one. What follows is the sexy, funny, touching story of two women who, in finding themselves, also find one another. (1-933110-31-7)

The Exile and the Sorcerer by Jane Fletcher. First in the Lyremouth Chronicles. Tevi, wounded and adrift, arrives in the courtyard of a shy young sorcerer. Together they face monsters, magic, and the challenge of loving despite their differences. (1-933110-32-5)

A Matter of Trust by Radclyffe. JT Sloan is a cybersleuth who doesn't like attachments. Michael Lassiter is leaving her husband, and she needs Sloan's expertise to safeguard her company. It should just be business—but it turns into much more. (1-933110-33-3)

Sweet Creek by Lee Lynch. A celebration of the enduring nature of love, friendship, and community in the quirky, heart-warming lesbian community of Waterfall Falls. (1-933110-29-5)

The Devil Inside by Ali Vali. Derby Cain Casey, head of a New Orleans crime organization, runs the family business with guts and grit, and no one crosses her. No one, that is, until Emma Verde claims her heart and turns her world upside down. (1-933110-30-9)

Grave Silence by Rose Beecham. Detective Jude Devine's investigation of a series of ritual murders is complicated by her torrid affair with the golden girl of Southwestern forensic pathology, Dr. Mercy Westmoreland. (1-933110-25-2)

Honor Reclaimed by Radclyffe. In the aftermath of 9/11, Secret Service Agent Cameron Roberts and Blair Powell close ranks with a trusted few to find the would-be assassins who nearly claimed Blair's life. (1-933110-18-X)

Honor Bound by Radclyffe. Secret Service Agent Cameron Roberts and Blair Powell face political intrigue, a clandestine threat to Blair's safety, and the seemingly irreconcilable personal differences that force them ever farther apart. (1-933110-20-1)

Protector of the Realm: Supreme Constellations Book One by Gun Brooke. A space adventure filled with suspense and a daring intergalactic romance featuring Commodore Rae Jacelon and the stunning, but decidedly lethal, Kellen O'Dal. (1-933110-26-0)

Innocent Hearts by Radclyffe. In a wild and unforgiving land, two women learn about love, passion, and the wonders of the heart. (1-933110-21-X)

The Temple at Landfall by Jane Fletcher. An imprinter, one of Celaeno's most revered servants of the Goddess, is also a prisoner to the faith—until a Ranger frees her by claiming her heart. The Celaeno series. (1-933110-27-9)

Force of Nature by Kim Baldwin. From tornados to forest fires, the forces of nature conspire to bring Gable McCoy and Erin Richards close to danger, and closer to each other. (1-933110-23-6)

In Too Deep by Ronica Black. Undercover homicide cop Erin McKenzie tracks a femme fatale who just might be a real killer…with love and danger hot on her heels. (1-933110-17-1)

Course of Action by Gun Brooke. Actress Carolyn Black desperately wants the starring role in an upcoming film produced by Annelie Peterson. Just how far will she go for the dream part of a lifetime? (1-933110-22-8)

Rangers at Roadsend by Jane Fletcher. Sergeant Chip Coppelli has learned to spot trouble coming, and that is exactly what she sees in her new recruit, Katryn Nagata. The Celaeno series. (1-933110-28-7)

Justice Served by Radclyffe. Lieutenant Rebecca Frye and her lover, Dr. Catherine Rawlings, embark on a deadly game of hide-and-seek with an underworld kingpin who traffics in human souls. (1-933110-15-5)

Distant Shores, Silent Thunder by Radclyffe. Dr. Tory King—along with the women who love her—is forced to examine the boundaries of love, friendship, and the ties that transcend time. (1-933110-08-2)

Hunter's Pursuit by Kim Baldwin. A raging blizzard, a mountain hideaway, and a killer-for-hire set a scene for disaster—or desire—when Katarzyna Demetrious rescues a beautiful stranger. (1-933110-09-0)

The Walls of Westernfort by Jane Fletcher. All Temple Guard Natasha Ionadis wants is to serve the Goddess—until she falls in love with one of the rebels she is sworn to destroy. The Celaeno series. (1-933110-24-4)

Change Of Pace: *Erotic Interludes* by Radclyffe. Twenty-five hot-wired encounters guaranteed to spark more than just your imagination. Erotica as you've always dreamed of it. (1-933110-07-4)

Honor Guards by Radclyffe. In a wild flight for their lives, the president's daughter and those who are sworn to protect her wage a desperate struggle for survival. (1-933110-01-5)

Fated Love by Radclyffe. Amidst the chaos and drama of a busy emergency room, two women must contend not only with the fragile nature of life, but also with the irresistible forces of fate. (1-933110-05-8)

Justice in the Shadows by Radclyffe. In a shadow world of secrets and lies, Detective Sergeant Rebecca Frye and her lover, Dr. Catherine Rawlings, join forces in the elusive search for justice. (1-933110-03-1)

shadowland by Radclyffe. In a world on the far edge of desire, two women are drawn together by power, passion, and dark pleasures. An erotic romance. (1-933110-11-2)

Love's Masquerade by Radclyffe. Plunged into the indistinguishable realms of fiction, fantasy, and hidden desires, Auden Frost is forced to question all she believes about the nature of love. (1-933110-14-7)

Love & Honor by Radclyffe. The president's daughter and her lover are faced with difficult choices as they battle a tangled web of Washington intrigue for...love and honor. (1-933110-10-4)

Beyond the Breakwater by Radclyffe. One Provincetown summer, three women learn the true meaning of love, friendship, and family. (1-933110-06-6)

Tomorrow's Promise by Radclyffe. One timeless summer, two very different women discover the power of passion to heal and the promise of hope that only love can bestow. (1-933110-12-0)

Love's Tender Warriors by Radclyffe. Two women who have accepted loneliness as a way of life learn that love is worth fighting for and a battle they cannot afford to lose. (1-933110-02-3)

Love's Melody Lost by Radclyffe. A secretive artist with a haunted past and a young woman escaping a life that has proved to be a lie find their destinies entwined. (1-933110-00-7)

Safe Harbor by Radclyffe. A mysterious newcomer, a reclusive doctor, and a troubled gay teenager learn about love, friendship, and trust during one tumultuous summer in Provincetown. (1-933110-13-9)

Above All, Honor by Radclyffe. Secret Service Agent Cameron Roberts fights her desire for the one woman she can't have—Blair Powell, the daughter of the president of the United States. (1-933110-04-X)